A Tale of Something New

D. S. McColgan

BOOK 1

A Tale Of Ltd

Published by
A Tale Of Ltd
Unit 133388, PO Box 7169
Poole, BH15 9EL
UK

www.ataleofbooks.com

Cover design by Lukas Lauener, instagram@lks_dsn
Map Art by KJ Reading, instagram@kjr.art
Illustration by instagram@winterofherdiscontent
Edited by Leona Skene, www.intuitiveediting.co.uk
Proofread by Phillipa Haskins

ISBN 978-1-7385050-1-2

This book is dedicated to the love of my life
as well as our little love that joined us along the way.

Heidenried
Krambach
Halfway Mark
Oberdorf
Peter's Farm
Church
Lindenbach Stream
Celebration Grounds
Uncle Bernd's Farm
Urs' Farm
The Little Mill
Liliana's Home
Road to Roinnenstadt

Every story begins with a decision.

Chapter One

Was that blood?

Liliana stopped abruptly. She clasped the rein tighter and hurried towards the spot where several trees had crashed into each other. Snow, already a few days old, crunched under her boots. The forest was silent. As she approached, she discovered more and more red spots on the ground and even on the branches. She slowly raised her head and immediately wished she hadn't. Which animal the parts hanging from the trees were from she couldn't say, but it was definitely dead. It looked like it had rained torn intestines, muscles and bones. To her horror, she also discovered shreds of clothes and human skin. Everything had remained fresh and nearly odourless; however, the mere sight of it made her slap a hand over her mouth and nose to swallow a bout of nausea.

The donkey on her side didn't fare much better. It brayed and jumped. Liliana stumbled sideways to the ground. The rein grated on her hand, and she had to let go in order to stop herself being dragged across the forest floor. As she struggled back to her feet, she saw the donkey disappear among the trees. Now she was all alone.

Liliana hesitated for a moment. Should she run after Donnie? No, as long as she found him before it got dark, everything would be fine. She took a deep breath before turning back to the bloody scene. The cold cleared her thoughts. There were wolf prints, but also tracks Liliana couldn't interpret. In the opposite direction, there was a kind of drag mark. Following it, she recognised sporadic outlines of hands, as well as bloodied pieces of fur and cloth that had stuck on sharp edges in the snow and protruding branches. She walked on, heart pounding, until she saw a bloody bundle on the ground a good thirty feet away. The closer she came, the more certain she grew. It was a person!

Liliana listened intently in the direction of the forest. The fear that the wolves might return – or whatever else had caused this carnage – sprawled across her skin. But there was no howling, no cracking sounds, no growling; not even the rustle of a mouse. The surroundings lay as silent and lifeless as the victim.

Father's warning voice resounded from her childhood days. *Never touch something dead if you don't know how it died.* He had taken the dead blue tit from her with a scowl and made Liliana scrub her hands until her skin peeled.

She knelt next to the curled-up figure. At first glance, all the limbs seemed to still be present, just not necessarily in their intended position. The entire body was blood-smeared and covered with wounds, bites and cuts. There was little left of the once exquisite clothes.

What if he wasn't dead? Could she bear the weight of never knowing whether she had left someone to die because of inflated fear?

Carefully, she touched his wrist, ignoring the throbbing in her own chest and focusing all her attention on her fingertips. Yes, there was a flutter. She slid forward to wipe the dark, blood-soaked hair out of his face.

'Can you hear me?'

He remained motionless. She checked again by holding her fingers in front of his nose. There, too, she found the barely perceptible breath of life. She couldn't leave him here. Even if he died on the way, she had to at least try to help him.

She wrapped her arms around his torso and lifted him. After a few steps, she had to put him down again. Struggling through the forest like this, bit by bit, Liliana was soon overcome by dizziness. The exertion, coupled with all the blood that had covered her chest, chin and arms, tightened her stomach. Her legs started to shake. Where was that stupid donkey?

'Donnie! Donnie! Where are you? Come back!'

Finally, she reached under the man's arms from behind and dragged him on like that. They would never reach the farm otherwise. Unfortunately, the tendrils, roots and saplings that protruded from the encrusted snow scratched his legs, leaving a scarlet line on the ground. She consoled herself with the observation that he was beyond any perception of pain.

When she finally approached the edge of the forest, the donkey appeared, as if he had been waiting for her.

Liliana scolded him with relief. 'You fool, I needed you!'

She was wondering if it made sense to heave the dying victim onto the donkey for the last stretch when she heard her name.

'What happened? I heard Donnie scream like mad!' Cedric squeezed through the bushes and rushed towards her. His eyes widened. 'You're covered in blood! Are you hurt? Who is that?'

'Cedi!' Liliana lowered herself to the ground next to the stranger. Her side ached as if a knitting needle were stuck there. 'We have to bring him into the house.'

Exerting all of her strength, she helped her brother place the stranger on Donnie. She wiped her forehead until it occurred to her that she was smearing even more blood on her face. She could taste it in her mouth already. Bite wounds ... rabies ... She quickly spat on the ground and pushed the thought far away.

As soon as they had reached the farm, Annelies came running. 'Merciful Light! What is going on?'

'Get Grandmother!' Liliana tugged at the wounded man and urged Cedi, with a nod, to lend her a hand.

The maid took one glance at the stranger and started her nagging. 'Where did you get him? From the forest? Are you crazy?'

'He's still breathing! We have to help him!'

'I am certainly not touching him!' Annelies backed away with her hands raised, as if Liliana had tried to slap her. 'You should get Priest Mathias! He's as good as dead anyway!'

Cedi hesitated but gave in to his sister's pleading looks. Together they carried the injured man to her room, and Annelies followed at a safe distance. Liliana ran to find Father's bottle of liquor. When she returned, she found Grandmother already with the others at the bedside.

Her hands on her hips, Grandmother asked, 'Why did you bring this dead body into our house?'

'He's not dead! We need to help him!'

'Oh, I don't know, dove ...'

'Imagine me or Cedi lying on that bed! You'd do anything to save us, wouldn't you?'

'Yes, yes, but ...'

'Are you that scared?' She looked around reproachfully and pointed to the wounded man. 'Look at him! We are his last hope! Here in the village, we haven't had a case of rabies in my whole lifetime.'

Annelies shook her head reluctantly, while Cedi seemed to wait for Grandmother's answer. She sighed. 'I don't think there's much we can do for him.'

'We have to at least try!' Liliana knew her grandmother well enough to know when she was about to relent. 'I'll get your ointments!'

She grabbed the bundle from Grandmother's chamber and ran back again.

'All right.' Grandmother took the bundle off her. 'Chamomile for cleansing, yarrow to stop the bleeding and ribwort to stimulate skin formation. Clean sheets for bandages. Move! This man has already lost far too much blood! But rub your hands with cider. Just in case.'

Since Annelies still refused to touch the dying man, she was sent to fetch Priest Mathias. Liliana started to remove the torn clothes from the body and clean the wounds. She had helped Grandmother patch up injured people from the village before and had believed she wasn't easily fazed. But now she felt weak on her feet.

Of course, Grandmother noticed and turned to her, using a stern voice. 'Go and wash that blood off! Thoroughly. With soap. Then get a bite of bread from the kitchen, dove.'

She nodded, took a gulp from the liquor bottle, and rinsed her mouth with another. Her throat burned as she stumbled out of the room.

'Hey, you're supposed to rub it in, not drink it!' Cedi shouted after her.

Outside, she bent over the small stream behind the oil press. In her twenty-two years, Liliana had never seen anyone in such a bad state. She washed her hands, her face and all her clothes. If her fingers hadn't gone numb, she would have enjoyed the cleansing cold.

In her wet petticoat, she staggered back to her room to get fresh clothes. There the stranger lay bandaged on a sheet on the floor, while Grandmother pulled on his outstretched arm, her foot in his armpit as a counter-lever.

Liliana dropped her pile of clothes. 'Grandmother, what are you doing?'

She heard a muffled snap, and Grandmother gently put the arm back. 'His shoulder was dislocated. That's what happened to Frederik last spring, if you remember?'

'He wouldn't stop whining,' Cedi interjected. 'At least this one knows to keep quiet.'

'Very funny, Cedi,' Liliana began, but Grandmother interrupted her.

'He needs proper stitches in some places. His torso has literally been slashed. Unfortunately, I'm no surgeon. And my eyes aren't getting any younger.'

'Then someone should get a surgeon!' Liliana said, slipping into fresh clothes.

Grandmother shook her head indecisively. She and Cedi grabbed the ends of the cloth and lifted the stranger back onto Liliana's bed. 'That would cost a lot, only for him to die on us anyway.'

'And if he dies because we didn't bother with a surgeon?'

There was a brief moment of silence, and the sounds from outside gained prevalence: the croaking of arguing chickens and a dull rumbling from the barn. Grandmother put a hand on Liliana's arm. 'We're already doing what we can. I've seen people die from far milder injuries. Today, the journey to the city and back would take too long.'

Liliana crossed her arms and said nothing.

'We'll put a compress of comfrey root on the arm here and the ribs. This looks contused, could be broken, who knows. As for the leg here, we'll need to put it back into the right position and fasten it in place. Cedric, find me two rods.'

When the two others were gone, she added quietly, 'If he survives the night, we'll ask your father to send someone to the city tomorrow. All right, my dove?'

Not taking her eyes off the stranger, Liliana nodded. Only after she could in good conscience assume that she had done everything possible for him, did she finally eat some bread and cheese. Then, lost in thought, she sat down at the weaving loom. Finding this stranger in the woods was undoubtedly the most exciting thing that had ever happened to her. Who was he?

Although she had few friends among the villagers, she would have quickly recognised one of them, even in this sorry state. In addition, the tattered clothes were of precious workmanship, with rich colours and engraved silver buttons. No one around here was dressed like that. He may have just been passing through the area. But that raised just as many new questions. Where did he come from and where was he headed? Had he been travelling alone? And if not, what had happened to his companions? Was he the only survivor? Had they thought him dead and simply left him behind?

When the others came in for lunch, Liliana hardly noticed. Because Priest Mathias was nowhere to be found, Annelies returned without him. Cedric, who had only just turned fourteen, was busy giving his account of the story. Meanwhile, Grandmother served gruel, which Hans and Jakob, the two farmhands, immediately shovelled into their mouths. Frederik and Father listened with the same sceptical lines on their forehead.

'Do we know who he is?' Father asked.

'No,' Liliana replied, and the others who had already seen the stranger shook their heads. 'I'd guess he's in his mid-twenties. His clothes were torn but too fancy for someone from around here.'

'Do you have any idea what might have happened to him?'

'No. There were wolf tracks. If it was wolves though, why would they leave him lying around and not just eat him? There were even bloody guts scattered in the trees! I've never seen anything so horrifying!'

'He must've met one of those monsters!' Annelies lowered her voice. 'I hear beasts roam the forest at night, horned and with wings. They drink blood and kidnap children.'

'You hear a lot.' Frederik rolled his eyes.

'I'm serious! My friend Lena has an aunt who almost fell victim to one. She saw a terrifying figure among the trees, whose eyes gleamed with malice in the darkness. In her village, several people have disappeared without a trace.'

This provoked another roll of Frederik's eyes, but Cedi shuddered with relish, and Jakob nodded knowingly.

'Enough of these old wives' tales,' Father grumbled. 'It was scavenging birds. Ravens will peck at a carcass, for example, and if they got too greedy and dropped parts or fought over them ...'

But Annelies wasn't cut back so easily. 'Two nights later, a sinister figure crept around Lena's house and sniffed around everywhere. The chickens didn't lay eggs for a whole week because they got such a fright!'

'Oh, come on,' Cedi interposed. 'Now that's made-up! I bet it was just an unlucky suitor who made his rounds at beautiful Lena's house, like a mangy tomcat. She should be glad he didn't sing.'

'Talking about suitors.' Frederik diverted the conversation. 'You told us about your uncle the other day, Annelies. His engagement broke off?'

He gave Liliana a meaningful look and she put on an uncaring expression, although she was tempted to kick his leg under the table. She had no plans of getting engaged to anyone's uncle.

'Oh, it was terrible!'

Annelies immediately picked up on this prompt and talked about a dispute over a long hair that the fiancée had discovered on a coat collar. Liliana sighed inwardly. It probably came from a horse. As long as Annelies held the attention of the table, the maid didn't care what kind of nonsense she spouted. But Liliana was bored with trivialities disguised as grave news. Usually, they weren't even very inventive. She would have preferred to immerse herself in one of her books, which touched her with their skilful narrative no matter how many times she'd read them already.

Soon, Father chased them back to work. In winter they had more leeway, yet there was a long list of tasks that needed doing every day. The harvest had been so successful this year that the men were still busy threshing. Liliana preferred not to go back into the forest for now and continued to weave until it was time to milk. She would look for resin for Grandmother's incense and pitch ointments another day.

In the evening, the family sat in the living room as usual. Since this was open to the kitchen, the heat of the stove spread well. In addition to carving, braiding, spinning and weaving, there was a lot of chatting and gossiping. Liliana gladly took this opportunity to disappear into her room and read. Father took pride in having a daughter who read, so she didn't care when Annelies and Cedi accused her of wanting to avoid work.

Although, this time, Liliana was drawn to her room not only by her books but also by curiosity and concern for the stranger. He was still lying there like a corpse. Relieved, she watched the blanket move gently up and down over his chest. She grabbed one of her books but kept looking up, because she knew the tale she read almost by heart. Before she set up straw sacks in the living room to sleep on, she'd fetch a warming pan so that he wouldn't freeze.

'Don't give up,' she said softly.

Chapter Two

As soon as Liliana awoke, she tiptoed to her room. In the dim light, the injured stranger looked even paler. She held her breath as she searched for his. So far, she had only seen three dead people up close: her grandfather, Uncle Tony, and her mother. The memory of her mother on her deathbed was already fading. The pictures of Grandfather and Uncle Tony, on the other hand, still resided clearly in her mind: the skin like wax, the limbs stiff and the faces empty.

No, the stranger was not dead. And as long as he was fighting for his life, she would too.

She intercepted Father before breakfast to make her request. If he made his decision before Frederik and the others could voice their concerns, he would stick to it. She didn't forget to mention that Grandmother supported the idea. After all, he had survived the night, and that was a good sign. Father agreed.

'Frederik is fastest on the horse. If you take over Cedric's work with the animals, he can replace Frederik. Annelies will just have to milk a little longer.'

Liliana first fed Donnie and the horse, Elisa, so that Frederik could start his journey as soon as possible. Then she took care of the cows, sheep, pigs and finally the chickens. She gratefully accepted Hans' help, and he joined her briefly during lunch break to muck out the stables. It was exhausting, but at least the movement warmed her. Every time she crossed the yard, she pricked up her ears in the hope of hooves clattering.

In the early afternoon, Frederik came back with the surgeon. Under Grandmother's watchful eyes, he loosened some of the bandages to look at the stranger's wounds. She relaxed a little when he praised their efforts so far. In the case of bite wounds, cleaning and then moist bandages were appropriate. However, he wanted to make an excision on the edge of the wounds in some places and suture the deep cuts. Liliana watched from the door. Finally, he wrapped a thick layer of sheets coated with egg whites around the broken leg.

'Immobilisation is important for healing. Although, um, that doesn't seem to be a problem right now. Was he in an unconscious state to begin with?'

Grandmother answered affirmatively, whereupon the surgeon continued, shaking his head. 'I treat patients every day, but I've never come across anything like this. The deep wound on the torso and the countless other injuries ... his survival borders on a miracle. We'll see if fate continues to favour him. If poorly managed, a single bite wound can turn into a death sentence. Keep an eye on his mental state as much as possible. He doesn't seem like a victim of rabies. Fever and nausea would be typical. But I have encountered a strange accumulation of infected people in the last couple of days. And you, um, never know ... so be careful with bodily fluids and abrasions, or open wounds on your hands. We don't want anyone to get infected.'

'If he had rabies, he'd be spitting and biting,' Liliana objected.

'In the last stage, and not necessarily. But as I said, his symptoms don't actually indicate such an infection.' The doctor collected his instruments and tins of medicine. 'When he wakes up, um, *if* he wakes up, he's going to be in a lot of pain. Should I leave something for that?'

'Yes please,' Liliana said emphatically, before anyone else answered.

The surgeon accepted his payment in clarified butter, linen and a few iron pennies. Then he climbed back on his horse. Liliana's find in the forest had upended the regular flow of things on the farm. Yet the excitement had also brought a welcome change to the daily grind.

After dinner, Liliana sat down by her bed, trying to get the stranger to drink something. His eyes remained closed, but he stirred and mumbled something, so she proceeded to gently lift his head and put a cup to his lips. At first, he seemed to swallow, but then he began to make panicked, stifled sounds. The gagging turned into wheezing and finally hissing.

Before Liliana knew it, the cup had rolled across the floor and the stranger was snarling and howling. His half-open eyes rolled in his sockets. Fortunately, the others were quickly on the spot. Father and Frederik pushed him down; Cedric threw himself on his feet. Nevertheless, the stranger resisted, continuing to make the sounds of an angry, drowning animal.

'Holy Light, help us! What's wrong with him?' Annelies entered the room and threw her hands in the air. Even the farmhands stuck their heads in.

Grandmother pushed past them. 'Dove, what are you doing? Don't put anything in his mouth if he's not conscious!'

'He seemed to be waking up ... I mean, he's moving!'

Grandmother replied with a stern look. 'I know you're eager to help, but you could drown a man if you're not careful!'

Shaken, Liliana watched the stranger still struggling against Father and her brothers. After a few moments, he slackened, presumably because he had run out of strength.

Once the excitement had passed, the room emptied again, except for Liliana, Grandmother and Father. Liliana heard the others' voices from the living room.

'Goodness!'

'He was growling like a mad animal!'

'I'm telling you, he's rabid! Maybe Liliana *should* drown him!'

Meanwhile, Father frowned. 'It's commendable that you want to help this stranger. But did you think about the danger you might've dragged in with him?' he asked Liliana.

'We've put him in *my* bed. If you're worried, just stay away from my room. Besides, he doesn't have rabies.' She looked at Grandmother, expecting her to agree.

'Dove, you heard the surgeon. We can't rule anything out. But it may well be that the whole experience was too much for his soul. Or he thought you were trying to end his life after all.'

'I don't just mean rabies,' Father continued. 'Whoever did this could ... come back.'

Liliana swallowed and kept silent. She hadn't considered that; at least not since she'd left the forest.

Grandmother went to prepare one of her herbal mixtures, and Liliana heard her working with the mortar in the kitchen. Father grumbled something into his beard and joined the others in the living room. Thankfully, he was letting the matter rest for now.

Liliana very much hoped that the stranger's wounds hadn't reopened. At least his leg was well fixed in place. She didn't dare have a closer look. Annelies liked to exaggerate, but Liliana herself had become a little anxious after this incident. If he did have rabies, it would in fact be more merciful to just end his misery. And should anyone have been infected ... No, that was highly unlikely. After all, they had taken precautions, and it wasn't like he had bitten anyone.

Grandmother came back with a stone bowl, in which she had already placed a glowing piece of coal. 'An incense mixture of meadowsweet, bedstraw, spruce resin, and juniper.' She placed the jar on the floor at sufficient distance from the bed. 'Soothing and purifying. To maintain vitality.'

Only when they were confident the stranger had calmed down did they leave the room. They locked the door, just in case. If he called for help, Liliana would hear it, seeing as she slept in the adjacent living room.

That night, she felt more restless than she had done in a long time. Pale moonlight squeezed through the cracks and gave the furniture surrounding her a life of its own. Normally, the wind blowing around the house intensified the cosy feeling of warmth inside. Now the usual background noises seemed threatening. The occasional scraping and mooing from the stables only fed her restlessness. She wished she could lie in her familiar bed. But the stranger lay there now.

When Father unlocked her room again the next day and peered through the door, along with Liliana, the injured stranger lay motionless, as on the first morning. The smell of Grandmother's incense mixture hung in the air. Despite Liliana's tiredness, she and Annelies finished milking in time for breakfast. In addition to the porridge, Grandmother had prepared tea with chamomile, lemon balm, and lavender, which she wanted to give to the stranger. Although nothing changed Liliana kept stopping by her room every time she had a break to eat. Once, when she entered the room and knelt beside the bed, he suddenly opened his eyes. They had a soft glow that she'd never seen before in an eye colour: brown with a golden undertone, a kind of bronze. Those eyes were fixed directly on Liliana, who was readying herself to quickly get out of reach should he lash out again.

'Thirsty.' His voice sounded like a rooster whose throat was being twisted. He could speak!

Relieved, Liliana called for Grandmother. She hurried over with Father and Frederik in tow. 'Have some of my soothing tea!'

Liliana held his head, and Grandmother poured him the drink. The stranger grimaced as if they'd given him bile. His eyes jumped from Grandmother to Father and back to Liliana.

'Where am I?'

'Our farm is located on the Lindenbach in Heidenried,' Liliana replied in a tone that she hoped was friendly and comforting.

The injured stranger let out a groaning sigh. Then he slipped back into unconsciousness. Grandmother took the opportunity to check on his wounds and his leg.

Hoping he would talk more and solve some of the riddles he posed, Liliana ran to him every free minute thereafter. But he didn't wake up until dinnertime. The servants took over cleaning the kitchen while Grandmother and Annelies dressed warmly to spend the last hours of the day over at the Mosers'. Once a week, the women of the village met there to chat, knit and sew together.

'Are you joining us tonight, dove?'

'I'd rather stay here in case he wakes up again,' Liliana said. She didn't want to miss that. She had found him, and she wanted to be the first to know what had happened out there in the forest.

'I don't know why we're even asking,' Annelies exclaimed from the front door, Father's lantern in one hand and a basket of wool in the other. 'She always has an excuse.'

Liliana didn't object but smiled apologetically and sat down at the loom. She could imagine exactly how the sewing bee would go. Annelies would talk about Liliana's find at length, making it sound as if she'd acted irresponsibly and risked her whole family getting rabies. The fact that the maid liked to wag her tongue didn't bother her much if it meant she wasn't getting interrogated herself. But the best option was to not be present at all.

A gush of cold night air swept in through the door when Annelies tore it open. As soon as the two women had left, Liliana scurried into her room, grabbed her book of fairy tales, and sat down next to her bed. Every time she turned a page, she looked up at the sleeping stranger.

Liliana really liked his features, even if they were sunken in his present state. She eyed the pale face, framed by dark hair. The tip of his nose seemed to be pointing slightly upward, and stubble began to grow on his chin and cheeks.

Suddenly, his eyelids fluttered, and his eyes snapped open. Was it the prancing flame of the tallow candle, or were they glowing with fever? She stretched out her hand to feel the temperature of his forehead. It felt cool.

Then his pupils dilated, and he panted out hoarsely, 'Don't touch me! Away! Away from me!'

Liliana, remembering the previous night vividly, hastily withdrew her hand and hurried back into the living room. Hans and Jakob were probably scrubbing the pots by the stream or had already retired to sleep. In any case, she found only father and Cedi. She beckoned them both over.

'He's behaving strangely again. But he doesn't have a fever, honestly!'

When she returned to the room with them, the stranger lay there in a deep slumber.

'Maybe you're making him restless, mooching about all the time. Let's just leave him alone.'

Cedi's assumption displeased Liliana. 'I just want him to feel that he's not alone. That someone is taking care of him.'

'We don't know what he's experienced,' Father said. 'In his head, he's still struggling to survive. In a way, that's true. When Priest Mathias is back, he needs to come over and have a look.'

Chapter Three

Despite Cedi's misgivings, Liliana stopped by her room the next day whenever the opportunity presented itself. Since it had been she who found the stranger, she felt responsible for him. She refused to believe that her presence was bothersome but tried hard not to wake him with loud noises or by touching him. Father let Cedi help with the winnow, so Liliana had to do the feeding of the animals. Father had built the winnowing machine himself after the concept had been explained to him by a traveller at the market. It helped them to separate the grains from chaff and dust. Hans came back to help her clean out the stables again.

The two farmhands had been hired at the same time. While Jakob, who had a fickle disposition, quickly became friends with Frederik and Annelies, Hans was the one whom Father preferred. He was a reliable bloke whose head was well screwed on, as Father put it. Liliana also liked Hans better. He was calm, not in a gruff kind of way like Uncle Tony had been – may his soul be united with the Light – but in a peaceful way. He reminded her of a tree that felt comfortable in its place and sprouted vigorously, thanks to deep roots.

'Do you think he'll make it?' Hans asked between two fork throws.

Liliana knew immediately who he was referring to. 'Hard to say. I very much hope so. Grandmother says we must pray that the wounds don't get infected.'

'And what will you do with him if he gets better?'

'I suppose he'll go home as soon as he's well enough. Wherever his home may be.'

'If he's rich, maybe he'll reward you.'

'Who knows ...'

'I'm sure you've already made up a hundred stories about what might have happened.'

'I don't have the slightest idea! He may have been part of a merchant convoy that was attacked by wolves. But that doesn't make sense, because wolves don't generally attack humans and our village is far from any trade routes. Even if they wanted to take a weird shortcut ... Or do you think he was on the run?'

'From whom?'

'From the henchmen of a neighbouring territory. Because he discovered a terrible secret.'

'Your find is strange, all right. But I don't think you've stumbled upon a world-shaking conspiracy.'

'Well, then he's just a servant who tried to assume the identity of his master and was exposed. His master chased him away, and now he wanders around begging for his sustenance.'

'In the middle of the forest?'

'Or maybe he's the son of a justice of the peace who made himself so hated with his arrogance that he was kidnapped and abandoned in the forest.'

'That sounds more likely.'

'Or he's a gleeman who dressed up for a play and got lost out here in his drunkenness after a wild night ...'

Hans shook his head, but Liliana saw the smile hiding under his straw-blond beard.

She grinned at him and returned to pondering. None of these ideas actually explained the carnage. Moreover, there had been at least one other victim who hadn't survived. Shivering, she suppressed the images.

After eating sour milk and bread with the others at noon, she snuck back into her room, feeling the need to reassure herself that he was still there and not dead. She meant to only take a quick look, but as she snuck away, he stirred and groaned. Since she wasn't sure what sort of state he was in, she paused and watched him closely.

'Where am I? Who are you?'

'Still on our farm, on the Lindenbach in Heidenried. My name is Liliana, and I live here.' She hesitantly approached the bed. 'May I put my hand on your forehead to see if you have a fever?'

'I don't have a fever. But everything hurts. I can hardly move.'

She got closer, and he remained calm. Almost reverently, she put her hand on his forehead and found his skin still cool. 'Grandmother's tea helps with all sorts of problems. And the doctor left this remedy here for the pain.'

She gave him both, and he swallowed willingly. Then she asked the question that had inspired all her speculations: 'And who are you? What were you doing in the forest?'

He closed his eyes, and at first, she thought he was falling asleep again. Then he opened them again with a lost expression. 'I don't know.'

'Can you tell me where you're from? Or what your name is?'

His gaze held on to her helplessly. 'I don't know.'

'Hmm, well ... I'm Liliana. What should I call you? You can choose something if your name doesn't come to mind.'

He took time to think. 'El ... just El.'

'El. All right.'

Before she could ask any more questions, he closed his eyes once more, this time apparently as a sign that he had talked enough. Liliana dashed into the kitchen to share the news. Only Grandmother was still there, stirring her pot. She had gotten hold of some chicken bones and boiled them overnight so that the marrow came off. Later, she would cook potatoes, vegetables and wild herbs along with it. That way, the broth became particularly nutritious and at the same time easily digestible. Liliana recounted the brief conversation she'd just had with the stranger.

Grandmother nodded thoughtfully. 'I've heard that people can lose their memory after an accident or other distressing incident. It'll probably come back on its own after a little while.' She tapped her forehead. 'Unless there's really something broken up there.'

Thanks to Hans' help, Liliana had a moment before she had to do the second feeding of the day. She set out to collect brushwood, resin, and speedwell. Although she felt uneasy doing so, she went back to the place where she'd found the stranger. Perhaps she had missed something that could give them further clues. The forest floor was only white in spots, like the fur of a flecked cow. Everything that had pointed to the mysterious attack except for the fallen trees had disappeared, or more precisely, been eaten by wild animals. Liliana tried to imagine wolves pouncing on their victims with such greed that intestines splashed up and got stuck in the branches above. And what if there really was something to Annelies' beast story? Fortunately, the rustling in the undergrowth and the occasional birdsong were back, so she no longer felt unable to breathe in the oppressive silence.

At dinner, Liliana repeated what the stranger had said. After all, he now had a name. Then the weather was discussed, and the whole table agreed that they were expecting another cold snap. Grandmother felt it in her bones, the farmhands and Cedric observed it in the animals' behaviour and Father smelled it in the air. The chicken broth was well received.

Armed with a portion of said broth, Liliana ventured to the stranger's bed after dinner. He awoke immediately and swallowed greedily, his gaze fixed on the bowl. There were so many questions swirling around in her head that she didn't quite know where to start. If he was missing his memories, he couldn't answer most of them, and she didn't want to overwhelm him.

'Do you remember me?'

He looked up briefly. 'Yes.'

The fact that he could remember newer things was a good sign.

'How's the pain?'

'Don't ask.'

Liliana would've liked to know if his curt manner was part of his personality or due to the pain he was in. To wake up in a strange environment, in this agonising state and unable to recollect anything ... No, she didn't envy him.

Once the bowl was empty, she gave him the medicine, and Grandmother came to look at his wounds. She loosened the bandages in some places, careful not to damage the skin that had already healed. She rubbed on some of the ointment containing the resin Liliana had collected. The stranger grimaced but made no sound.

'That's my grandmother,' Liliana said. 'She's nursed many people back to health.'

Since he lay there quietly afterwards, Liliana stayed in the room. She was eager to talk to him more, but he kept his eyes closed, exhaustion on his face. So she sat down with her book, in front of the wardrobe. It was a precious, carved piece of furniture that Father had given to her mother after their wedding.

'How did I get here?'

Astonished, she looked up. His eyes were still closed, but it seemed he felt her presence in the room. 'I found you half-dead in the woods and brought you here.'

A pause followed, during which Liliana watched him over the edge of the book. What a peculiar way of speaking he had ... Although she understood him clearly, the melody of his sentences sounded strange to her ears. His lips formed the words with precision, as if every single one of them deserved to be heard.

'Be honest, what are my chances?'

'The fact that you survived the first few days is amazing. If you keep going like this, I'm sure you'll make it.'

A hint of a smile appeared on his lips. He opened his eyes and slowly turned his head to look at her, quietly grunting with pain. 'What … are you reading?'

The bronze colour of his eyes still fascinated her. 'Oh, this? A collection of fairy tales.'

Another pause followed while they studied each other.

'You like books?'

'I do. Would you like me to read you one of the stories?'

'Yes, please.'

Liliana cleared her throat. 'Most farmers struggle with reading. While I am by far the best reader in the family, it probably still sounds bungled to trained ears.'

The stranger gave her another smile to acknowledge her efforts and closed his eyes. Liliana began to read. She hadn't read out loud in a long time. No one here shared her enthusiasm for books. Why would they? There always seemed to be gossip to share, and after a day of hard work, most people in the village didn't want to overexert their tired brains. For them, books were an expensive and superfluous possession. When Cedi had been younger, she'd taught him to read. As with many other activities, her little brother started on it with great zeal, only to lose interest after the first few strides. Reading to someone who may be well educated made her nervous. But she soon found her rhythm. As intended, the stranger relaxed. Distraction was a good antidote to pain.

Chapter Four

The following day was baking day. Liliana and Annelies prepared several loaves of bread with sourdough, which had to be kneaded for a long time before baking. It was strange how quickly normality had returned to the farm. The stranger in Liliana's room was already as much a part of the daily routine as the cattle in the stables. She had fallen into the habit of seeing him before or after a meal. He started to stay awake for longer periods, especially in the evenings. This worked out well for her because in winter the family spent more time indoors after dark.

She fed El more of the chicken broth, from which an appetising cloud of steam rose. Her nose would no longer have recognised the room as hers. The smell of the stranger, with his bandaged wounds, and the smoked herbs had settled as a thick layer over everything else. Since he hadn't had any other scary attacks, they could probably rule out rabies. Liliana was very relieved about this.

'What's the first thing you remember?' she asked him after he'd finished drinking.

El stared at the ceiling with a blank expression. 'Pain. Blood. Darkness. Then this room here. You.'

'Do you have any idea what could have happened to you out there in the forest?'

'No.'

'Where did you come from? Why were you there?'

He was silent for some time, after which Liliana apologised. 'I don't mean to torment you with my questions! All this just makes me wonder. It was a real bloodbath. I also found wolf tracks, but could wolves do such a thing? Even a few felled trees ...'

She broke off. If she'd understood Grandmother correctly, what the others had called rabies could've been the wild despair that the experience had triggered in him. If so, it wasn't wise to conjure it up again too soon.

'In any case, you are safe now. We'll take good care of you. You already know Grandmother. Then there is my father, my brothers Frederik and Cedric, Annelies, who is our maid, and the farmhands, Hans and Jakob.'

Tilting his head slightly to the side, he finally looked at her. 'No mother?'

'My mother died shortly after Cedi's birth. I was eight years old.'

'I'm sorry to hear that.'

'Of course, I wish she was still here. But that's life. She taught me how to read, by the way. At least the beginnings of it.'

'Is that why you appreciate it so much?'

'I've never thought about it like that, but yes, I guess so. I inherited her books. Do you want to see them?' Without waiting for an answer, Liliana opened her chest in the corner. She got out the books one by one and piled them up next to her. 'I have fifteen.'

El nodded and let his eyes fly over the titles. So, he could indeed read, and very quickly at that. 'Your mother liked fairy tales and travel novels. Had she always lived on a farm?'

'No, not from birth.' Liliana's hand rested on her precious stack of books. 'She married my father against the will of her family. I have never met that family. They didn't even attend her funeral. They probably live somewhere in the south of the territory, because her father, my grandfather, was a fabric merchant.'

'What was her maiden name?'

'Zumbrunn. My mother's name was Emma Zumbrunn. You—'

'Liliana!' Annelies' voice could be heard all over the courtyard. 'Are you coming? Help me with the loaves!'

She carefully put her books back. Annelies was the only one who got audibly upset with Liliana when she neglected her tasks because she was chasing fairies or visiting exotic countries in her imagination. While the others laughed about it or simply accepted it, Liliana suspected that Annelies' lack of understanding was joined by feelings of jealousy. While she, Annelies, had to work on someone else's farm, Liliana lived with her own family, who treated her leniently. Father usually assigned the lightest work to her, and Grandmother often took her aside to show her how to make herbal concoctions. Since Annelies couldn't change her circumstances, she expressed her displeasure in targeted impatience and frequent complaints.

After the bread, it was time for milking. Annelies had forgotten her anger and was chatting away again. She was looking forward to cradling her sister's infant after church tomorrow. She also promised to ask whether anyone in her home village knew who this stranger could be.

At dinner, the conversation turned to the chickens. One of the older laying hens looked badly battered after a skirmish. Cedi said he would take extra care so that she wouldn't starve to death at the bottom of the pecking order. Liliana ate fast and then grabbed some soup for El.

Grandmother joined her. She only loosened the bandages in certain places, so as not to impair wound healing. The ribwort extract had left dark discolouration, but there was no nasty inflammation or suppuration. In some places, the skin already looked rather healthy.

No sooner had Grandmother lit her herbs and left, than Father came in. He patted a few wooden rasps off his trouser leg.

'Thought I'd drop by ...'

El made an effort to sit up, but Liliana shook her head. Instead, he contented himself with a pained smile.

'I would like to express my deep gratitude for the hospitality and excellent care. I cannot, at least in my current state, give anything in return. Should I ever be in a position to do so, I shall of course repay you for your generosity.'

Surprised, Father exchanged a glance with Liliana. He was visibly confused as to how one should react to such courtesy. 'No need, uhm ... I just wanted to see how you are.'

'Grandmother is very pleased with his progress,' replied Liliana.

'Well then ...' Although he only went back to the adjoining room, Father nodded a formal goodbye. Liliana suppressed an amused grin.

Sighing with exhaustion, El put his head down and immediately turned to Liliana. 'I would also like to thank you ... You said you found me half-dead in the woods. Why didn't you just leave me there?'

'Why?' Liliana sat up straight. 'I couldn't do that! Once I knew there was still life in you. I mean, if I'm ever injured in the forest, I hope that others take pity on me and won't leave me to die.'

He didn't say anything, just looked at her as if she'd said something extremely curious.

'By the way, I didn't find anything else around that spot in the forest. There are no clues I could give you. Except perhaps your buttons.' Liliana had put them at the bottom of her closet. 'Here. They were on your clothes. The rest of it was burned by Annelies. There was hardly anything left anyway, and we thought you might have rabies.'

El briefly studied the buttons held out to him. 'I don't see anything special about them.'

'Well, I think they could be made of real silver. And there's a fine engraving with a ... leafless tree, perhaps?'

'You can keep them. As partial compensation.'

A little disappointed, she put the buttons back. Other than that, she had nothing to show in connection with his person. 'Do you have a family?'

'Probably.'

'Brothers or sisters?'

'Maybe.'

Why did she feel like she was running up against a wall every time she tried to help him recover his memory? Perhaps he felt the same way; for him, it had to be even more frustrating. Liliana pulled out the book from the night before and started reading aloud. It didn't take long before she heard him breathe more calmly.

Chapter Five

Hans squeezed onto the bench next to Liliana. The many bodies kept the village church warm. The sermon offered everyone an opportune break in the work-laden week. Before it started, there was always a lively exchange among the villagers, so Priest Mathias had put together a makeshift gong with a brass bowl and a wooden spoon. Liliana was particularly fond of the short stories he included in his preachings to illustrate the point he was trying to make. He usually warned them against moral corruption or admonished them to support each other in need. Today, he spoke about the power of prayer.

'Never forget that the prayer of a pure soul can work wonders,' he said.

She also liked the singing, despite the wrong notes that crept in. The last song served as the starting signal for a new competition of converging voices. Liliana mostly waited around while Grandmother gave advice for all kinds of ailments and Father was dragged into conversations from several sides. Her brothers chatted over the heads of the others with their comrades. She heard the word 'stranger' several times and knew that the news of her find in the forest had spread like spurs in the wind. What had Annelies told the women at the sewing bee?

When the church finally began to empty, multiple villagers approached her.

'Where did you find him?'

'What does he look like?'

'Will he survive?'

'How can you be sure he doesn't have rabies?'

She was glad when Hans quickly took her by the hand and led her outside. All of a sudden, the church had become too stuffy. 'I bet we'll have visitors today,' he whispered.

Indeed, half the village passed by their farm in the course of the afternoon. Grandmother happily accepted eggs, apples and other bribes that were offered as an excuse to satisfy curiosity. Meanwhile, Liliana tried in vain to shoo away all the heads that were stuck in her room.

'Shhh, you're waking him up! He's still recovering!'

El kept his eyes closed the whole time, but she was convinced that he was aware of the uproar. Uncle Bernd and Cousin Valerie were invited to stay for dinner. Of the girls in the village, Liliana liked Valerie most. She was a simple soul but treated everyone with kindness. Together, they helped Grandmother prepare potatoes with beans and cured meat. Since Annelies would not return from her family's village until later, the farmhands took over the milking.

During the meal, Priest Mathias showed up and was also given a plate. In this smaller setting, Liliana enjoyed the feeling of community.

'I'm sorry I couldn't come earlier,' Priest Mathias said after giving thanks for the meal. 'What's important is that we all pray for the stranger. The Holy Light can heal everything if it sees fit to do so.'

Liliana took the opportunity to get his opinion on a remark made by the surgeon from the city. 'The doctor said that there has been an unusually large number of rabies victims. Did you know about that?'

Priest Mathias looked at her thoughtfully. 'I didn't want to spread panic, so I haven't commented on it yet. But yes, that's one of the reasons I want to see your mysterious stranger. I spoke with other priests about the increasing number of deaths in the area. Some report rabies, others speak of possession.'

'Is there nothing you can do about it?'

Priest Mathias sighed. 'Fortunately, no one has caught it here in the village. Those affected lash out, drool, roll their eyes, suffer from convulsions, cramps, fever and pain. They tend to be unresponsive. In addition, they display bouts of rage and impaired perception. Most of the time, they run away and wander around, or they are killed because they hurt themselves as well as others. The other priests report that blessings of healing only aggravate the symptoms.'

'Our stranger is definitely responsive and behaves normally now,' Liliana said hurriedly.

After the meal, Priest Mathias took a look at El. He decided that their stranger didn't have rabies and said a short prayer at the end of the bed. Liliana smiled complacently as he praised the good deed the family had done. Then he pulled out a ritual knife from the expanse of his robe and made a cut into the outer edge of his left hand. He smeared a drop of blood on El's forehead. She noticed how El's body stiffened, even though he pretended to be asleep. But she kept this observation to herself. Everyone bowed their heads until Priest Mathias had finished.

'If his condition deteriorates, call on me so that I can commend his soul to the Light.'

It was getting late by the time everyone had left, and Liliana was finally able to bring El some tea and food. She fed him silently; he needed the respite. When she wanted to leave, he held her back.

'Who was that man dressed in white?'

'You mean Priest Mathias?'

'Why was he here? Why did he recite that incantation? What has he done to me?'

Puzzled, Liliana approached the bed again and knelt so that they were at the same height. He looked at her with clear eyes, but his jaw remained tense.

'That wasn't an incantation. On the contrary. He prayed for you and gave you a blessing of healing. It means you ought to have more strength now.'

As far as Liliana understood, a blessing of healing did not heal in the same sense that herbal remedies did, which, depending on the composition, triggered a specific effect in the body. A blessing of healing strengthened one's vitality. Therefore, Priest Mathias used the blessing only when there was a hope of recovery. Otherwise, he would end up prolonging the suffering. Grandmother had always believed the two arts complemented each other perfectly.

'Hm.'

'Have you never seen a priest before?'

'Apparently not. And if I did, it wasn't a pleasant experience.'

Most villages featured a church, and if they didn't have their own priest, as they did in Heidenried, one came by regularly for special occasions or the odd sermon. Liliana didn't know anyone who had never been to church. Then again, most city dwellers probably found little room in their busy lives for what they dismissed as useless superstition.

'Have you never been to a church before?'

El cleared his throat. 'Won't you read to me today?'

She regarded him thoughtfully. The fact that he found it uncomfortable to answer her questions only made her more curious. At the same time, she didn't want to press him in case he stopped talking to her altogether. Finally, she gave in and leaned back against the box.

'I thought you'd want to recover from all the turmoil.'

'Exactly.' He smiled.

Returning his smile, Liliana took a book out of her chest. 'I'm sorry you've been disturbed so much today. Rarely does anything as exciting as your appearance happen around here. At least we now know that you are not Heinrich's niece's fiancé.'

'At least we know that much,' he sighed.

Chapter Six

Two weeks had passed since Liliana had brought the stranger home. She noticed that she'd not only become accustomed to his presence but was enjoying the time spent at his side. Although he couldn't remember anything from his own life, he boasted a wide range of general knowledge. As he was conscious longer and longer, they were also able to talk more extensively.

El didn't seem to know Heidenried or the surrounding villages, except for Roinnenstadt, the city they were subjected to for governance. She got one of her mother's books out, which contained a sketched map of the continent. It consisted of six territories. Roinnenstadt was located at the northwestern tip of the Highlands, which bordered the Moorlands in the north and the Lowlands in the west. There were also the Harshlands, the Lakelands, and somewhere out there at the southwestern end of the continent, the famous Silver Coast jutted out into the sea.

She asked El to point his finger on the map, to where he thought he might be from. But he just shook his head. On the other hand, the names of the larger cities of the Highlands seemed familiar to him, and he knew how to describe most of them, too. He could even name the four ports of Trinago and the major festivals in Jasnok – and these places were far beyond territory borders.

That didn't necessarily mean he had been there in person. He could have collected this information from books and hearsay, like Liliana herself, because crossing a territorial border without a trading permit was strictly forbidden. If he'd done that, it would make him either a chosen merchant who had been separated from his goods and his escort ... or a fugitive from the law. The latter would explain his peculiar way of speaking, but Liliana decided to keep these speculations to herself. They were just speculations, after all.

El also began to move more. When Liliana brought him food, he propped himself up, and while she was talking to him, he sometimes stretched his stiff limbs. Once, she heard a dull thud in the middle of the night. Fearing another kind of attack, she grabbed the lantern and cast a cautious glance into her room. El had slumped at the end of the bed. A cold breeze poured in through the only window, and snowflakes scurried in. The winter covering had been removed somehow. Just when a snowstorm was approaching, El had opened the window! Was the air too stuffy? Had he developed a fever after all and wanted to cool down? Or had he tried to break out?

She hurriedly helped him back to bed and set about locking the window. She spoke quietly but clearly to him.

'Why are you trying to get up? You're still much too weak. If I hadn't heard you, you'd have frozen to death here on the floor!'

El just mumbled to himself, '... much better ...'

'Even if you feel much better, your injuries still have a lot of healing to do!'

Back on her temporary bed, Liliana curled herself tightly into her woollen blanket. The blizzard pounced on the house and shook it furiously from all sides. How long would it last?

The morning was not recognisable as such. Armed with the storm lantern and still wrapped in their blankets, Liliana and Annelies went milking. Normally, the animals were allowed outside even in winter. But now Father made sure that they all remained safely inside and were well cared for. Most of their sheep were already showing signs of pregnancy, as well as one of the cows.

Later, while eating, they learned from Cedi that the old laying hen, who had recently lost a quarrel, had disappeared. He insisted that the hole in the fence hadn't been there the night before. Maybe the other chickens had chased her away? Cedi searched for the hen for a while in the snowy flurry, although she'd probably been caught by a fox or frozen to death by then.

Other than that, the day felt like a very long evening. The fire was burning in the stove, and everyone spent as much time as possible in the living room. Hans helped Annelies with dairy processing, Grandmother simmered herbal tinctures, Jakob sat at the loom, Frederik carved spoons and Liliana mended worn-out clothes. Father was at the spinning wheel and retold some of his adventures. Liliana always loved to hear the story of how he and Mother had met. Their paths crossed at the annual summer market in Roinnenstadt, where they both sold goods with their respective fathers.

El slept the whole time and didn't wake up when Liliana gently nudged him to give him something to eat and drink. Since he was breathing deeply and everything else seemed to be in perfect order, she left it at that. It wasn't until the evening that Grandmother came to check his wounds and wash him. He woke up when they loosened the bandages. Seeing as his injuries had already healed surprisingly well, they also unwrapped his upper body. The terrible tear over the abdomen and chest had almost completely closed over with scar tissue.

'We couldn't have hoped for better progress,' Grandmother said appreciatively. 'We needed a miracle, and that is what we got! There hasn't been any bad suppuration or inflammation. Priest Mathias is a true master.'

'I feel much more alive.'

El propped himself up, showing a sleepy smile. Liliana couldn't help but smile back.

'I'm happy to hear it.'

When she set about cleaning him with warm water, he said he could do it himself and asked for the washcloth. Liliana thought it appropriate to leave him alone. But Grandmother placed her hands on her hips.

'The broken leg remains secured, but your belly is almost healed, and you seem to be much more cheerful. It's time for you to start eating properly again!'

'Yes, madam,' replied El. His expression didn't give away whether he wanted to be polite or if he was teasing her.

Grandmother just snorted and sent Liliana to get soup, bread and butter. El sat up in bed and, under Grandmother's scrutinising gaze, obediently devoured everything. 'Thank you very much, that was certainly very … nutritious.'

Meanwhile, Liliana rummaged around in the chest she kept in a corner of her room. She'd just come up with a new idea that might help El's memory. She found the simple cloth in which she wrapped her mirror.

'Here.' She exchanged the empty bowl in El's hands with the mirror. He looked at the angular shape of his face and rubbed his stubble. His eyebrows had a natural curl, and even with a neutral face, he looked as if he was refraining from making an ironic remark or studying something fascinating in the distance.

'And?'

'I'm sure I must've looked more appealing than this.'

'No, I mean, doesn't your own image trigger anything? Any memories of who you are?'

'If you are asking whether I recognise myself, the answer is no. Maybe if I were properly shaved …'

He returned the mirror, and Liliana took a quick glance at herself. In the face looking back at her, she saw round cheeks that tapered into a pointed chin. The blue of her eyes looked rather grey in the dim light. Her lips were chapped, but despite the season, she boasted a healthy, rosy complexion.

'And?'

Surprised and somewhat caught, she looked up. El grinned. Grandmother remarked that she still had some work to do and left. Silence ensued, accompanied by the squeaking of the loom and the voices in the living room. The wind outside had finally subsided.

'This mirror belonged to my mother,' Liliana said. 'I also inherited her comb and a few nice ribbons and dresses.'

El listened attentively, although Liliana couldn't imagine him being particularly excited by ribbons and dresses.

'My mother also instilled it in me to comb my hair every day,' she continued her chatter. 'And to put oil on the tips to keep it supple.'

'But you always wear your hair in a braid?'

'Of course. A woman with loose hair will not be seen as ... the reputable sort.'

'What a shame ...'

She packed the mirror away to hide a flattered smile. Sometimes, she wished she had Valerie's golden head of curls instead of her nut-brown hair. Still, she couldn't complain; after combing, it fell over her waist with a rich shine.

Since the window had been opened at night, the air in her room was fresher. Nevertheless, she feared that the herbal smoke would never completely disappear from the cracks. She turned back to El and took the opportunity to ask the question that had been swirling around in her head all day.

'There's something I need to know. Don't you feel comfortable with us?'

'As comfortable as one can feel with strangers. You saved my life. What more could I want?'

'Last night ...' Liliana lowered her voice, although it was unlikely anyone was listening to them. 'I found you by the window on the floor. Why did you get up?'

His lips narrowed and he put his arms around his tightened knee. 'I'm not sure, myself.'

'Do you have nightmares?' Dreams could contain clues about his person and would, at least to some extent, explain his strange behaviour.

'It's hard to say at which point exactly they deviate from just dreams.' El sighed, without further elaboration.

Liliana hadn't shared her worries with anyone yet, but after seeing the angry fear in his eyes and his disturbing conduct at times, Annelies' beast no longer seemed so far-fetched. She would never forget the scene she'd encountered in the forest.

'Annelies told us about a beast that is supposed to make the forests unsafe,' she began cautiously. 'I know it sounds crazy, but ... could it be that it wasn't wolves, or not *just* wolves, that attacked you?'

El sat motionless, as if he hadn't heard her. Had she gone too far with this question? Sooner or later, he would have to face what had happened to him.

'I don't remember wolves or a beast,' he said flatly.

'If it's too soon, I understand.' She rose with a reassuring smile. 'Let me know if there's anything I can do for you ...'

'You're already doing a lot.' He became more animated again. 'It's very boring to only be in bed. I'm glad you're taking the time to talk to me.'

'The pleasure is all mine.'

Liliana had taken this phrase from one of her books. It seemed fitting, since she'd never found such a willing listener; not only in terms of reading out loud, but also when it came to her sometimes whimsical thoughts. El found everything interesting. To him, conditions that others accepted as unwritten fact seemed remarkable. Could it be due to his memory loss? Or because he came from a completely different background?

Chapter Seven

The storm had walled them up so much that they needed to shovel their way to the stable and barn. Urs, the neighbour on the other side of the road, asked for help because his roof had collapsed in one place. Father helped him, along with Hans, while Frederik chopped wood with Jakob and carried out some overdue repairs on their farming equipment. Under normal circumstances, it would've been washing day, but the stream was not visible under the cover of snow. Cedi found an opportunity to stuff a piece of ice down the back of Liliana's dress, which slipped down her skin, cold and disgustingly wet. In return, Hans got him with a huge snowball in the head.

El sat up in bed more often, even though he was still weak. By now, they had removed most of the bandages. He wore Father's old shirt and a pair of patched-up trousers from Frederik. Both were a bit too short for him. Once, when Liliana brought him food, she had sat down next to him on the edge of the bed. Grandmother had recommended they remove the last bandages soon and that he should move again, despite the broken leg, to get his blood circulation going. So she lifted his shirt to look at the wound on his torso. But he grabbed her wrist and held it.

'Has no one ever taught you that you can't just undress a man?'

She raised her head and realised that he was looking straight into her eyes. Her lips moved without her thoughts being able to keep up. 'I just wanted to see the, uh, the bandage and the wound. I didn't think you …'

Throughout the entire span of their acquaintance, he had needed her help most intimately. But this one question shifted the meaning of physical closeness between them in a way that made her blush.

She felt his cool touch on her skin for a moment longer before he gently released his fingers. Then he laughed and pulled the shirt over his head with some difficulty. 'I'm only kidding.'

Liliana didn't know where to look any more. He'd alerted her to a boundary that hadn't existed before. As if reconquering a piece of land through his increased independence, he had set new landmarks and left her disoriented.

With a pounding heart and fumbling fingers, she fiddled with the bandage. As soon as the scars were visible underneath, she got up, assured him that everything was just fine, and hurried out of the room.

She couldn't remember her next task and sat down at the loom to keep her hands busy. Of course, she understood that he wanted to do things like changing clothes and relieving himself on his own as soon as he was able to do so. But he could've expressed that wish differently. Had he deliberately embarrassed her because she had acted too intimately with him? Perhaps he had left a family behind and the memory of it gradually rose inside his conscience. A fiancée or a wife even ... children ... The thought made her chest tighten. His behaviour and his refined language made him appear older than he looked. Whether he was in his mid-twenties or already around thirty, the women from the sewing bee would undoubtedly describe him as being *of prime marrying age*. And a man like him would have no trouble winning over a woman from a distinguished family.

Annelies finally got her out of her restlessness by asking for help with milking and dairy processing. As a hired farm maid, Annelies was primarily responsible for the latter. She cleaned the milk and put it aside in shallow bowls. Once the cream had settled on top, she continued to work with the butter churn to separate the lumps of butter from the milk. She then pressed the kneaded butter into moulds. Liliana gratefully helped and threw herself into a conversation about Frida, who was expecting a calf.

When Annelies and Liliana sat down with the others for dinner, Grandmother immediately sent her to help El to the table. Liliana tried not to let anything show. Thankfully, all eyes followed El as he carefully sat down on the bench. After a short prayer, Cedi gushed away.

'What do you think of our farm? Will you be out of the woods soon? What are you going to do to find your own home again?'

'I am confident that I will soon be restored to my former health, thanks to the excellent care I enjoy here.'

Cedi gaped at him with open bewilderment, and the rest of the family members exchanged glances as well. Liliana didn't know whether to laugh or rebuke them. They reacted to El's formal language just like Father had.

'Regarding my supposed home ...'

'Eat! Eat!' interrupted Grandmother.

'Liliana says you still can't remember who you are?' Annelies shook her head in disbelief. 'I'd hate that! Suddenly forgetting my loved ones ...'

Meanwhile, everyone watched the way El held the spoon in his long fingers and let the soup silently disappear between his lips.

'You won't get anywhere like that!' Jakob blurted out, and everyone laughed.

'You've just never seen proper manners before,' Liliana said. El continued to spoon his soup serenely.

'If this is common among rich people, I'm not surprised that we never get to see our nobles. It takes them all day to spoon a single bowl of soup!' Frederik grinned broadly, and Liliana gave him a punishing look. Did her family have no decency?

Then Hans cleared his throat. 'Our life here must seem meagre compared to what you're used to.'

El put down his spoon before he spoke. 'Not at all. I can't remember anything. I have nothing to compare it with.'

Grandmother took this opportunity to give him more soup. Cedi also got seconds. Soon after, El asked to be excused to lie down again. Liliana and Annelies supported him. The latter hurried back to the dining table, while Liliana lingered indecisively in the doorway. She gnawed at her lower lip.

'Do you have everything you need?'

'Everything is fine, thank you.'

Her heart sank. But when she turned to leave, his voice held her back.

'Wait. Tell me a little more about your village.'

Hesitantly, she turned to him and asked what he wanted to know.

'What is it like to live here?'

'I have no reason to complain.' She wrapped her arms around herself and took a few steps towards the bed. 'Everyone has their assigned jobs to do. We help each other out whenever needed. Sowing is followed by the harvest; the harvest is followed by storing and sowing again in spring.'

'But?'

'No buts. It's always the same. We are lucky to have enough to live on and even a little extra. We sell that in the city.'

'What if you're not working?'

'Then we go to church. Now and then, we celebrate. Personally, I like to read. Or I ...'

'Yes?'

'I replay the stories in my head. What if, in the end, the robber isn't killed but begins a new life?'

El blinked kindly at her. Somehow, she'd arrived next to the bed.

'What would happen then?'

'There are so many possibilities. Perhaps he ends up in the Harshlands, where there are said to be many robbers. Or he sails across the sea, to a distant place where there are only robbers.' Although it was just a made-up example, Liliana could see him jumping off the boat on a strange new shore. 'And whoever is most cunning becomes the Robber King. Thus, the robber has to prove himself to gain respect. Maybe his usual tricks won't work because everyone there already knows them. Or maybe he'll rise up to the challenge and duel the Robber King in a competition of wits.'

'That sounds exciting.'

She replied by shrugging her shoulders, whereupon El pushed himself up on his elbow. There it was again, that captivating look in his eyes.

'And what about *your* story?'

'What do you mean?'

'Where does that lead?'

It was a curious question; a question that no one had ever asked before, because the answer was a given. Only El, probably coming from somewhere out there, could think of a question like that.

'If I'm lucky, I'll find a nice husband with much farmland, have children and learn how to bake bread that never gets hard. Our fields and livestock thrive, and we live in excellent health to an old age.'

'And that is what you are hoping for?'

'Well, I think Father secretly hopes I might marry someone from the city or one of the towns. Someone with more money. That I'll marry into the status that my mother left behind, so to speak. But to say that would kind of imply that Mother should have stayed there.'

'What about you? Would you seize the opportunity if it arose?'

'I don't know. I think it's a shame that the world is so big and I've seen so little of it.' She finally settled down on the floor. 'When the wind blows over the golden fields in summer, I think I want to stay here forever because there couldn't possibly be a more beautiful place than this. But did you know that in Dimas, all the streets are illuminated by colourful lights at night? And in the Lowlands, a sea of poppies turns the landscape red during summer? The ships sailing from the Silver Coast are meant to head for a distant island out in the sea, where golden donkeys with humps and snakes with horns live.'

Her last words made El laugh. 'So that is what you dream of. The colourful lights of Dimas and horned snakes.'

'Pfff ...' Liliana pouted playfully. 'Why am I telling *you* this, of all people? You've probably seen more of the world than I ever will.'

'Probably. And I can't remember any of it.'

'I'm sure it'll come back to you eventually.' She hesitated. 'Please don't tell anyone. But sometimes I wonder ... if life here in this village really is all that fate has in store for me.'

In this respect, El's unexpected appearance seemed like a hint, a kind of call. Didn't he offer the opportunity to break the boundaries of her narrow world? Lying on her bed, all composed, he hardly reminded her of the half-dead bundle they had carried in here a few weeks ago.

'Why are you asking, anyway?'

El grinned innocently. 'For the same reason you enjoy sounding me out, I imagine.'

Now Liliana found herself smiling, too. The tension in her shoulders had loosened, and the room seemed to warm up. 'What about your story? It's playing out as if we'd started in the middle. So far, the end *and* the beginning are missing.'

He sighed. 'In other words, I don't have a story. Only an isolated scene.'

'You could see it as the beginning of a new story. A blank sheet of paper on which to place your quill.'

'I like that idea.'

Chapter Eight

From then on, El was brought to the table for every meal. While the rest of the family continued to comment on his manners with jokes and teasing, Liliana, without intending to, began to imitate his upright posture and his genteel way of touching everything at the table with care. The icy weather remained for a while, and Grandmother instructed the women to melt snow in a pot to do the laundry. Liliana asked her how long a femoral fracture would take to heal and was happy to hear that a total of ten weeks or more would usually be expected. They hung the laundry in front of the oven, as outside it would have immediately frozen.

Father found a stick for El, to enable him to walk. Liliana showed him around the farm little by little. She let him name all the animals and, although it wasn't difficult for him, he eyed them all in amazement, as if he was seeing them up close for the first time. Only the horses seemed familiar to him. Liliana promised that he'd be allowed to try horse riding as soon as his leg was restored.

Finally, she showed him the mill that Father had designed. The stream was channelled into a gully at the top, which split into two. One side powered the flour mill, the other set beaters for flax and linseed in motion. Each section could be opened or closed with a simple board to regulate water flow.

'Grandmother swears by the linseed oil we make here. She needs it for her remedies. It preserves the effects of the herbs and is also said to make skin and hair beautiful. In here, the mashed flax seeds are heated on the wood stove and the mass is pressed through the cloth while still warm. The oil is also well-suited for producing paint. Women from all around the area of Heidenried come here to process their flax.'

Since El praised the construction and showed a lot of interest, Liliana went to get Father. He answered every question with obvious pride, and she watched for the first time how the two men talked on an equal footing. In addition to his natural authority and profitable business, it was this technical understanding Father was recognised for in the village. Liliana had inherited his imagination, but not when it came to spatial constructions.

Concomitant with his regained mobility, El began to insist that Liliana move back into her room; after all, he was doing much better. But Liliana wanted none of that. His leg needed the even surface of a proper mattress. This argument turned into ongoing banter between them.

One evening, as she came back from the outhouse in the dark, she found El sitting on the bench in front of the house. She asked if he was cold, and he answered, 'Not at all. In fact, I've decided to sleep out here, seeing as we can't seem to resolve the situation with your bed.'

Liliana laughed, shaking her head, and slipped into the house. She snatched her blanket and went back outside.

'Here.' She threw the blanket over his shoulders and felt the bench for moisture. Surprisingly, the wood was dry. She sat down next to him, grabbed one end of the blanket and pulled it around herself. 'I won't let you sleep alone in the cold. Either we both go in or we both stay out here.'

El made a half-suppressed chuckling sound. 'You can be quite stubborn, you know.'

'Not at all,' Liliana said. She moved closer to him, not just in jest, as she felt the warmth escape from her body with every breath.

'I wanted to look at the stars. Clear winter nights like this one are rare.'

The sky stretched over them, so speckled with stars that Liliana thought it might start raining lights any moment. What a sight indeed!

El pointed up with his free hand. 'There is the hare. And that is the diamond. Do you see this elongated triangle? That is the tip of the big sickle. Its handle points westward. This allows you to orient yourself at night. Once you have found the North Star as well, you cannot get lost.'

Liliana looked from the stars to his shimmering eyes and back. By now she'd become accustomed to his strange pronunciation and liked to listen to his voice. Could he be a sailor? Who else would need to be able to follow the stars at night? But they were so far inland ... Was he a hunter, who often spent the nights under the open sky? Perhaps he had killed game to which the noble family laid claim and had therefore been punished.

El cleared his throat, and Liliana noticed that she was staring at him, lost in thought. She couldn't see his face well enough to read it. So, she smiled apologetically and instead looked at her knees peeking out from under the blanket. They sat close together, and his leg touched hers on the side. As soon as she became aware of this touch, a pleasant tingling sensation spread through her body. She didn't really know what to do with it. She would've liked to put her head on his shoulder. But he would probably have found that presumptuous.

Instead, she blew on her hands and rubbed them together. She began to talk about the coming spring, which so far didn't fancy showing its face. El seemed absent-minded, which was unusual for him, as he was usually anxious to give her his full attention.

When another pause followed, she mustered the courage to move on to a more personal subject. 'Do you think that ... you might be married, and your wife is waiting for you somewhere? It must be heartbreaking to lose the love of your life without knowing what has become of him.'

This question brought El back to the present. He flinched slightly and cleared his throat. 'Honestly, I don't know. But I doubt it very much.'

'Why?'

'Hm.' He glanced sideways at her. Then he straightened up on the bench and leaned forward, his elbows resting on his knees and his chin resting on his hands. Liliana held on to the blanket, tightened by this movement, so that it wouldn't slip off her shoulder.

'Hm?'

He sighed. 'If a woman was waiting for me, I should miss her, shouldn't I? Even with my memory gone ... One would think that a deep bond like that could not simply disappear.'

Liliana smiled to herself. She leaned forward, too, so that their faces were on the same level. 'Unless your dear wife is a tyrant, and you're relieved not to be under her thumb any more.'

Accompanied by a slanted grin, his eyebrows darted upward. 'Am I giving off that impression?'

'Or you cheated on her, and she kicked you out ... or ran away because she's eager to take revenge on you for your infidelity.'

'I'm glad she can't see us like this then. Or else she might make you the prime suspect.'

Liliana laughed. Her soul felt so light. There was something magical about this moment. She could have sat on this bench forever. But when, despite the shared warmth, she began to tremble, they rose in wordless agreement.

She supported El on the way inside. More time must have passed than she'd assumed. Except for Hans, everyone had gone to sleep. He sat in a corner of the living room and looked up briefly as they entered. Liliana saw in his gaze that he was upset about something. She felt El tightening his shoulders next to her. Then Hans turned back to the figurine he was carving. It wasn't like him to make a big fuss about personal matters.

While Liliana helped El to bed and got ready to sleep herself, Hans took his good time to put the tools away and shuffle out of the room. Maybe he'd fallen out with Jakob, and because they shared a room, he wanted to wait until the other farmhand had fallen asleep.

The more El moved, the more often voices were raised – especially those of Frederik, Jakob and Hans – to point out that he was well enough to help out with the farmwork. The dining table was usually the place where such matters were discussed.

Frederik addressed his remark mainly at Father. 'He seems to have enough strength by now.'

'Although he has hardly any skill that is useful to us,' Hans remarked, without looking up from his plate.

It annoyed Liliana that they were talking about El as if he wasn't present, and she wanted to rebuke the two of them. El beat her to it. 'Of course, I'm happy to help where I can if I'm instructed accordingly.'

Liliana, who wanted to spare El as long as possible, turned to Grandmother to hear her assessment.

'As long as you do work sitting down and take breaks in between, I don't see a problem.'

'I can weave with you,' Liliana volunteered.

'I'll show you how to carve a bowl,' Cedi added. 'It's not that hard.'

'Do your work first,' Father grumbled into his beard.

Since Liliana had planned on weaving until the second milking anyway, she grabbed El right away. He clearly had never operated a loom before.

'We've carded, combed and spun all the linen beforehand. I've got the loom ready for you. During weaving, the warp threads, which have been stretched lengthwise, are connected to the weft threads. With your healthy leg, you can step on the pedals here, so that the warp threads are moved up and down. You move the shuttle through the shed, which is this gap here. Keep going until you run out of space. Then you need to roll the woven fabric up at the end. To do this, loosen the beam by pulling on this string. And then you spin the wheel down there. I'll help you.'

El worked so slowly that Liliana found it difficult not to take the shuttle off him and sit down herself. She tried to remember how Grandmother had taught her to weave. Father had built the loom, like many other pieces of equipment on the farm, himself. When Mother was still alive, she had tried out different dyes and combinations of materials, most of which were now forgotten. Liliana still had a tiny jacket that her mother had made from rabbit wool dyed with elderberry.

'Would you like to see some of my work?'

Gratefully, he put the shuttle aside. 'Yes, please.'

She led El into her room and opened the closet. In addition to Liliana's clothes, the family kept ready-woven linen, sheets and blankets in there.

'These fabrics are intended for sale.' Liliana gestured to the top compartment before spreading out two kitchen towels in front of his eyes.

'Those are ...' She cocked her ears to make sure no one happened to pass by the door. Apart from Valerie and Grandmother, no one had ever seen her finished pieces. 'They belong to my dowry.'

'What is a dowry?' El inspected the cloths in astonishment.

Liliana couldn't help but giggle. If he'd never met a priest before, he probably didn't know much about their wedding customs.

'Every bride does her part to contribute to her future household. As girls, we work on it from an early age. Bed linen, tablecloths, pillowcases and the like.'

She met his gaze and her stomach twisted. 'What do you think? Do you like them?'

'A bride is a woman who attaches herself to a man to form a new family, is that correct?'

'Yes, through marriage. At their wedding, we call the woman a bride and the man a bridegroom.'

He smiled and looked at the intricate embroidery around the edges. 'In that case, your future bridegroom can consider himself lucky.'

Liliana would've liked to pursue this train of thought a little longer, but footsteps approached, and she hastily put the cloths back. As promised, Cedi had come to teach El how to carve wood. He sat down with him in the living room and explained in detail how the piece of wood was to be worked. He'd already rubbed the surface with a knife to smooth it and marked the intended hollow with a charred stick.

As soon as El picked up the rounded knife, Liliana discarded the idea of him as a hunter and leaned towards the assumption that he must be some kind of scribe who had never learned any craftsmanship.

'No, no, no,' Cedi took the knife off him. 'You have to press the piece onto a hard surface so that you can use proper force. And then hold the knife like *this* in your hand. Work from the centre to the outside.'

Cedi sat down next to El on the bench, and Liliana watched the two of them as she cut potatoes, cabbage and carrots for dinner. Grandmother had been called to a farmer's wife, who was in labour, and had taken her whole collection of tinctures and ointments with her. When Annelies fetched Liliana for milking and Cedi went to feed the cattle, El remained on the bench with his carving. On their return, they found him engrossed in his work, and after dinner, he immediately resumed. Liliana praised his efforts, while Cedi instructed him to chop off the corners with the small axe and touch everything up with the wedge-shaped carving knife. He tied a leather strap around his thumb for protection. El tinkered around until his bowl was finished, and the rest of the family retired to their rooms to sleep.

'It's turned out to be quite the passable bowl,' Liliana said just as Hans entered the room.

He held his arms behind his back and approached her. Clearing his throat, he cautiously held out the figurine he'd been working on the night before.

'This is for you, Liliana.'

'Oh, how pretty!' She accepted it with surprised thanks. The candlelight and the warm glow of the embers in the stove cast vivid shadows on the wooden girl. She wore a long braid and a wide skirt. Liliana ran her fingers over the smooth wood and was amazed that he had managed to create such fine details.

'I didn't know you were this gifted.'

Hans smiled. 'If you like it, I'll be happy to make another one for you.'

'Of course I like it!' Liliana continued to turn the wooden girl in her hands to examine her from all sides. How much work and effort he must've put into it!

'I'd better lie down.' El rose from the bench. He looked tired, and Liliana offered to help him on his way to bed. But Hans turned her attention back to the figurine.

'It's made of stone pine. Meant to be good for the heart and ensure restful sleep.'

'Yes, I've heard that, too. Grandmother filled a pillow with shavings for herself.'

'And look here, she's holding a book in her hand.'

'Is that me?'

Hans nodded contentedly. Liliana looked at the girl again and tried to recognise herself in it. The wide cheekbones, perhaps? No, a carving couldn't be that accurate, could it? Only then did she notice that El had limped past them.

'It turned out beautifully.' Liliana looked up at Hans and smiled at him.

'Thank you.' He grinned, embarrassed. 'I think so, too.'

'I have to show this to the others tomorrow.' Liliana hugged Hans and wished him a good night's rest.

Then she hurried to her room, where El was already lying on the bed. 'Why didn't you wait? I was going to help you.'

El sighed in a disgruntled mood, his eyes fixed on the beams in the ceiling. 'As you can see, I didn't need your help.'

'I would've been there in just a minute. Look at the pretty figurine Hans made for me!'

Enthusiastically, she held out the gift to him, but El didn't move at all. 'I've seen it.'

'Can you guess who it is? Hans carved *me!*'

'That was to be expected.' El still talked to the ceiling.

'Why was that to be expected?'

And why couldn't she shake the feeling that El was angry with her? She lowered her outstretched arm and instead looked for a suitable place to put the figurine. When she finally laid it in the chest with her other treasures, El turned to the side and looked at her through narrow eyes.

'If you're done here, I would like to sleep.'

Chapter Nine

Over the next few days, El accompanied Liliana around the farm as best he could and had her explain how the animals were cared for. Beneath the remnants of snow, the earth began to stir and put out its green feelers. Liliana had decided to bring El to church with them. She kept badgering him until he agreed to be there the next Sunday. Knowing that he felt uneasy about it, she explained to him what to expect as she tressed her hair into a wreath of braids. Frederik had lent him a better shirt and his razor blade for the sermon. Without the stubbly beard, El seemed to feel more comfortable, and Liliana noticed how his sharply cut jawline showed.

Small clouds scurried across the sky, creating a patchwork of light and shadow over the landscape. Liliana's wide skirt blew around her legs. Because there was usually someone dawdling at the entrance, chattering churchgoers lined the way to the church. Liliana perceived their curious glances from afar. El leaned on her for his first outing away from the farm. The closer they got, the faster he began to breathe.

As they climbed the steps to the church, he suddenly staggered and clung to Liliana, who almost fell over with him. 'I'm not feeling too well. I have to lie down.'

'You're so close.' She signalled to Cedi to hold El from the other side. 'You can sit down inside.'

They were already swarmed by curious bystanders who wanted to know if this was the stranger, if he was feeling better, and why he wasn't sitting down.

The people in the back pews moved their heads and their nosy voices echoed from the church. Liliana barely heard El's voice amid all the talking.

'I feel weak. I'd like to go back.'

She and Cedi turned around, and the three of them moved a little away from the church. Fortunately, only the family followed them.

'El isn't doing well,' Liliana explained. 'I'll take him back. The rest of you can stay.'

But Father frowned uncomfortably, and Hans put his hand on her shoulder. 'I'll take him. You stay. You always like to listen to Priest Mathias.'

'Oh.' Liliana hesitated. 'All right then.'

Hans slid between them. His strong arm wrapped effortlessly around El's torso. The latter looked slender next to him, although he was half a head taller. If necessary, Hans would probably even be able to carry him.

They separated, and the sermon began a little late after the commotion. Liliana found the mayhem of the churchgoers more overwhelming without Hans, who normally never left her side on Sunday mornings. She'd been so close to showing El that nothing threatening was happening here, apart from the endless pushing and chattering. Priest Mathias shared some well-formulated thoughts about not putting their hearts on the fleeting luxuries of the world. He also exhorted them to stay away from animals and people who behaved strangely or aggressively, and to pray that they would be spared from the rapidly spreading plague of rabies.

After he finished, Liliana made her way over to Valerie, who was sitting in the far corner. She climbed over the bench and plonked herself down next to her cousin. Apart from Grandmother, Valerie was the only person Liliana sometimes confided in. She was honest and didn't judge anyone. In addition, she was the only one who rarely drew even the most obvious of conclusions from what was said.

Liliana let her gaze wander back and forth so that she'd notice if someone was paying too much attention to their exchange. 'What would you say if a girl ... if a woman likes someone even though she knows very little about him.'

'I like most people, even if I don't know them very well,' Valerie said.

'What if that someone is a handsome man?'

Valerie bowed her head. 'Looks alone aren't a good reason to like someone.'

'He could also be interesting, clever and entertaining, and have refined manners.'

'Then I'd like him, too.' Now Valerie smiled. 'Is he from one of your books?'

'Not quite,' Liliana replied, immediately throwing in another question. 'What about you? Is your father still trying to set you up with the widower, Peter? Or what was the name of that other fellow from Krambach?'

'No, not for a long time. Since Mother has taken ill, he's no longer in a hurry to get rid of me.'

Liliana squeezed Valerie's hand. 'I'm sorry about your mother. She just won't get better, huh?'

'At least she's still with me. You were too young when yours left you.'

How much happier the world would be if everyone had Valerie's gift of seeing things in a positive light. Liliana felt a pang of guilt. Since El had appeared, she hadn't visited her cousin even once.

Her alertness must have waned because she didn't notice Karina until she was standing right in front of them. The girl was a lot younger than Valerie but still liked to hang around her.

'Are you looking forward to the Spring Celebrations?'

'Sure.' Valerie greeted her friend warmly, and Liliana also attempted a friendly face.

'I can't wait! My mother is sewing a new dress for me. Do you know what you're wearing? Have you promised someone a dance yet?'

'I'm going to wear the same dress I wore last year,' Valerie said, 'only with a new bow and a scarf that I'll need to finish knitting. No one has asked me to dance, but that certainly doesn't mean I'm going to be bored that night.'

Liliana hadn't given the Spring Celebrations any thought yet. They were in three weeks' time. Besides the Harvest Festival, it was the most exciting event of the year for the whole village. She very much hoped that El would still be around then. She wanted him to see Heidenried from its best side.

'And you, Liliana?' Karina giggled and continued to speak, not waiting for Liliana's answer. 'I've seen your stranger. He's not quite back on his feet yet, huh? A handsome man, if it weren't for that long scar on his face.'

Liliana found her last remark strange. El's whole body had been scarred from the attack he'd miraculously survived, but those scars had already healed so well that she barely noticed them at all. Karina must have been among the curious crowd at the church entrance. How closely had she looked at El? Liliana crossed her arms.

'What?' Karina nudged her. 'I'll dance with him, anyway, if he asks me.'

Grandmother calling her over at that moment was great timing, and Liliana abruptly said goodbye to the other girls.

At home, she helped Grandmother as usual with the Sunday dinner: meat dumplings and winter vegetables. She'd seen to El on her return and found him quite irritable. Had something happened between him and Hans on the way back? Or was it because of his fainting spell in front of everyone at the church? In any case, Grandmother didn't seem worried. This was to be expected if he overexerted himself after weeks of being bedridden.

El claimed that he had recovered enough to come to the living room for dinner. As she handed out plates, Liliana told him about Priest Mathias' sermon. Then she called everyone to the table. As soon as she caught Frederik's gaze, she knew he wanted to address a topic she wouldn't like. What had he been chatting about with his friends today?

'Father, don't you think it's time to marry Liliana off? She's already twenty-two and not getting any younger.'

Liliana stopped chewing and glared at her brother in disbelief. Had he gotten wind of her conversation with Valerie? His incessant hints had been annoying enough. Did he have to be so forward when everyone was listening?

To make matters worse, Father nodded in agreement, and even Grandmother made a face of approval rather than indignation. 'Were you thinking of someone in particular?'

'Not necessarily,' Frederik said.

At least Annelies was not here to make ridiculous suggestions for possible marriage partners. Liliana wished herself far away. Her cheeks and ears glowed. Hoping for some kind of reaction, she watched El out of the corner of her eye. What exactly she was hoping for she didn't know, only that it was more than this non-involved expression.

Cedi grinned. 'I think we should leave Liliana be. If she wants to die as an old spinster surrounded by nothing but books and skinny goats ...'

Jakob spat cabbage across the table with laughter, while Hans silently pondered his plate, as if he weren't listening.

'Shut up!' Liliana snapped at her brother more forcefully than intended, which earned her Grandmother's reproachful wagging finger.

'It was a joke!' Cedi defended himself. 'You never talk to anyone. Are you surprised men don't chase after you?'

'Is that unusual?' El finally said. 'Not being married at twenty-two?'
Everyone turned to him.

'Or at least engaged.' Frederik stuffed himself with dumplings and continued with his mouth full. 'In our village, Liliana is the oldest girl who isn't promised to anyone. Except for Valerie ... The early ones start at fifteen.'

'I was not aware there is some kind of age limit to getting married.' El casually shook his head and said into the silence that followed, 'This morning, someone mentioned visiting the city?'

'Next Saturday, we will sell some goods at the market,' Father confirmed. 'It would make sense for you to come along and look around for relatives or acquaintances ... or work that suits you.'

El nodded but said nothing more. Was he worried about his future? Liliana had one last idea to nudge his memory, which she hadn't implemented until now.

After all the dishes were washed, she offered to show El the place where she found him. He agreed, and Liliana fetched Donnie so as not to tire El out. In the forest, the birdsong had increased. Snowdrops and crocuses greeted them in passing. The air smelled of a mixture of mould and fresh shoots. Although El looked like it wasn't his first time on a mount, Liliana pulled Donnie by the rein. He could be unruly at times.

Having returned to the place once before, she found her way easily. With her help, El carefully slid off the donkey and looked around. Liliana pointed to the spot with the fallen trees. 'That's where I found blood and body parts. I followed the tracks all the way over there, to the thicket where you were lying.'

El swept his gaze over the ground and trees and then tilted his head back, as if hoping the heavens might give him a sign. He crossed his arms and kept kneading the same place on his upper arm with his right hand. Pain reflected on his face.

'Is everything all right?' she asked.

Startled, he swung around and stared at her in confusion. 'I think I've been betrayed. I fought for my life, thought I was dead. I remember only vague sensations. But other than that ... nothing.'

He swallowed. 'I have nothing. Absolutely nothing.'

Liliana stepped up to him and put her hand on his so that he'd stop squeezing his arm like he meant to bruise it. No matter how misunderstood she sometimes felt by her family or how unnoticed by the villagers, she had never felt as lost as he looked just now. Her heart swelled with compassion. She wanted to assure him that everything would turn out well. But it was wiser to let him finish.

'How can it be that my memory is completely empty? I'm a stranger to myself. Who am I? Don't I *want* to remember?' He shrugged helplessly. 'Do you know what it's like to have nothing? No home, no friends, no family, no life, no meaning?'

Liliana continued to stand quietly next to him.

'I can't expect you to understand. I have had a lot of time to think. Maybe too much. This image came to me, and it won't leave. I'm floating on an unknown lake. A shadow lurks beneath the surface. I can't see it, but I feel it is there. If I could see the shadow, maybe I would know what to do. But it simply continues to circle down there. And I'm drifting without an oar and waiting ... waiting for it to strike.'

Shuddering, he closed his eyes. Liliana leaned forward and hugged him. Whether it was the right thing to do, she wasn't sure, but he didn't resist. She felt his breath in the movement of his chest. The clarity with which he described his inner world was astonishing. No one around her could put their feelings into words in such eloquent ways. She would hold him for as long as he needed it.

After a while, the tension in his body subsided. The birds continued to chirp their songs from between the branches. When he broke away from the embrace, his gaze was fixed on the ground.

'You must excuse me. It wasn't my intention to tell you all my ...' His voice faded as he slowly looked up. He seemed to look for something in her face. Then he cleared his throat.

'Shall we go back?'

Liliana helped him onto the donkey. Didn't he realise that he wasn't alone? He didn't have nothing; after all, he had *her*.

Chapter Ten

Father steered the cart through the main gate into Roinnenstadt. What had begun with a fortress on the hill and the jetty on the river gradually grew together until the whole slope was crammed with narrow streets and wonky houses. Father had been persuaded surprisingly easily to take Liliana along with him in addition to Frederik and El. Long before dawn, they had packed linen, carvings, butter and cheese, grain and leftover vegetables onto the wagon and harnessed the horse, Elisa.

To Liliana, the city was both stimulating and thronging. Everything was busy and colourful. She imagined what it would be like to live here; to observe constant foot traffic in front of her window instead of swaying green trees, and to constantly hear noises and arguments from the neighbouring houses. On the other hand, she could go to the theatre, marvel at the goods in the shops, or drink tea with elegant ladies. What she liked most was that people from places she had only ever heard of arrived in the city daily.

While she tried not to get in anyone's way, El behaved as if the flow of people was none of his business. Despite his walking stick, he stood serenely like a rock in the current. Grandmother had allowed his leg to be freed from all restraining measures, as long as he promised not to put his full weight onto it.

'Does anything seem familiar to you?' Liliana asked over the clatter of hooves and rattling wheels.

El blew out air through pursed lips. 'Not really.' He looked with mild interest in every direction. 'So this is Roinnenstadt. Who's pulling the strings here?'

Frederik, who had overheard them, exchanged a puzzled look with Liliana. 'Well, if you have a complaint, you go to the justice of the peace. He settles disputes and decides whether any changes to the law proposed by the people should be implemented. He is also in charge of the street guard.'

'The justice of the peace, huh?'

'Yes. In Heidenried, however, he has little to no real say. The street guard rarely bothers to get out into the countryside. Where we live, the community rules.'

Looking at Frederik thoughtfully, El asked, 'And where does the money end up that your father is paying to enter the city?'

'In the pockets of the street guard.'

'Nonsense,' Liliana interjected. 'Everyone just badmouths them because they're the face you see when you hand your coins over. But all of the taxes are collected in the city treasury. And a goodly portion of it goes all the way up to the noble family. They live somewhere on their own in their fancy castle, which needs to be financed somehow.'

El nodded contentedly. Father came back, grumbled under his beard about the shocking increase of the tax, and steered the cart to the market. It had already begun, as the sellers all raced to get the best spots. Many had travelled a shorter distance than them, and travelling merchants often stayed in the city for several days. Those who wanted to set up on the market square itself had to pay a tax again, but not those who set up on the long street from the square to the pier. As a result, only precious products such as spices, fine cloth, handicrafts, and the like were offered on the actual marketplace. Among the peasants, the upper street in the immediate vicinity of the square was popular. The lower street was occupied by those who came from the river and didn't want to carry their goods far due to convenience or lack of time. Therefore, they had to settle for a place in the middle, despite having left in the early hours of darkness.

Frederik set about arranging the goods nicely and spreading the linen over the side wall of the cart. The farmers who came to the city with their wains also used them to display their wares. Surrounded by haggling voices, Liliana took El aside and handed him the silver buttons she'd kept for him.

Money only passed through her fingers when they went to market. The coin she saw most often was the iron penny. Twelve iron pennies made one copper groat, and twelve copper groats equalled one silver thaler. Accordingly, she estimated the value of the three silver buttons to be over four hundred iron pennies. That was a large sum, and the reason she hadn't told the others about it. Frederik would've wanted to keep them as payment for the additional costs. Father might have been more generous, but she didn't want to cause any quarrels. Flashing in the mild sunlight, the buttons actually resembled inflated coins.

'Here. I know you wanted to leave them to us, but I think you need them more right now.'

El didn't object but thanked her warmly. 'I'd like to have a look around.'

As she watched him disappear into the crowd, she felt a sting in her chest. He would come back, wouldn't he?

The couple who lined up next to them carried baskets of fish and crayfish. From here she could see neither the Roinne nor the pier, but she knew that the boats also had to pay to dock in the city. Transport on the river was cheaper and particularly suitable for heavy goods or large quantities. It was even possible to transport upstream by towing the boats with a rope pulled by animals or people on the shore.

Soon thereafter, Father went to get leather and replace some tools. By noon, Liliana was very pleased with the sales they were making. Then, suddenly, they seeped away, and she began to worry that they might spend more than they earned on this visit to the city. The couple with the crayfish next to them seemed to have similar concerns and began to argue about the cost of shoes and nets.

In addition to the familiar fumes of the chickens, pigs and sheep that were sold, the smell of already roasted meat and spices wafted over from time to time. Unfortunately, buying food prepared by someone else wasn't something Father would ever consider. So she unpacked the bread they'd brought and shared it with Frederik.

Having taken care of Elisa as well, they grew bored, and Frederik said he wanted to stretch his legs. He'd probably know a few of the other farmers who offered their yields for sale. Liliana was left to herself. She watched the maids buying leeks and chickens for the kitchen of a rich gentleman, and the wives of the craftsmen who touched everything but bought nothing. Now and then, she saw dirty children running by or an especially fashionable figure pattering through the crowds. She imagined where they came from and what stories they had to tell.

'I just had to come by myself after my cook had so much praise for you!' Liliana looked up in astonishment and almost didn't recognise the man who had addressed her. She opened her mouth, but El was faster. 'No need to be modest. I hear your vegetables are the best on this whole market. And once one has tasted your butter, there is no going back. May I take a look at this beautifully carved piece?'

Puzzled, Liliana reached for the appointed bowl. El wore an elegantly cut men's tailcoat with a wide collar and clean, lightly coloured trousers. He inspected the bowl carefully and announced, 'Perfect in every way. Just like the young lady who sells them.'

Liliana noticed several heads turning towards them. El winked at her. Heat climbed up her neck.

'The linen, too, please.'

She quickly complied with his request and presented her cloth. El ran his fingers over the fabric and nodded appreciatively. 'How much will this cost me?'

She named the price, and El let a handful of iron and copper pennies clink into her hand. In the meantime, a group of marketgoers formed around her cart. El sighed loudly. 'If only I knew where my footboy is hiding! Put the goods aside for me, and I will instruct him to pick them up later. He's short with a full head of ginger hair. Have a wonderful day!'

With that, he left, and Liliana suddenly didn't have enough hands to serve all the potential buyers. Luckily, Frederik had noticed what was going on and came running. When she finally got around to looking for El, he was nowhere to be seen. Father couldn't believe his eyes when he returned, and they had sold their entire stock.

'That means we can leave early for once.'

Liliana continued to search the crowd for El. Surely, they weren't going to leave until he was back? Where was he? Had he found something? Family? Friends? She got onto the cart to see better. A runaway chicken fluttered around the knees of passers-by. There, a dark thatch of hair wiggled through the crowd, and here someone strutted past in a wide men's coat ... but she didn't recognise any of the faces. What if he didn't come back? What if that short exchange earlier was the last time she would ever see him? She hastily pushed the thought away.

'Are you looking for someone?'

There he stood, just below her on the side of the wain, his elegant clothes hidden under a brown cloak. His voice was almost drowned out by all the noise around her.

'El!'

He extended a hand to help her down. As soon as her feet touched the ground, she hugged him so tightly that he gasped.

'You're here!'

'What's the matter?' He grabbed her shoulders, held Liliana at arm's length, and looked at her in surprise.

'I wasn't sure if you'd come back. Have you found your family?'

'No.'

'Then where did you get the fancy clothes?'

'Oh ...' He grinned. 'A single silver button helped me with them. Someone lost badly in a game of dice. And the winner squandered the clothes, unaware of what he truly could have asked for them. They are a little too wide for me, but appearance is the first step to finding a well-paid position.'

'Did you find one, then?' Liliana held her breath.

'Not where I've asked so far. It's difficult without references. If I had a letter of recommendation ...'

'So no one knows you?'

'Neither the street guard nor the people at public houses recognised me. There currently seems to be an unusually large number of missing people. Asking about that has proven to be a fruitless effort.'

Listening in on his last words, Father grumbled into his beard. Liliana suspected she knew what was going on in his head. He didn't want to throw the stranger out without the prospect of a source of income, but at the same time, he had to conserve his family's resources.

El took Liliana by the elbow and stepped a little further into the market crowd before continuing in a lowered voice. 'However, I found what I was looking for in other respects. Everyone seems to know the domicile of the Zumbrunn family.'

'Really?' He could remember a name she had only briefly mentioned once? 'Why are you telling me that?'

He looked at her for a moment and shrugged. 'You said you've never met your mother's family. This surprises me, especially seeing as today clearly isn't the first time you and your father have been to the city. If it's because you're too shy, I'm happy to accompany you.'

'Wait, Mother's family lives *here*?'

Liliana looked over at Father, who was already harnessing Elisa. He'd never told them that Mother's family lived in Roinnenstadt! She knew that her parents had met at the summer market, but as the daughter of a merchant who travelled long distances to acquire and sell his precious fabrics, she could have lived anywhere on the continent.

She swallowed her reproaches for the time being and instead spontaneously called out to Father over passing heads. 'El would like to show me something briefly. We'll be back in no time at all!'

She took El's hand, and he led her limping but unerringly through the hustle and bustle of the market. Where had his walking stick gone? Her heart was pounding. Perhaps she'd admired the house where her mother had grown up from the outside on previous occasions without even knowing it. She couldn't decide what weighed more heavily in her mind: the fact that, despite her pleas, Father had never told her where Mother's family lived, or that they had never tried to get into contact.

They turned into a side alley and Liliana heard footsteps catching up. Frederik pushed through the foot traffic. 'What's this? Where are you going?'

El hurriedly let go of her hand, and Liliana crossed her arms. 'We want to see the house where Mother's family lives.'

'Why?'

She eyed her brother indignantly. This was not the reaction she'd expected. 'You knew they lived in Roinnenstadt?'

'You didn't?'

'No!' Liliana released her arms. Evidently, Father had treated her and Frederik differently in this regard.

Her brother made a sullen face. 'It's not worth your time. Come, Father is waiting.'

'I'll decide for myself after I've seen it.'

She continued to march straight ahead but stopped at regular intervals to let El catch up with her and correct her if she'd taken a wrong turn. Frederik followed them, muttering to himself. The closer they got to the fortress walls on the hill, the cleaner the facades got. Even the rubbish in the gutter decreased, although it was still as busy as everywhere else in the city. The rich could afford to pay someone to sweep their doorsteps.

El and Frederik stopped at the same time, looking at a certain house on the left side of the street which seemed to be making room for itself by pushing its neighbours aside. It was four stories high. Each floor had several windows and protruded a little further outward than the one below it. Despite the low rays of sunlight only reaching the roof, the white of the outer wall shone coolly between black-painted beams. Behind a rounded gate, Liliana suspected a small courtyard for carriages. A narrower door for people on foot was built into the gate.

El took off the cloak and put it over his arm. With his new tailcoat, he fit right into the picture. 'Do you want me to knock?'

'Don't do it!' Frederik looked at Liliana insistently. She suddenly understood.

'You've been here before, haven't you?'

'Not just me, both of us.' Frederik sighed. His gaze remained scowling. 'You were an infant, and I was too young to realise what it was all about. But I remember Mother's tears on the way home. She probably wanted to introduce us or hoped for some kind of reconciliation. We weren't even allowed to cross the doorstep.'

'Maybe they've changed their minds, now that we're older. Do they even know that Mother died?'

'Bah! Of course, they know. And still no one came to the funeral. It's better this way, believe me.'

A passing coachman whistled them out of the way, and they stepped to the side of the road together. Poor Mother ... Liliana didn't want to cause bad blood. Nevertheless, she peeked through a crack in the gate, hoping to catch a glimpse of the inside.

She jumped back as the door in the gate sprang open. A young woman with an apron, crisp and white like the wall of the house, stepped out with an empty basket in her arms. Liliana backed away and collided with Frederik, whereupon the maid nodded at them gruffly.

'Do you need anything?'

'We desire to speak with the master of the house.' El's clear voice pierced through the noise of the street. He hinted at a stiff bow.

The maid's gaze jumped confusedly between him, Liliana, and Frederik. 'You are ... together? Wait here.'

She withdrew to wherever she'd come from. Liliana bit her lower lip. Should she leave? She felt torn between El's serene posture and Frederik's grim expression. Presumably, Mother's family didn't deserve any offers of friendship if they couldn't be bothered to show up even at the funeral … But when else would she get the opportunity to meet her grandparents or any of the cousins she might have?

Again, the door opened, and an elegantly dressed woman appeared. Liliana's heart jumped. The hazy memory of Mother suddenly took on a clear form. Those big blue eyes, the wide cheekbones and that pointy chin … even details she had forgotten, like the long earlobes or the way she pursed her lips when she was unhappy about something. Baffled, Liliana took a step back.

But no, this was not her mother. This was a version of her that lacked softness despite plump curves; a version that ate six sumptuous meals a day, frowned too much and didn't do any manual labour.

The woman immediately turned to El, 'The old master of the house is asleep, and my husband is absent today. If you want to talk to him on business matters, try again tomorrow.'

'May we come in for a moment?'

She looked at Liliana more closely and puffed. 'You … I don't have to ask who you are.' She now spoke very slowly and clearly, as if she believed Liliana to be partially deaf. 'There is nothing for you to get here!'

Liliana still gaped at the apparition. Her *sister* … yes, of course. Mother hadn't often talked about her, but she now remembered. Jana was her name.

El coughed, and the aunt's head spun around. 'Do I have to assume that you are not here on your own behalf but as an advocate for these peasant children?'

He smiled, unimpressed. 'That would be correct.'

'And who exactly am I dealing with, if I may ask?'

'I just wanted to see where my mother grew up,' Liliana finally managed.

Aunt Jana grimaced. 'It's not convenient right now. To be honest, it won't be convenient tomorrow or any other day either.'

Didn't she care what had become of her niece and nephew? 'Did you know that Mother died fourteen years ago?'

'What difference does it make? For us, she died long before that.'

Speechless again, Liliana opened her mouth. How could she be so cold-hearted? 'But …'

'The lady will be able to at least share a few memories with us, won't she?' insisted El.

'If I do, will you leave without causing an incident?'

'Yes,' Liliana hurriedly promised, whereupon El nodded next to her. She didn't want to come here a second time anyway. 'Yes, please tell us what she was like. As a girl, I mean.'

'There was no need to bring an advocate with you,' snorted Aunt Jana, who certainly would have been much more hostile without El's presence. 'Fine, then …'

She stood in front of her locked townhouse with her arms crossed over her stout chest and waited. Liliana took a deep breath and continued. 'What do you remember? What was she like when she was young? What made her happy?'

'Disobedient.' Aunt Jana rolled her big blue eyes. 'As an older sister, Emma should have been a role model for me. But no, she preferred to climb rooftops and collect stray cats from the streets. Our parents often locked her up in her room.'

'And later?'

'Later, with her foolhardiness, she tossed away every privilege she was born with. Served her right. My father always preferred her, slipping her books and other souvenirs and even taking her with him on his travels a couple of times. Until she fell in love with that destitute oaf.'

'That oaf is our father and a respected man in our village community,' Frederik mumbled next to Liliana. 'We've never had to beg for a single speck of dust from you or anyone else!'

The aunt ignored him. 'As soon as our father found out about their secret trysts, he wanted to realise the marriage that had been arranged for her – to the son of the captain of the street guard. He said she had to choose between her family and her lover. She made up her mind, and he disowned her. End of story.'

'What a needless punishment!'

Aunt Jana met Liliana's angry words with malice in her voice. 'All the better for me. *I* have married a clever man who will soon take over my father's business and trade licence. There is nothing you lot can do about that, legally.'

Frederik grabbed his sister by the arm. 'Come on, we've heard enough.'

They were about to leave, but Aunt Jana called El back. Now that she no longer perceived him as a threat, her curiosity took over. 'There's something familiar about you. Have we met before?'

El stopped too hastily, and his mouth twitched in pain before he turned around with an emphatically dignified attitude. 'I couldn't say for sure. What makes you think that?'

'Is it possible that you have some kind of connection to the noble family?'

'The noble family?' He raised his eyebrows.

'Do you know them?' Liliana asked.

'Nobody *knows* the noble family.' Aunt Jana made no effort to suppress her conceited smile. 'But a selected delegation appointed the new justice of the peace last month, and we were invited to be present as guests. As always, they appeared veiled and announced major changes. You should have seen them! The almost white, perfect skin. Their fashionable style, the elegance of their appearance ...' She kept looking at El, hoping to discover a detail about him that would indicate whom she was dealing with. 'You can always tell when people move in finer circles.'

By this, she probably meant to say that the people of the city liked to flaunt their wealth through the way they dressed. It wasn't impossible that she'd met El, but why did no one else remember him? She probably only raised the question to draw attention to the social divide between herself and her sister's offspring.

'If you can remember where you think you may have seen me before ...' El pressed the arm with the cloak closer to his body.

Aunt Jana frowned and thought for a long time. A loudly yapping dog chased a smaller playmate around the corner. 'No, I cannot remember. What was your name again?'

El's features hardened. 'Have a good day.'

Chapter Eleven

'I warned you,' Frederik murmured as he climbed past her to his usual place beside Father at the front of the cart. 'To them, everyone who doesn't move in their high society is scum. Does this stuffed goose even know where the food on her precious plates comes from?'

Liliana kept silent. Inwardly, she agreed with Frederik. She had never felt poor until she was portrayed as such by an aunt who should've been happy to see her. They worked hard but never starved. This woman had no idea what real poverty looked like. Those who owned land had a livelihood. They continued to expand the farm and their livestock annually. She could only imagine how conceited the nobility had to be when rich city dwellers already acted like this. Only a select number of merchants were granted the precious permission to travel across borders. And Aunt Jana sure was smug about theirs.

Father drove off. El sat opposite her and leaned against the wall of the cart, lost in thought. Did he feel discouraged about his search? He would have to try another city, Thomlin in the northeast or Hohburg near the southern mountains maybe. Or even across the border? No, her aunt, who must have encountered more travellers, had associated his manner of speaking with the upper class rather than with another territory. What if he actually was related to the nobility? She couldn't quite see him as a haughty nobleman. In addition, those nobles certainly would have turned the whole territory upside down if they had been missing a high-ranking member. She could, however, see him as a high official, as someone who managed possessions and kept registers.

Both started a question at the same time, and she let El speak first. He propped himself up on one knee and leaned forward. The bronze in his eyes expressed sympathy.

'Are you disappointed?'

'About my relatives?' Father had wanted to save her from being rejected like this. That was why he hadn't told her how close Mother's family lived; the family that *should have been* family. Perhaps only her aunt was so ill-disposed. They hadn't been able to talk to anyone else. Perhaps she'd somehow intercepted the news of Mother's death and never passed it on. On the other hand, her grandfather – the old master of the house, as she'd called him – surely could've made contact all these years if he'd really wanted to.

'A little. I mean ...' She shrugged her shoulders in resignation. 'At least now I know. And I did hear a thing or two about my mother that I hadn't been aware of before.'

'She must have been a very interesting and strong-willed woman.'

Liliana returned El's smile. 'I think so, too.'

The books that her mother had left her were gifts from her grandfather. She pictured Mother as a child, dangling her feet from the roof, reading about the adventures of a Velusian pirate and petting stray cats. As much as Liliana appreciated Grandmother and her wisdom, she, like the rest of the family, knew no other life and wasn't interested in what was happening beyond the nearest villages. If, on the other hand, Mother were still alive, she would understand Liliana's longing for adventure.

'Do you think my aunt was right?' she asked. 'Could you come from her kind of circle?' And could it be a twist of fate; an invitation to take up Mother's legacy somehow?

But El shook his head. 'None of what she said stirred any memories in me.'

They made good progress until one of the wheels got stuck in the mud. In springtime, the rain and melting snow softened the paths. Elisa frothed in frustration, and Father ordered her to stop. They climbed down and elevated the cart together to drag it onto firmer ground. That would have been much more difficult on the way to the city. Although perhaps the cart slipped precisely because of the lack of weight.

Journeying onwards, Frederik shared with Father what he'd picked up from the other farmers and traders. Rabies had hit the city even harder than the population out in the countryside. As a result, the rules on meat and livestock had become stricter. Furthermore, all kinds of taxes had been raised, which had caused general resentment. Something was in the air, he concluded.

Liliana looked at the rolling hills that wobbled past them. She'd hoped that the visit to the Zumbrunn family home would revive her connection to Mother. But the very fact that she had broken away from them and started her own new family was what had shaped her life the most. Other than her love for Father, what had made her give up her status? Perhaps it had been a relief for her to leave behind the cold-hearted austerity of her parents' home. Or maybe she hadn't truly expected Grandfather to carry out his threat and cut her off completely.

It wasn't until Frederik called out to Father to go faster that she noticed the fierce clouds rolling up behind them. Not only did they bring the prospect of getting soaked, but they also darkened the sky, advancing nightfall. Just as they spotted the village in the distance and thought they'd won the race, a whang sounded, and the side on which Liliana sat dropped. She clung to the edge as the wain skidded. Luckily, Father had the presence of mind to stop Elisa before they smashed into a tree.

'Holy Saints!' Frederik jumped off and assessed the damage. 'First we get stuck, and now the wheel is broken!'

Twilight chose this exact moment to fall upon them. Father began to loosen Elisa's reins and handed them over to Frederik. 'We're not far from home. There's a spare wheel in the barn.'

Frederik nodded and swung himself onto the horse. The lantern that Father lit was no match for the rapidly descending darkness. Meanwhile, Liliana looked for a tree trunk by the wayside. El sat next to her while Father paced up and down. Treetops concealed the lightning that illuminated the sky above them. Apart from a couple of drops, the rain passed them by. The forest remained calm. Then Liliana heard a distant howl and shivered.

'Did you hear that?'

Father stopped with a concentrated face, and El tilted his head, listening. Was she imagining it, or was the howling getting closer? Nervously, Liliana pulled her knees closer to her body. Why didn't the others say anything? Again, the darkness howled, and Liliana felt anxiety simmer in her stomach.

She moved closer to El, who in turn sat up straight, stiff as a board. 'Where's Frederik?'

'Stay calm,' muttered Father under his beard. 'The rumours that wolves attack people to eat them is nonsense. Wild animals rarely dare to get close to humans.'

Before Liliana's eyes, the images of shredded flesh in the trees and wolf tracks in the snow flickered. 'And what if it's the wolves that spread rabies? Priest Mathias warned us to avoid wild animals. The disease is said to make them particularly aggressive. If we get bitten ...'

Father stood next to her. 'And how do they get into the city? There's many cases of that wretched illness there, too.'

'Maybe they infect other animals, like sheep or dogs, for example, who then pass it on.'

The howling sounded again, and this time, she heard growls from several directions. She jumped up and peered into the dark gaps between the outlines of the trees and bushes. Her heart was pounding, ready for flight.

'Father? What do we do? We have nothing to defend ourselves!'

'That won't be necessary—' Father faltered. The first pair of yellow eyes glowed out of the darkness. He lowered his voice. 'Slowly ... Don't run, Liliana!'

Why did they have to be stuck right after dark? Liliana looked around in panic. The only thing they were left with was ... 'Let's hide under the cart!'

More and more pairs of yellow eyes appeared. Gradually, the lurking wolves drew their circle tighter. With bated breath, she moved towards the cart, fumbling backward with her feet, not daring to look away for a second.

Father followed her step by step. Even he seemed worried. 'They're getting closer and closer,' he whispered. 'Why?'

'El, what are you waiting for?' Liliana had reached the still-upright side of the car and grabbed the wooden frame. 'If we turn it over, we can—'

'Wait!' El straightened up. He sounded strangely serene. 'That won't be necessary.'

Bewildered, Liliana spun around and saw him facing the lurking shadows. He rose to his full height and – growled back!

Liliana's hair stood on end. Had he gone mad? What in the name of the Light was he doing? She watched his figure from behind. An exceptionally monstrous animal broke away from the ranks and stalked so close to El that she could see the bristled fur and teeth sticking out of its drooling mouth in the dim circle of the lantern. It readied itself to jump, remained in the position, and put its ears back.

For an unbearably drawn-out moment, Liliana waited for the attack. But it never came. The animal whined and withdrew. As if on command, the pack dispersed and disappeared into the night.

Liliana listened intently into the forest. It crackled and rustled in the undergrowth for a while. No one spoke until a howl rang out from a safe distance. Still shaky, she walked towards El, who was standing there with his back to them.

'What was that?'

He didn't react, and Liliana approached, still as cautiously as she'd acted in the presence of the wolves. She couldn't imagine how frightening this confrontation must've been for someone who, possibly, had been mauled by wolves not long ago. 'El?'

She tugged at his sleeve. 'El!'

'What?' He looked down at her blankly.

'What was that?'

'I ... didn't feel aggression but curiosity from them. I figured, if I intimidate the pack leader, they might leave us alone.'

She stared at him, disconcerted. Had the impending danger left him cold? Who came up with an idea as strange as growling at wolves? They might just as well have interpreted it as a challenge! She looked from him to Father, who was still standing by the cart. As he lifted the lantern, his half-lit face clearly showed how eerie he found this strange episode.

'I don't think they would have backed away from me or Liliana,' he remarked, turning to El.

'Maybe they would have,' El replied with a half-hearted shrug. 'It was an instinctive reaction.'

Father looked over at them as if waiting for another growl, or a sign of rabies, perhaps. 'If it wasn't aggression,' he said slowly, 'then what attracted the wolves to us?'

El avoided his gaze. 'I'm unsure.'

'Why don't you have a guess?'

There was a tone in Father's voice that Liliana didn't like. When El, apparently lost in thought, looked out into the dark forest and answered no longer, she plucked at his sleeve again. 'Is everything all right?'

He flinched. 'Yes ... Yes, thank you for asking.'

'Weren't you afraid of the wolves? After what ... what happened to you?'

'No. I trusted my instincts.'

Finally, the sound of clopping announced Frederik with the spare wheel. The wain was soon ready to drive again, and Father urged Elisa to great haste. Deep folds dug into his forehead. They spent the last part of the journey home in silence.

Chapter Twelve

El tried his hand at milking and helped as much as he could with feeding. His gait gradually became steadier. The sheep would soon have their lambs, and Frida, who had been dry for eight weeks, was about to give birth to her calf. She had separated herself from the other animals and behaved restlessly. For hours, glassy mucus flowed. When the amniotic sac appeared, Liliana excitedly brought El into the stable. The calf's front legs came first, and after the rupture of the amniotic sac, the head became visible. Moments later, the calf slipped onto the straw. El watched the mother intently as she licked the newborn, which soon made its first attempts at standing and walking. Cedi named the calf Nima, and seeing as no one objected, it stayed that way.

Father wanted to wait until the soil dried a bit before sowing wheat. However, they had already started with garden beans, garlic, radishes, carrots and an intercrop for green manure.

'You spend a lot of time with him,' Hans said in a lowered voice. He loosened the beds with a rake and hoe so that Liliana could remove the weeds. Further back, Cedi planted seeds and tubers. Without the delicate rays of the morning sun, Liliana's hands would have quickly turned stiff from the damp, cold earth and the plants covered in dew.

'What do you mean?'

'At some point, he will remember his family and return to his own home.'

'Maybe he doesn't have one any more.'

'Even so ... Someone like El won't stay here. He can't build a new life with us. He knows nothing about livestock and agriculture. He speaks differently, eats differently, thinks differently.'

'Being different is not bad. I'm different, too, in some ways. You forget that my mother didn't grow up here either.'

Hans shook his head vehemently. 'You're still one of us. You grew up in the countryside. We don't know anything about El, except that he's different.'

'That he's friendly. And well read, attentive, imaginative ...'

And that he might have held a very respectable position before he lost his memory. However, the elegance of the rich and important didn't quite suit someone who growled at wolves in the forest at night. Had the experience in which he almost died had some kind of strange impact on him? In any case, he wasn't a madman, and he didn't have rabies either.

With a casual but powerful blow, Hans stuck the hoe into the ground. Liliana couldn't tell if he was worried or indignant. 'He could be a criminal!'

'Or the escaped victim of a deceitful intrigue.' Undeterred, Liliana continued to pluck weeds and throw them into the wheelbarrow.

Still shaking his head, Hans picked up the hoe again. 'Not everyone who is friendly is also trustworthy. I don't want to accuse him of bad intentions. But don't get caught up in something you might regret later. The world out there isn't as romantic as you imagine it to be. Why do you think your mother turned her back on that breed of people?'

Liliana looked up at him. 'You like life here, don't you?'

'Why not? I like working outside. I feel comfortable with the animals, and I know I can count on everyone else when I need help. I like the smell of hay and the open sky above me.'

'It sounds like your life wouldn't look any different if you could make it up as you pleased.'

Hans grinned at that. 'My dream is to build a house on my own stretch of land. I want to pass something on to my children and grandchildren. Something I created with my own hands.'

As they continued to work, she watched his practiced, rhythmic strokes. Hans was proof that one could be satisfied with little. True, being able to admire something created by one's own hands was a reward in itself. Spoiled people like Aunt Jana would never understand that, just as they wouldn't know how to enjoy the peaceful setting surrounded by fields, streams and trees. Was that what had encouraged Mother to stay? The modest reliability of the people in the countryside and their connection with nature? Or had she died young because, despite her love for Father, she could never be happy in the daily grind of peasants?

The Spring Celebrations were now an ongoing topic. Liliana told El about the many competitions that would take place and the dance in the evening. Cedi never got tired of talking about the ball game with which the Celebrations were opened. This year, he was finally old enough to participate. After dinner, he explained to El how it was played.

'The goal is to kick the ball, meaning the inflated pig's bladder, into the church of the opposing village. We start at the centre stone denoting the halfway mark between Krambach and Heidenried. Every man from the village can take part, and everything is allowed!'

'Except for manslaughter,' added Frederik, who stood up from the table. The farmhands had already retired, and Annelies was washing the cooking pot outside.

'Except for manslaughter!' Cedi nodded enthusiastically. 'Last year's losers slaughter a pig, and the winning village keeps it as a festive roast. Sadly, we lost last year. But this time round we are definitely going to win!'

Father remained seated for once – he had been even more silent than usual since the incident with the wolves – and joined the conversation. 'Just don't take your brother as a role model. He dislocated his shoulder last year.'

'Martin, that fat beast of a man, threw himself at me just as I was about to grab the ball!' shouted Frederik from one of the other rooms.

'Are you in?' Cedi nudged El with his elbow, whereupon he looked questioningly at Liliana. She shook her head.

'Well then,' El said with a grin, 'why not? …'

Liliana threw her hands in the air. 'Grandmother! Tell him this is a stupid idea!'

But Grandmother laughed. 'He's already moving quite freely. After the game, we'll know if everything has grown back properly.'

'Or everything will have to heal all over again! Father?'

'El is a free man. If he wants to throw himself into battle for the pride of the village, I won't stop him.'

'Then you two can nurse him back to health afterwards!'

Liliana trudged to her room but left the door ajar and listened to the men's voices discussing which opponents one had to be particularly wary of. Now and then, Grandmother would chip in to mention a violent game from a past year, after which she had run out of bandages to hand out.

Meanwhile, Liliana opened her closet. She owned several aprons, two work dresses, a Sunday dress, and three beautiful gowns that had once belonged to Mother. Despite the simple cuts, the material was exquisite, and they seemed too precious to wear more than once or twice a year. Since she had also inherited Mother's petite figure, they fit very well, although Liliana was probably taller. In any case, she didn't mind showing some ankle. Where might those dresses have been made? Mother could well have acquired them on one of her trips.

She decided she'd wear the light blue one – she wanted to save the silver one for a special occasion, and the pink one she'd worn last year – so she spread it out on her bed. Then she noticed a movement behind her. El appeared in the doorway.

'Pretty,' he remarked approvingly. 'The delicate shimmer stems from woven silk threads, I take it?'

'I'll be out again in no time.' She'd hoped he wouldn't see the dress until she wore it and quickly grabbed it again.

'No, no.' He raised his hands defensively. 'It is high time for me to move into the living room. You've given up your bed long enough for me.'

'Fine.' She tidied the dress away. Seeing as El remained in the doorway, she turned to him, arms crossed in front of her chest. 'I don't understand how you seriously think you'll take part in this game when you're only just able to stand on your own two feet again!'

'Don't worry, I'll take care of myself.'

His voice sounded unusually soft, and her anger melted away. A feeling came over her, as if she needed to urgently tell him something that had slipped her mind. He returned her gaze for a while, and an exciting kind of dizziness stirred in her. She wished he would name what was happening between them. Instead, he interrupted the tension by clearing his throat, and abruptly broke away from the doorframe.

'Good night, then.'

Liliana hadn't noticed just how comfortable her own bed was compared to the straw sacks until she slipped into it. The second thing she immediately noticed was a smell. She wouldn't have been able to describe it, but she knew it was El's smell. Lulled into it, she fell asleep quickly, and when she awoke, she was sure they had spent time together in her dreams, too. It was still dark and quiet in the house, yet she couldn't fall asleep again.

When she thought she heard a noise in the living room, she got up. It was probably nothing, but she would take the opportunity to see if El slept well on the straw sacks. She walked carefully in the dark so as not to bump a toe or wake the others by making a loud noise. Gently, she leaned over the makeshift bed. It was empty. She straightened up and peered around. Where was he? Should she look for him, or should she go back to the warmth of her covers?

Then the front door opened, and a figure illuminated by the moon entered. Liliana was startled, although she knew who it had to be. He dabbed his face with the bottom of his shirt.

'El?'

He flinched and dropped the hem. 'You're awake?'

'Some kind of noise woke me. I couldn't fall asleep after that. What about you?'

With the door, he also closed the moonlight away. She straightened up and stepped closer to see more than just his outline. He ran his fingers through his dark hair.

'I had to relieve myself.'

Liliana felt for his hand, which was damp, and began to rub it between her hands. 'You're very cold. It's not raining outside, is it?'

'No, I washed myself briefly by the stream.'

'Why? In the middle of the night?'

She recognised a shrug and set about rubbing his other hand as well. 'Come, wrap up in your blanket!'

But when she went to get the blanket, he held her back. 'Liliana.'

His hand rested on her shoulder. Through the fabric of her undershirt, her skin began to burn in a strangely pleasant way. 'You realise that next time we go to Roinnenstadt, I'll stay there, don't you?'

She swallowed and nodded slowly. 'What are you going to do? You haven't found anyone who knows you. We don't know what kind of work you could take on either.'

'Don't worry about me. I will find something. I would like to follow up on your aunt's suspicion, in case she was right after all. And if not, I'll move on ... If I stay here, I may never find out who I am and where I come from. And I don't want to be a burden to your family any longer, now that I've recovered.'

'You're not a burden. No matter what you do afterwards, you're always welcome here in my bed.'

His eyebrows darted upward. An amused tone vibrated in his voice. 'How am I to interpret that?'

Liliana caught her breath. Somehow, two different strands of thought had treacherously intertwined. 'That sounded ... I mean, you're always welcome here and ... I'm happy to give up my bed for you if you need one ... Unless you prefer straw sacks.'

He laughed with a delight that made her knees buckle. She felt his hand on her cheek, his fingers gently stroking towards the back of her neck. 'I know very well what you mean.'

Her heart reared up as if wanting to break away with excitement, like a wild mare. They were so close together that her chest almost touched his. His fingers reached the back of her head and stayed there for several heartbeats. She looked expectantly at his face, where the bronze eyes glowed warmly. When she felt his breath on her lips, she opened them just a little.

Suddenly, he backed away. Liliana could physically feel the emptiness in front of her. She shrank back. Had she completely misjudged the moment?

El retreated so far into the shadows that she couldn't make out his expression. She only heard him tentatively clear his throat.

'I should … get some sleep.'

'Oh.' Confused, she searched for something appropriate to say but couldn't think of anything useful. 'I thought …' Yes, what exactly *had* she been thinking? That he wanted to kiss her? When it came to love, all of her knowledge came from books. 'Me, too. I should be sleeping, too.'

She wrapped her arms around her middle and crawled back into her room. Had she imagined that he liked her back? Would a man who had no interest in her behave like that? Hardly. What, then, prevented him from expressing his affection? She didn't sleep a wink until dawn.

Chapter Thirteen

On the morning of the Celebrations, the whole farmstead vibrated with tension.
Even the animals scratched, squealed and bleated excitedly. Grandmother served
a sumptuous breakfast, which Liliana thought was unnecessary; after all, there
would be a proper feast in the evening. But the others all greedily stuck in.

A little later, the family set off and met with the other villagers, who were
pouring in from field and house. It was a proper parade, led by the dead pig and
its bladder. The young men hooted and goaded each other while high-spirited
children jumped around their legs. Priest Mathias placed two ropes at equal
intervals from the centre stone, so that the parties would remain separated
before the start of the game. He was given the honour of throwing the ball in
the air when the time came.

A cheerful sun shone down on the players, who gathered on both sides. The
air was clear and cool but would soon warm up. Of course, Liliana's brothers
immediately pushed to the front row. Frederik rolled up his sleeves, Cedi danced
excitedly on the spot, Hans clenched his fists and Jakob pulled his shirt over his
head and flexed his muscles. Even Father stood there, legs wide apart, and El
cracked his fingers and neck. Liliana groaned inwardly. If only this turned out
well ...

Priest Mathias had wisely taken his gong with him, which he struck several
times to make himself heard. 'You all know the custom. Are you ready?'

Eager shouting filled the landscape, and as soon as Priest Mathias threw
up the ball, the groups collided with each other like two stone walls. In the

"

beginning, there was chaos, and no one knew where the ball was. The players pushed each other to the ground and arbitrarily tugged at limbs they believed belonged to the opposition. Finally, one of them fought his way free and stumbled off. Unfortunately, it was someone from Krambach. The spectators rushed out of the way so as to not be overrun.

Liliana, who was standing by the side of the road with Annelies and Grandmother, reluctantly began to be engrossed in the game. 'Quick, stop him! Grab that man!' Her voice was drowned out in the general tumult.

Because the game could last for several hours, it was important for the participants to manage their stamina well. Liliana noticed that some of the people of Krambach went on their way to their own village right from the start. They were probably lining up in front of their church to guard it. She doubted that her own team had come up with any tactics. Whether they could make up for it with enthusiasm and sportsmanship remained to be seen.

After the ball had changed direction several times, the crowd now quickly moved down the path to Heidenried. Liliana suggested to Grandmother that they climb the nearest hill, so that they could keep track and follow the game without having to rush back and forth themselves. Annelies and a few other women from the village joined them. From a distance, the event was reminiscent of an odd anthill whose ants couldn't decide where their place was. The ball almost came back to the centre stone, and then moved back to Heidenried. So far, the people of Krambach had not made it to the church, but it seemed only a matter of time before they broke through.

Then the ball flew out of the pile in a wide arc. A lone player grabbed it and dashed off. Liliana narrowed her eyes. 'That's El!'

She gathered her skirt and ran down the hill to Krambach. It was a long way to the village, and when she got to the first farm she held her side, panting and looking around for the players. No one in sight yet! She took a shortcut across a field that hadn't been cultivated yet, and when she saw the church, she leaned against a fence. She tore off her thick woollen scarf and, in addition to the noise of mooing and ringing of cowbells, heard approaching screams. Where were they?

One of the barns suddenly spat out El – and, a little after, a mob covered with straw and dirt. Fluttering chickens dispersed in all directions. El headed for the church and started his final spurt. But the opponents, positioned in front of it, were already waiting for him. He let the first one stagger into thin air with a jerky turn and skilfully avoided the second one, too. Then all the rest threw themselves at him. He fell to the ground and tossed the ball out of reach at the last moment, before he was buried under the mass of bodies.

'El!'

Worried, Liliana shot off. She thought they'd lost the ball, then Cedi jumped out of nowhere and caught it. Neither Liliana nor the people of Krambach had seen him coming. He ducked between two players and kicked the ball under the legs of another ... right through the open church door.

Cedi threw his fist in the air and cheered into the incredulous silence of the players and gathered villagers. With disappointed grumbles, the men of Krambach rolled out of the tangle under which El had disappeared. Meanwhile, the large mass of players that had been chasing El came to a slippery halt.

'We won!'

'What the—'

'Did you see that?'

Liliana hurried past them towards the spot where El lay motionless in the mud, holding one arm in front of his face for protection. She dropped to her knees beside him. 'El? Are you still alive?'

'I think so.' He coughed, sat up cautiously and rubbed his head. Relieved, Liliana threw her arms around his neck. He groaned but indulged her. 'We won?'

She released her embrace. Her dress was now just as muddy. 'Yes!'

His face glowed with excitement. Despite his exhaustion, Liliana had never seen him so lively. He laughed and brushed the tangled hair out of his forehead.

His gaze lingered on her lips, where it left a painfully tingling sensation. In his eyes, she saw the same longing that had gripped her from head to toe.

He leaned forward, and the world stopped.

'El, that was fantastic!'

Cedi's voice wedged between them. El turned his head away. Liliana also caught herself quickly this time and covered her racing heartbeat with a bright laugh. The world resumed its usual course. Cedi held out his hand to help El up.

'I've never seen anyone run so fast! At least not since Frederik knocked down the wasp's nest from the oak tree.'

Other players found their way over to congratulate Cedi and El on their efforts. Frederik patted El on the back and, with Jakob's help, hoisted Cedi high up in the air. Surrounded by revellers, they carried him back to their village. Everyone was bursting with joy and dirt. El shook hands here and there and was eyed curiously from all sides. Eventually, they met Hans and Father, who had skinned his knees and elbows. Grandmother scolded him as if he were her little boy again.

On a fallow meadow at the foot of the hill where the church stood, tables and benches had been set up, and a stone circle had been built for the fire. The sunny afternoon had smaller competitions and games in store. Children fought with sticks, jumped over wooden posts, aimed slingshots at a straw doll and twisted colourful bows into ribbons. Whole families massed in tugs of war. Hans won a cheese wheel in horseshoe-throwing and a wreath of sausages in arm-wrestling.

Liliana watched the hustle and bustle with El from the sidelines. It smelled of hay and damp earth, sweaty bodies and soon of smoke. This was the sign for Liliana and Annelies to get the two huge semolina cakes with dried plums that they had baked the day before. The men joined them, in order to slip out of their muddy clothing. Liliana also wanted to take the opportunity to put on her blue dress. But first, the cows needed milking.

Once the most urgent tasks had been done, and everyone was freshly dressed up, they set off together for the evening part of the Spring Celebrations. El provoked astonished looks and whispers with the attire he had acquired in the city. A queue had formed for the pig on the spit, with its fat hissing into the embers. Liliana's stomach gurgled impatiently, and she joined the line.

Frederik sat down to eat with his friends, and the rest of the family followed him, except for Father and Grandmother, who were already engaged in conversations elsewhere. By the time it got dark, there was nothing left of the pig. But there was still plenty of beer flowing. Someone revived the fire with extra wood, and it flickered happily into the starry sky. Liliana loved this atmosphere. Everyone was chatting, warming themselves by the fire. The children chased each other around the benches until tiredness caught up with them. When the first chords of the music sounded, she felt a hand on her arm.

'Will you dance with me?'

Liliana looked up at Hans and back down at her plate. 'Maybe later. Let me finish my food first.'

She'd hoped El would ask her to dance. But perhaps the situation was too unfamiliar to him, and she would have to take the initiative. That one brief moment after the game had given her a boost. This time she was sure he'd been very close to kissing her. If Cedi hadn't interrupted them ...

She ate the last piece of pork and watched the circling couples. Among them was Mathilde, whose name Frederik had mentioned suspiciously often of late.

'Well?' She nudged her brother from the side. 'Why aren't you with your beloved?'

Cedi was immediately in on it and pinched his brother on the cheek across the table. 'Well? Well? What are you waiting for?'

'Oh, stop it!' Frederik slapped his hand away, and his siblings laughed teasingly.

She caught El's gaze. Since they had changed into their fancy apparel, he conducted himself even more reservedly than usual. Did he feel out of place?

She took a deep breath and said loudly, 'Now I feel like dancing! El, are you coming?'

But he shook his head distractedly. Was he lacking something? A group of youths rushed past their table, laughing and screaming. She waited until they had moved on before she tried again.

'Would you like to eat some more?'

'No, thank you.'

'Do you want me to get you another beer?'

'No, thank you.'

She raised her arms theatrically. 'What's wrong with you? You don't want anything.'

He mumbled something inaudible, and Liliana frowned at him. Didn't he enjoy the Celebrations? She would try again later. 'Fine. Frederik, will you dance with me?'

He also waved her off. Liliana could have bet he was waiting for the end of the current song, to see if Mathilde separated from her dance partner.

'Cedi?'

'Me?'

'Yes, you! The way you were celebrated today, girls will soon be throwing themselves at you. You'd better step on your sister's toes a bit before you embarrass yourself with them.'

Cedi shook his head, but Liliana didn't give in and dragged him onto the dancing ground, where she showed him the steps one by one. After three or four rounds, he had memorised the movements. Liliana grabbed his hands and spun around with him. He stuck the tip of his tongue out of his mouth in concentration. The realisation of how quickly her little brother was growing up put Liliana in a nostalgic mood. Hadn't he been hiding behind her skirt only yesterday because a ram snorted at him angrily? And now he had won the village game and learned how to dance.

At the end of the fourth song, she finished the lesson. As soon as she let go of Cedi, a group of giggling girls approached. She sighed. Maybe Frederik was right, and she was getting too old for all this. She gradually moved away from Cedi, and the girls immediately showered him with questions about the game. Liliana looked for Valerie among those present. She found her cousin next to Uncle Bernd by the fire and beckoned her over.

'Did you miss the ball game? I couldn't see you anywhere!'

'Yes, and of course this time we won. Everyone says it was very exciting.' Valerie sounded mildly disappointed. 'Mother needed me, but now she's sleeping.'

Liliana felt too much zest for life tingling in her toes to stand still. So, she took Valerie by the hand and led her into the circle of dancers. 'Madam ...'

Valerie smiled and they hopped into the sequence of steps together. 'Who have you danced with?'

'Only with Cedi. Hans asked me, but I was still eating.' Between two turns, Liliana glanced back at the table, where El was still sitting with a stony expression. How come none of the other girls tried to approach him? El probably scared them off with his distant air.

'And you?'

'With Peter. And with Jakob.'

'Jakob?' This was an unexpected development. 'Has he ever even spoken to you before?'

'A few times,' Valerie replied. 'He's quite nice. It's just that he speaks a little too fast for me.'

'His thoughts can be jumpy.' Liliana chuckled. Not only her feet but also her heart bobbed up and down to the music. The dress swayed around her legs, and loose strands from her pinned-up braid flew into her mouth. She blew them away, laughing.

During a break between two songs, she looked over at El again, and their eyes met. Liliana waved, but he turned away. She tilted her head closer to Valerie and whispered, 'Now, let's see if I can't get our stranger to dance after all …'

Then she marched in a direct line towards him. Still slightly out of breath, she reached the table, and placed her hands on the tabletop in front of him.

'El, come, dance with me!'

'I'd rather not.'

He avoided her gaze. Why did he squirm like that?

'Why not?'

Finally, he looked up. He appeared overwhelmed. 'I … can't.'

'I'll teach you!'

Liliana leaned over the table, balancing her weight on her hands. She didn't understand how her enthusiasm could leave him cold. Was he afraid of embarrassing himself in front of the villagers? Who cared about their opinion anyway?

He backed away. 'No, thank you.'

Just as she was about to double down, a harsh voice broke through the general noise of the festivities. It was one of Frederik's circle of friends.

'Look at her! She's gonna climb on his lap any moment now!'

'I bet she's seen everything already,' roared another.

'And she liked it! She can't get enough!'

Loud laughter broke out on the benches, and embarrassment flushed her face. What did these drunkards care? And why did El have to treat her like this? Would a single dance be so bad? Before any other comments followed, Liliana turned and fled towards the fire.

She was close to walking home alone. Her eyes burned. She blinked, feeling humiliated. This wasn't how she'd imagined the evening would go. It was supposed to be a wonderful night, one he would never forget. One that would keep him from leaving her behind when he ventured out there. She couldn't let him go just like that. At last, she'd found someone who showed genuine interest in her thoughts, who was well read and well spoken, who awakened that warm feeling in her bosom – someone who could show her the world.

Liliana stopped sharply and straightened her shoulders. No, she wouldn't let her good mood be spoiled, not by a grumpy El and not by Frederik's uncouth friends. She spotted Hans, who was toasting with Father. At least there was a man who wasn't too fine to dance.

On the way to Hans, she almost bumped into someone else. It was Peter, who hastily apologised and gave her a nervous smile. 'Ah, Liliana. May I ask you to dance?'

She was too astonished to refuse his request. Since he didn't pick up the rhythm right away, it took a moment for them to find each other. Liliana examined him secretly. Uncle Bernd had given up trying marry Valerie off because of her mother's illness. But that didn't mean that Peter was no longer looking for a replacement for his dead wife. There was hardly a better opportunity to do so than the Spring Celebrations. She couldn't say exactly how old Peter was; too young not to marry again, and yet too old for Valerie, she thought. Aside from towering over most men, he was as unremarkable as a man could be. If all of the faces in the village were mixed into one, the result would be Peter.

He complimented her on her dress and asked how she was doing and who she was getting along well with. Presumably, he knew as little about her as she did about him. Liliana replied politely, trying not to think about El. Still, the empty seat on the bench where he had been sitting all this time was disheartening. Peter held her so carefully that she barely felt his hand on her back. Fortunately, he dismissed her before she started to get antsy.

Liliana searched everywhere for El, but he was neither at the fire, nor around the tables, nor in any other group of chattering villagers. Unsettled, she stared into the silent darkness of the surroundings. He must have grown so tired of the hustle and bustle that he'd made his way home without a word. A bitter taste settled on her tongue. She wrapped her arms around her chest. For a moment, she felt abandoned, despite the many happy people around her. As she was shivering without her scarf in the progressing night, she decided to dance one last time with Hans and then end the day.

She quickly tracked him down, and his fervour was reassuring. He sometimes missed the mark but quickly found the sequence of steps again. For the first time since they had known each other, Liliana asked him about his family and the village where he'd grown up. She learned that Hans was one of ten children his parents had struggled to feed. He held her a little tighter than she was used to, creating a brisk tension for dancing and whirling her around almost without any effort on her part.

When she said goodbye for the evening, he offered to accompany her. Liliana was happy to be distracted from her feelings by conversation on the way home. She stumbled on the stony path a few times before her eyes got used to the lack of light, and Hans was there to support her every time. They discussed the ball game, and Liliana shared tactical ideas she'd come up with. Passing the edge of the forest, they heard distant cracking.

'I only hope Annelies' beast doesn't show up now,' Liliana remarked amusedly. 'If so, we'll quickly find out whose legs are more tired after today.'

Hans stopped and sought her gaze. 'You know ... I've never met someone like you.'

'That's putting it nicely.' Liliana slowed her steps only briefly. She knew that most people in the village found her dreamy nature odd.

Hans hurried to walk beside her again. 'I mean it nicely, too. Actually, more than just nicely.'

All of a sudden, Liliana's stomach tightened. His voice had changed tone and reminded her of Uncle Bernd's dog, Timmy, when he rested his head on her leg with his big, brown eyes, hoping for a treat from the table. She quickened her step. Had they almost arrived at the house yet?

'Liliana ... I don't know how to tell you this ...'

She laughed tensely and swung her legs with even more urgency. Whatever he had to say, she had an uneasy feeling that she'd rather not hear it. Although she loved her home, she felt that she'd already given in to the call of the big wide world. She jumped over the creek and rushed to the door of the main house before he could get his words in.

'You can give it some more thought tomorrow,' she said, holding the door open for him.

'Can't you guess what I'm trying to say?'

He entered hesitantly, and Liliana almost dragged him through the entrance. 'No. Maybe. I don't know … I'm going to bed now. Good night!'

In her panicky haste, she forgot to check whether El had already fallen asleep on the straw sacks.

Chapter Fourteen

An overtired group greeted her the morning after the festivities. Annelies yawned incessantly while milking. In the living room, they met Jakob and Hans, who were groaning and stretching their overused muscles. Frederik gazed at the wall in blissful half-sleep, and Cedi hung over the table with a pale face, as if he would quite like to throw up but couldn't quite muster the strength to do it. Even Grandmother, who held out a mug of herbal tea to him, looked at least a decade older overnight. Only El and Father were nowhere to be seen.

'Does anyone know where El is? Or Father?'

'Your father had something pressing to discuss with the neighbours, dove. I'm sure he'll be back soon.'

'And El?' Liliana asked hopefully. But Grandmother shrugged her shoulders as she filled bowls of oats for Liliana and Annelies.

They sat down, and Liliana was careful not to get too close to Cedi so that he wouldn't fall over or empty his stomach on her lap. The fingers of her free hand scratched over a dent in the tabletop. It was an uncomfortable feeling, not knowing where El was. Should she be worried? Where else would he go? Had he set off alone to the city without saying goodbye? That seemed unlikely.

'Where could he be? Didn't he say anything to anyone?'

'Hmm, who?' Frederik, who was resting his chin on his hand and hadn't touched his food yet, looked up in astonishment.

'El! The injured stranger who has been with us this whole time?'

'Oh, him ... I saw him disappear into the dark with Marie last night.'

Liliana coughed. She felt as if she'd just swallowed gravel. The two farmhands also raised their heads, and Annelies opened her mouth in shock. Only Cedi continued to show no signs of life.

'Marie?' Liliana's voice soared an octave higher. 'Are you sure?'

'Yes, yes, Marie. Everyone in the village knows her.'

The gravel had landed in her stomach and turned into lead. She pushed the gruel away and lowered her head, so as to not let the others read her face. The tenacious mass spread from her stomach into her limbs, her thoughts and her heart, until everything about her felt heavy and miserable.

'For a fine fellow like him to get involved with someone like Marie,' Annelies remarked.

Marie of all people … the only girl who didn't show her face at the sewing bee either, ever since the village had found out how willingly she let all sorts of men look under her skirt.

The voices blurred, and so did the table and the living room before Liliana's eyes. Everything bent and contorted, as if reality had to reshape itself to absorb what she'd heard. How could she have been so wrong about him?

She barely noticed Father entering and throwing his cloak over his shoulder. There was a hard line around his mouth. 'Frederik, Hans, Jakob, Cedi, you're coming with me. Liliana, you will see to Uncle Herbert with Grandmother. Annelies … you're free until tomorrow morning. Go and visit your family.'

A moment of silence followed. Lone neighing echoed from the stable. Cedi whimpered and raised his head. 'Leave me be …'

Father grabbed him by the collar and dragged him out of the door. A little later, Cedi staggered back into the room with bright, frightened eyes and dripping hair. Everyone gawped at Father, who was standing in the doorway with an iron face.

'Was that necessary?' Grandmother chimed in.

Father paid no attention to her. 'Today, no one stays at home. You've heard what you have to do!'

The farmhands rose and even Frederik suddenly seemed completely present. Liliana, on the other hand, did not move.

'Liliana!'

'Grandmother doesn't need me!' she blurted out irritably. Couldn't Father choose another day for his bout of authoritative posturing? She felt like bursting into tears.

Father looked as if he wanted to rush up to her and grab her as well. Had she been a son, he wouldn't have held back. 'You will do what I tell you to do! And stay there until everything's done!'

Liliana jumped up and ran to her room, where she threw herself on the bed and sobbed quietly. Why did it hurt so much? How could El do this to her? Did he have no feelings for her at all?

A little later, Grandmother came and stroked her hair comfortingly.

'I'm sure he has his reasons, dove.'

For a confused moment, Liliana thought she was talking about El.

'Come on, you can tell me what's on your mind along the way.'

Liliana wiped away her tears. Maybe getting away from the farm wasn't such a bad idea. She didn't want to be here when El came back from his nightly adventure with tousled hair and dreamy eyes. And Marie ... of course she had to prey on the only man far and wide who didn't know of her reputation.

She wrapped herself tightly in her scarf and followed Grandmother, who had already packed her bundle of herbal medicines. For the first bit, they wandered in silence. Her legs still weighed heavily. Nevertheless, she put one foot in front of the other. Without a horse, it was a long way to Oberdorf, where Uncle Herbert lived with his family, but Father had claimed that he needed Elisa himself. His behaviour was strange, yet Liliana was too busy with her emotional whirlpool to care. Even the first butterfly that fluttered in front of her face could not distract her. Around noon, they crossed the forest just before Oberdorf, and Liliana finally broke the silence.

'El is the absolute worst! After everything we've done for him, he's spending the night of the Spring Celebrations with Marie! I should have left him in the forest!'

Marie had snuck into all the images she'd made up in her mind. Now this hussy would stroll arm in arm with El through the streets of an exciting city, dance closely with him in the moonlight, and ride towards new adventures beyond the territorial borders ... Or maybe she had just opened Liliana's eyes. Perhaps he was a selfish, rich cad, whose profound words had been nothing but empty husks from the start.

While Grandmother looked at her from the side, Liliana tightened the scarf around her shoulders and stared at her feet. 'What do all these men see in Marie? Is she so stunningly beautiful that it doesn't matter how many others she's had ... and will have still? She's so dull! She can't even spell her own name.'

'It's a mystery to me, too,' Grandmother said helpfully.

'What's wrong with me? Am I not good enough?'

'You're more than enough, little dove,' Grandmother assured her. 'It just takes the right person to recognise that.'

'And if that person doesn't exist?'

'There's always someone. Or even more than a single someone. You know, sometimes we're the ones who don't see what we truly need.'

Liliana wasn't sure if she was ready for Grandmother's wisdom, so she kept silent. Uncle Herbert seemed astonished to see them, and Grandmother took him aside for a moment. Presumably, they were talking about his gout. Then he invited them in and had Liliana sweep the house. She worked the floors as if this unbearable stinging in her chest were their fault. Afterwards, she helped Aunt Charlotte bake and fed the animals. Cedi's prophecy that she would grow old all alone, surrounded only by books and goats, was already beginning to come true.

When they had an in-between meal together, Liliana sat down next to Grandmother and quietly asked if she really had to stay.

'I don't think they need our help that much. I'd rather be alone. We can't stay much longer anyway if we want to be back before dark.'

Grandmother agreed. 'I think we've completed your father's assignment to the best of our abilities.'

They quickly made their way home. Something pulled Liliana back; perhaps the prospect of losing herself in a book, perhaps the self-tormenting need to see how El would act. When they entered the homestead, it was suspiciously quiet. There were no sounds of anyone working or talking, only the clucking of the chickens, occasional snorting from the barn and the babbling of the stream. Liliana pushed open the front door and looked around.

'Where is everyone?'

Out of the corner of her eye, she noticed someone creeping silently into the room behind them. She whirled around and stared at El while Grandmother leisurely put down her bundle.

'There he is, the absolute worst,' Grandmother said. She shuffled away, remarking that someone had to do the milking.

Meanwhile, El walked up to Liliana, running his hand through his hair. He was still wearing the elegant clothes he had worn the night before; they looked crinkled now. Was she mistaken, or was there something different about him? His posture more upright, his movements more targeted?

'I need to talk to you …' He sounded excited.

Her heart was pounding in such a way that she couldn't determine the feeling that went with it. Her voice sounded shrill in her ears. 'I don't want to talk to you!'

She gathered her skirt and wanted to rush past him, but he grabbed her by the wrist. His touch threatened to etch a hole in her skin.

'Let me go!' She snatched her arm away more forcefully than necessary, trudged into her room and slammed the door in his face.

'How now?' He knocked on the wood that separated him from her. 'Liliana, it's important! My memories are back!'

She faltered. His memories? Anger and disappointment struggled with her longing to be close to him and her rising curiosity. On the spur of the moment, she pulled the door open again. He took the opportunity and slipped in before she could change her mind.

'I know everything,' he disclosed. 'Who I am, where I come from, why I was injured in the forest. It was my brother. He set a trap for me. Seeing as he doesn't know I'm still alive, I can use that to my advantage. It's too dangerous now, but when it's all over, I will come back to get you … if that's what you want.'

'Is this the same story you told Marie?'

'Marie?'

Liliana gasped. The leaden lump in her stomach wanted to come out. 'Don't play dumb! Frederik saw you two leave together last night!'

El shifted his weight and crossed his arms. He gazed at her suspiciously. 'Did he?'

Liliana would have liked to push and kick him, but she suspected that the difference of strength between them would make any such attempts futile. 'Yes, don't even try to talk your way out of it! I know exactly what happened between you.' Her eyes burned treacherously again. 'And I thought I knew you!'

His jaw tightened. 'Well, you don't.' Something sinister settled on his features. A warning glowed in his eyes.

'Then go and tell her your tale about your brother's betrayal, and all that!' She clenched her fists. 'You deserve each other!'

He blinked in surprise. 'What?'

'Why try to get to know someone first? No, it's all about looks, isn't it! I thought you were different. But stupid me only imagined there was something between us!'

El burst out laughing. It began as a cheerful chuckle and ended in a relieved cascade of laughter. Frustrated, she wiped her eyes. 'Why are you laughing?'

'You don't think I slept with her, do you?'

Hearing it so outrageously straightforward out of his mouth robbed her of her senses. Her cheeks flushed. Her eyelids fluttered uncertainly. She turned her head away, hoping to get a hold of herself.

'Are you jealous?' He was still laughing to himself.

She felt an intense need to hide. Everything was spinning in her head. She didn't understand what was happening. Could it be that she was wrong again? What should she believe now?

'I assure you, I didn't touch Marie ... at least not like this.' He put a finger under her chin to lift it, and his lips gently touched hers. The sensation shot through her like lightning. Then he took her hand and put it to his chest. She could feel his heartbeat, fast and strong.

'You're the only one who has this effect on me. If you knew how good you smell, you'd know there is no reason for you to be jealous.'

How good she smelled? His kiss still tingled on her lips and made her want more. She looked into his shimmering eyes, and she believed him.

This time, he hesitated because he was waiting. He was waiting for her consent. He didn't want to impose himself on her. Yet, if she gave him a sign, any sign, there would be no holding back for him.

Those eyes were the cliff on which she staggered. It was her decision. Would she take the plunge into the abyss? She couldn't see the ground from here, couldn't guess what came next, where it would lead.

She clawed her hand into his shirt and pulled him close. He greedily returned her initially awkward kisses. His hands ran over her curves as if he had to constantly reassure himself that he wasn't dreaming. Liliana was completely consumed by him, his tongue, his mouth, his taste.

Then he pulled away again and clasped her face with both hands. They paused, forehead to forehead, to catch their breath.

He was panting softly. 'Do you want to ...? With me ...?'

In response, she pressed her body to his, and he shuddered.

The tension between them reminded her of a rainstorm she had experienced as a child. The heat had accumulated throughout the day. Insects buzzed through the air, nervous with anticipation. Under the open sky, Liliana was at the mercy of the forces of nature. She had watched, fascinated, as the clouds piled up with menacing speed, feeling the deep rumble of the thunder to her bones. She had respect for the storm but was not afraid. The tension grew until it was almost unbearable. Then came the redeeming rain. Liliana welcomed it with open arms and danced to the drumming of the drops surrounding her.

Chapter Fifteen

When the storm had cooled down, Liliana snuggled up to El.

Although she knew his body well, this time she had discovered him in a completely different way. She knew exactly where to find each of the already fading scars and stroked the healed-up wound on his upper body with her fingertips. How wonderful it was that she found him, that he had come into her life. How great, how sweet, how delightful ...

El's head rested on one of his arms and he stroked her with his other hand, from her shoulder to her neck. Liliana closed her eyes and smiled blissfully. She wished this moment would never end.

'I have to leave soon. If you want to come with me, I will get you later. But first, I have to right some important matters.'

He seemed more confident than Liliana had seen him before. The knowledge of who he was must have given him new courage.

'Are you going to take revenge on your brother?'

Sighing, he withdrew his hand and sat up. 'It's not about revenge. It's about creating stability. My home is a dangerous place for someone like you. For me, too, as it turns out. But much more so for you.'

'What do you mean? Where is your home?'

He slipped into his trousers and pulled the shirt loosely over his head. 'I'm getting some water. I'll be right back.'

Had it been up to Liliana, he could have stayed undressed a while longer, but she remembered that Grandmother would not milk the cows forever. And the others should have returned long ago. What was this mysterious task Father needed to do so urgently?

She stretched comfortably and snuggled under the covers. Some places were still throbbing with unaccustomed soreness. Nevertheless, her body felt relaxed and full of life at the same time. According to his own words, El was already thinking about a possible future together. He wanted to come back for her. Liliana grinned into her blanket. What such a future might look like remained open for now. There were too many questions bouncing around in her head. Where was his home? Why did El's brother want to kill him? Was El even his real name?

Considering he'd meant to be right back, he stayed away for a long time. So Liliana finally got up and collected her clothes from the floor. Water would have been handy indeed, but she couldn't wait here endlessly. Just as she came out of her room, she heard strange noises from outside, angry shouts, footsteps and scraping, as if a whole crowd had gathered out there. She hurried into the living room and grabbed the door handle but couldn't move it. Had someone locked her in the house?

'El? El?' She pressed all her weight on it. Still nothing happened. Her stomach tightened. 'Grandmother?'

The clamour from outside grew louder. Something wasn't right; something wasn't right at all! She turned around and hastily crossed the house, towards the back door. Fortunately, that one did open. She rushed past the stable and barn.

As she skidded around the corner, she ran into an angry mob. Liliana knew most of the faces from her village. They had armed themselves with knives, shovels, rocks and pitchforks. What was going on?

She stood on her tiptoes to look over their heads. Everyone glowered grimly in the direction of the mill. Then, suddenly, she could make out El, who was retreating further and further back. He had raised his hands defensively and was talking to the crowd, who threw insults at his head. Along with the insults, stones flew through the air.

'Monster! Monster!'

'You murdered one of us! You're going to pay for that!'

'Leave, unholy creature!'

'You have no business here! We're not afraid of you!'

'Stop! Stop it! What are you doing?' Her voice broke; she was unable to drown out the angry cries.

Feverishly, she pushed the men aside and tried to make her way to El. But there was no getting through. They had pushed him back so far he almost touched the wall of the mill, and began to surround him on all sides. One stone hit him in the stomach, another in the face. His cheek was bleeding. What had gotten into all of them? Where were Father, Frederik and the others?

'Stop!' she heard El's voice. 'I'm going! I'm leaving as soon as ...'

The sun was only half a ball on the horizon. The long shadows and the reddish light of the twilight made everything look like a bad dream. To her horror, Liliana spotted Frederik and Hans, who stabbed at El with a skewer.

'Hans! *No!*' Liliana screamed so loudly that her lungs threatened to jump out of her throat, along with her screams.

Then the sun sank. The cold that began to spread was too malicious to be attributed to the coming night alone. It reached out and wrapped itself around everyone's limbs. Liliana gawked spellbound at El, whose eyes glowed bronze in the semi-darkness. The shadow around his feet was moving. Anxious neighing and bleating came from the stable. The mob held their breath like a single being.

'Back!' El's voice turned into a deep growl. The teeth in his mouth grew to abnormal length.

What? How could this be? Liliana struggled to think clearly. *What is he?*

At first, everyone looked intimidated. Then Hans jumped forward and thrust his spit into El's ribs – or at least, where his ribs should have been. El moved so fast that Liliana barely followed, and before anyone, including Hans himself, could react, blood and shreds of flesh shot out of his throat. With a gurgle, the farmhand fell to the ground.

El stood menacingly above him. His hands were dripping claws. 'Back, I said!'

But the crowd charged at him with hatred. He roared, and mighty black wings shot out of his back. One huge leap, and he was up in the air, disappearing into the cloudy night sky.

Liliana gasped as if she were drowning. Someone ran off to find Grandmother, but the way Hans was bleeding, death would come quickly and inevitably. Liliana trembled uncontrollably. In her panic, she sucked in more and more air, but it wasn't enough.

He had killed Hans. They had chased him away. He was a monster.

She trembled even more violently until her whole body shook uncontrollably. Her knees hit the ground. She was cold, so cold. Around her, the chaos of rushing legs and shovel handles began to spin. She was suffocating.

They had chased him away. He had killed Hans. He was a monster.

Her field of vision shrank from the outside in. She thought she heard her name, but soon all sounds broke off and a piercing, high-pitched tone filled her head. Everything went black. The only thing her senses still perceived was the smell that clung to her. *His* smell.

He was a monster.

Chapter Sixteen

Liliana saw herself from above, sometimes from the side or even from below, as she lay on the bed stiff with dread. Grandmother, who poured tea for her; Father, who encouraged her to eat; Annelies, who complained about the lack of help; none of it concerned her.

Hans and Marie were buried. Liliana remained motionless in her room. She didn't know if it was Tuesday or Saturday; if three days had passed or three weeks.

Valerie came to see her, but Liliana didn't understand any of the questions she asked. Before leaving, she opened the window so Liliana could hear the birds chirping and the lambs frolicking. When had the lambs arrived?

A patch of sunlight stuck to the opposite wall. Muffled voices and the smell of cooked food spilled over from the kitchen. Liliana watched as the spot moved further up and turned orange, then red, and then disappeared. After some time in the dark, she discovered a new, pale spot further down, which replaced the old one. Thankfully, the two didn't meet. Otherwise, one surely would have killed the other. Liliana turned around so she didn't have to see the spot of light any more.

'Eat a little, dove.'

Liliana counted the knots in the ceiling boards. This time it came to fifty-six, plus forty-eight cracks.

'Get up and move! Get some fresh air. You're pale as death.'

Death? Where? Here, in her bed?

'Liliana, you're worrying us.'

She dreamed of a thunderstorm, whose lightning struck all around her until the whole landscape was bare and charred.

At some point, Grandmother lit incense in her room, and something stirred inside Liliana. She sat up jerkily. Bright dots buzzed around her head like angry bees. And already she felt herself slowly tipping back onto the bed. She stared at Grandmother in a daze.

Please, don't!

'You've come back to your senses ... my herbs are working.'

'Away ...'

She didn't want the images, conjured up by the smell, in her head: her past self, watching over the stranger, caring for him, talking to him, laughing and opening her heart. What a naive young thing this Liliana was.

The smell subsided, and she was able to breathe again. The emptiness was back.

'Liliana, we need you.' Father's face hovered over her. 'There is so much work to do. And with one farmhand less ... He was a diligent worker, may his soul rest peacefully in the Light.'

She was scooped up. Wobbly, the room passed her by. Then, she sat on a bench in the evening sun, a chicken on her lap. It clucked and spread its feathers. It pecked at her finger.

'Ouch!' Liliana shooed the chicken away and began to cry. When she stopped, she had forgotten why she'd started in the first place.

In the kitchen, she found a hard loaf of bread and bit into it. After a second bite, she left the bread and went to the stable. Wasn't it time to milk the cows? Annelies looked up from her chair in amazement when Liliana grabbed an empty jug.

'You're up again?'

Liliana nodded and got to work. From then on, she fit seamlessly into the daily rhythm on the farm. The regimented work schedule gave her security. She didn't say a word, but no one complained. The vegetable patches needed to be prepared, and the sowing had to be cultivated. Liliana could almost believe that everything was back to the way it had been before. But the strange weakness did not want to leave her limbs.

Chapter Seventeen

The news of the monstrous incident in Heidenried had spread to the city, because one afternoon two men from the Roinnenstadt stood in front of the main house and talked to Father. Liliana kept her head down and shuffled past them into the stable, where Annelies was already listening at the door.

'Do you know what they want? I bet it's about ... *you know!*'

Liliana sat down with the milking chair to prepare Viola's udder.

As if she needed to counterbalance the lack of reaction with her own excitement, Annelies continued to comment on what she could spot between the cracks. 'That's the doctor who came to treat *his* wounds. And the other one, such a bighead! Look how he writes everything your father says down. Before you know it, people will be travelling from afar to see the place where that beast was hosted!'

A sharp pain pierced the back of Liliana's head. She took the jug between her knees and focused on the feeling of the cool metal beneath her fingers.

'Wait ... I think now they're talking about the increased cases of rabies. Your father is shaking his head. If only it had been rabies ... Are they stupid? Claws and wings growing out of his back. There's no way that was an illness! Oh, here comes Frederik!'

Suddenly, her brother's raised voice boomed through the wooden wall. 'A delusion? Two of ours are dead, by goodness-and-Light! You can ask anyone here. We all saw it with our very own eyes. Do you want to declare the whole village crazy?'

Annelies listened for a moment. Then she scurried over to Liliana. Muffled male voices approached the stable.

'... will not allow this. My daughter has been through enough! She's not doing well.'

'We should talk to everyone who shared this strange experience.'

'Is she sick? If it's, um, contagious, we should keep an eye on every conceivable symptom. What if the whole village comes down with it?'

The pain in her head increased, and so did the dizziness. She staggered to her feet and knocked over the jug. Milk spilled over the strawy ground. Annelies gasped.

'I'm telling you, that bite wound Marie had was not normal. Some kind of evil magic was at play, not rabies! Leave my daughter alone!'

'It would be extremely useful for my report.'

'She can't tell you more than we've already explained!'

'You're not going to turn violent on us, are you?'

'Look, uh, we can take her statement another time ...'

A short silence and the scraping of feet followed the doctor's imploring voice. Footsteps moved away.

Annelies picked up the jug, with an accusatory look at Liliana. 'If you feel unwell, go lie down,' she whispered.

Liliana felt for the wall, half blindly, and sank against it. She clasped her upper body and waited for the pain to subside. Meanwhile, Annelies took on her unfinished task.

The next Sunday, Liliana didn't feel even a sliver of desire to go to church. She didn't want to be around people, and certainly not around people who would reproach her because of the calamity she'd brought upon them. Still, Grandmother tried to persuade her.

'You can't hide forever.'

In the end, she began to dress and feed Liliana like a small child. Liliana surrendered simply because resisting became too exhausting. Grandmother sneaked her past everyone, through the aisle, while she stared intently at the ground. Why was the church filled with hissing and whispering, instead of the usual loud babble of voices? Priest Mathias didn't even need his gong to make himself heard.

'Ulrich here would like to have a short word with everyone again.'

Until he got up and went to the front, Liliana didn't even realise the priest was referring to Father. He was not a man of lengthy speeches, but when he did speak, the village listened.

'We're all relieved that we didn't have any incidents this week. Paul reported a sighting, but he confessed this morning that it was probably the shadow of his dog with a long branch in its mouth.'

The odd laugh rang out from the benches. Father was trying to ease the anxious tension. Liliana only now noticed that some peasants had clubs across their knees, and there were pitchforks leaning against the wall.

'Please report if something seems suspicious. Also, if possible, don't leave your house when it is dark outside, and stay away from strangers. Priest Mathias should have consecrated every house in the village with a protective blessing by now. It'll prevent all evil from entering uninvited. In the event of an attack, we will ring the fire bell as discussed.'

Liliana sat petrified on the bench. In her head, there was rushing and thundering as if she were standing under a waterfall. So the village expected him to come back and take revenge for having been chased away? Were there any other monsters like him? Did they think he could gather allies, and attack the village with an army of demonic creatures?

'How do I know whether I should barricade myself in my house because of a vampire or run out and help because of a fire?'

She listened despite the soaring dizziness. Had she heard correctly? *Vampire*?

Frederik turned his upper body and shouted back, 'It's quite simple: if something's smoking, it's a fire!'

This remark also earned muted laughter.

'We can ring the bell continuously in the event of a fire and ring with short pauses during an attack. Is that acceptable? It doesn't mean that we won't help each other out when we see someone in need. But, as Frederik said, be clever. Use your eyes.'

Father paused and bowed his head. All of a sudden, the church turned very quiet. 'It's ... um ... We regret that we've brought this misfortune on everyone. We wanted to show mercy to an unfortunate soul. I certainly wasn't the only one who thought vampires were nothing but tales from ancient times. From the bottom of my heart, my condolences to Marie's family. We have lost our faithful farmhand and a good friend. You have lost a beloved daughter. Whatever comes our way, we must stick together.'

He sat down again, and Liliana felt like boiling water was running through her veins. If only the others knew the whole truth. If only they knew how far she had gone with *her* mercy ...

'Why doesn't the city send us any help?' someone objected rather belatedly.

'As if the justice of the peace cares what happens out in the countryside!' Uncle Bernd rumbled. 'The residents of Roinnenstadt are comfortable. As long as there is something to buy at the market, they see no reason to act. This investigator the judge sent us can stick his mass hysteria up his arse! When I see a demon, I know what I'm dealing with.'

'This hysteria thing is now making the rounds,' said another voice. 'The innkeeper at the intersection to Roinnenstadt kicked me out because I wanted to share our story. They say we're all not right in the head. Not even my brother in Niederenthal wants to believe me because, you know, vampires aren't real.'

'No more investigators! He already knew what he wanted to believe and what he didn't want to hear.' Frederik slapped one hand into the other. 'He's used his report to make us look stupid.'

Murmurs of agreement followed, until Priest Mathias, who had been about to begin his sermon, put his hands on his hips. For the first time in her life, Liliana heard a hint of anger in his voice. 'Don't let anyone talk you out of what happened. But believe me when I say the heretical city people can't protect you from creatures of darkness! Only the Light can defeat them ... you should have reached out to me, before confronting a vampire!'

An embarrassed silence settled over the meeting. Frederik sat down. Priest Mathias sighed with resignation and yielded to his sermon, but Liliana didn't understand any of it. Her inner noise drowned out everything else. What had she done? Would more deaths follow? She couldn't possibly have guessed the consequences of her actions. Still, she was numbed by the feeling of having betrayed everyone.

'Liliana!'

Father's voice snapped her out of her thoughts. The church was empty except for the two of them. He was standing right in front of her, his face wrinkled in concern.

'It wasn't your fault.'

Liliana nodded and shook her head at the same time, which resulted in a sort of circle. She didn't know whom to blame, just as she didn't know which was the biggest loss. Not only had she lost a loyal friend but also her heart, her dreams and her belief in goodness.

Weeks later, the fatigue still hadn't left; if anything, it had increased. Although Liliana slept more than usual, she never felt refreshed. Working and sleeping was all she did. She couldn't even bring herself to read. But since she hadn't talked to anyone since Hans' death, she continued to keep her worries to herself. Once, when she staggered from the stable directly into her bed, Grandmother followed her.

'Dove,' she said gently. 'You know what's wrong with you, don't you?'

Liliana scrambled up the bed until she sat with her back against the wall. She didn't really care. Nevertheless, she looked at Grandmother quizzically.

The old woman sighed and stepped closer. 'You're pregnant. Why don't you tell me who the father is?'

Grandmother's words hovered ominously over her head. A part of her had suspected it. She felt so foreign in her own body. Almost overnight, her breasts had swollen up. She began to rock back and forth, hot tears running down her face. Something terrible was crouching in her chest and wanted to crawl up her throat out of her mouth. She whimpered and choked and whimpered again.

Grandmother brought her a bucket. But it wasn't that kind of gagging. Her soul choked. She couldn't digest the misery she had brought on herself. Liliana opened her mouth in a grotesque grimace to make way for what needed to come out. When nothing happened, she cried out in despair. She grabbed the bucket and spat furiously into it. Her stomach continued to bubble and ferment but wouldn't let go of its contents. She threw the bucket across the room and clasped her knees. In this position she stayed, until all the lights went out and the farmhouse fell silent.

So that was the punishment. A monster seed was growing in her womb, as a testimony to her transgression. She had gambled away her life with one single foolish decision. Liliana gritted her teeth until it hurt. She should have died instead of Hans. He hadn't done anything wrong. She'd been blinded by her infatuation and had trusted a stranger she barely knew.

The gagging returned. She would not bring this monster into the world, even if it cost her life. What did she have to lose? Her reputation would be ruined as soon as her condition came to light; as soon as the village knew what she had done. She'd be excluded, stoned, or burned alive. Or maybe the monster would eat her from the inside, like a wasp larva, until she was completely hollow. And then, when it had eaten her up and gained enough strength, it would fall on her family and her village.

She swallowed her tears and rolled out of bed. Her bare feet were a wild drumming on the wooden floor. The kitchen – a knife, any knife, as long as it was sharp enough. What did Grandmother use to cut pumpkins? As if possessed, her fingers raced over the cabinets and holders. There! She grabbed the knife by the handle with both hands and pointed the tip at the lower half of her abdomen. Her hands trembled; her knuckles wanted to jump out of her cramped fingers. She held her breath and aimed.

'Liliana!'

Dim light fell on Father's face, making his eye sockets and his cheeks under the beard look sunken. The next moment, he had grabbed her forearms and snatched the knife from her with a directed movement. She gasped.

'Never, *never* do anything like that again! Do you understand?'

Although the fright spoke from his raspy voice, it had a calming effect on Liliana. Her muscles slackened. He took her, led her to bed and sat down on the floor next to it. There he stayed until dawn.

As if nothing had happened, she left for the barn on time for milking, and Father didn't waste any words on it either. But from then on, the big knife was nowhere to be found.

Chapter Eighteen

Liliana had never known such nausea before. It drowned what little vitality she had left in her. From morning to nightfall, and even in the middle of the night, she was sick to her stomach. She wanted to vomit as soon as she smelled, saw or even heard someone fiddling around in the kitchen. The farm was filled with foul smells, in every room, in every corner. Dung and sweat lurked everywhere. Even her own smell was repulsive, so badly so that it made her cry a couple of times.

At first, she blamed the evil little creature inside her. She still refused to speak. Because if she did, she would have had to answer certain questions; especially one specific question. This didn't prevent Grandmother from chatting at her and reassuring her that these symptoms were unfortunate but not unusual. Since that night with the knife, Liliana had often thought about how she could induce an abortion without drawing too much attention to herself. Grandmother would have known how to do it, but Liliana couldn't ask her because she only assisted in such undertakings if the mother's life was in danger. And how could Liliana convince her of that without confessing whose child she was carrying?

When the boundless nausea set in, she had no strength left for such plans. Every day was a battle against her own body. She drank Grandmother's tea blend of chamomile, mint and lemon balm, vomited on an empty stomach, and dragged herself to the stable, where she took countless breaks during her work. She'd hoped to hide her condition from the rest of the family for a while longer. But after a whole month of stomach upset, even Cedi grew suspicious. She heard him whispering to Annelies as she left another meal in a hurry. Later, Grandmother arranged for everyone to gather at her bedside.

'You may have guessed already what's going on with Liliana. But I believe she'd rather tell you herself.'

Liliana had to get a grip of herself. Apart from the one word with which she'd begged Grandmother to stop with her incense, this was the first time she had spoken at all since Hans died. Her throat rasped unpleasantly. 'I'm pretty miserable because I ... I'm expecting a child.'

Meaningful glances and curt nods were exchanged. She saw the unspoken question on their faces and felt her hands twitch nervously.

'From Hans, isn't it?' said Cedi, who couldn't stand the silence. 'I saw you two dancing and going home together on the night of the Spring Celebrations. You know, before he ...'

She nodded, grateful not to have to utter the lie herself.

'He always liked you,' Annelies sighed, and Jakob grumbled approvingly.

Liliana lowered her eyes. She was sweating and shivering at the same time. Did they really believe this, or did they dismiss their suspicions because the alternative was too heinous? Even Grandmother, to whom she had confessed her feelings back then, showed no emotion.

Anxiously, she made them promise not to let any of this be known in the village. Then Grandmother chased everyone out of the room. Only Father remained. The disappointment that Liliana could read in his posture hurt. Had he suspected it since the incident with the knife? He took a breath, hesitated, and finally left, shaking his head wordlessly. She knew how much he had wished for something better for her, and she regretted taking that wish away from him, as much as she regretted her own shattered dreams. The lie weighed heavy on her chest. But as long as no one guessed the truth, Liliana would take it to her grave.

She realised that the first trimester had to be over the day she got a craving for butter. Summer had moved in without her noticing. Father had hired a new farmhand. His name was Walther, and Liliana found everything about him annoying.

Now that her head was no longer foggy with constant nausea, she began to think more deeply about her situation and how she might limit the damage she'd done. She knew that the longer she carried the being, the lower the chance of a spontaneous miscarriage became; assuming that her case progressed similarly to a normal pregnancy. Her stomach was starting to bulge slightly, and she poked it, wondering if there was some kind of poison she could drink. Or maybe letting herself get beaten up, or throwing herself and her stomach against the edge of a table, several times, would do it? What kind of creature had taken up residence there? Suddenly, she felt like crying, and pushed those thoughts aside.

It was a small jab, little more than a twitch, with which the unborn made itself known for the first time. She wouldn't have recognised it as such if she hadn't felt it a second time immediately thereafter. It was alive! The apples she was collecting tumbled out of her apron. Startled and rather shaken, she expected to feel claws on her abdominal wall next. Nothing of the kind happened. A smile crept to her mouth and froze as soon as she noticed it. She looked at the apples, blurring with the grass on the ground. The red didn't mix with the background to form a new colour but formed prominent streaks – just like the absurd, loving feeling that had appeared alongside her anger. She sat down in the shade under the tree and put her hands on her stomach.

'What are you?'

There had to be something of her in it, too. After all, it was her child. Could she dare carry it to term without knowing what it would be? Could she, on the other hand, kill a helpless being? For it was helpless, she no longer doubted that; enclosed and completely dependent on her, the mother. She didn't feel any evil intent radiating from it, only the tender beginning of a new life. But what about the villagers and her family? Would she put everyone in even more danger if she let the child live? Or would the others kill her, if they found out what kind of child it was? Perhaps she deserved to die of the consequences of her stupidity. And yet ... she was reluctant to take it all upon herself. How could she have known all this would happen? And the unborn: what was its crime? Could she kill it before it had even had a chance to prove it wasn't like its father?

Listening to the humming of the bees and the chirping of cicadas, she chose life. The little creature hadn't done anything. If that were to change, she would act accordingly. Then, killing it would be self-defence. Perhaps it was precisely this deep respect for all life that had led to these tragic events in the first place. But Liliana had discovered a stubborn streak in herself. After all, she was her mother's daughter. And if she was the wrong one to make that decision, fate shouldn't have left it up to her.

She leaned against the tree and picked up the apples. It was time for her to take charge of her life. This was her secret, and she was on her own now. Reality wasn't made for dreamers.

Liliana arrived at Peter's farm slightly sweaty. If it hadn't been for the mild wind sweeping over the fields, the midday heat would've been unbearable. The farm consisted of a single building, in which both the house and the barn were situated. Liliana knocked, and when no one answered, she tried to enter the barn. On the right, there was a stack of hay, and the left side housed the animals that were now grazing outside in the pasture. A few chickens hopped around her, hoping she'd brought grain for them. She went back to the house and entered after knocking again. Maybe Peter was in the field, shearing grass. A dry day like today was perfect for it.

She glanced into the narrow rooms. As with her home, the living room was directly adjacent to the kitchen. Next to it, there were two other rooms; a bedroom and one that served as a kind of storage room. The smell of dust hung in the air, and it was eerily quiet. What might it be like to live here? Peaceful, by the looks of it, but also lonely. The unexpected squeaking of the front door made her wince.

'Is anyone here?' she heard Peter ask.

'I'm sorry! It's me, Liliana.' She stepped quickly back into the living room and stroked a loosened strand of hair behind her ear in embarrassment. 'I wanted to talk to you, but I didn't know where you were ...'

'I just went to the neighbours to help out with a fence ...' Surprise resonated in his voice. He wiped his earthy hands on his trouser legs and continued to look at her, wide-eyed.

She cleared her throat in the awkward silence. 'I have a suggestion. What I'm telling you now is not common knowledge, so no matter what you think of it, promise me that you won't tell anyone anything ... until it gets out.'

He nodded, but she insisted. 'Promise!'

'I promise.'

When she took a deep breath, the air felt oppressive and stuffy in her throat. She continued to speak before her courage abandoned her. 'I wanted to suggest that we ... Well, you and I, we could get married.'

Peter's chin dropped, and his eyebrows jumped in the opposite direction. His hands stopped the rubbing motion and hung motionless on either side. The sounds of quarrelling chickens came in from outside.

'You are childless, and your first wife died last year. I, on the other hand, am expecting a child without a father.'

He closed his mouth, still speechless, while her words slowly sank in. She wanted to make herself as small as possible. Instead, she continued to babble. 'I know we hardly know each other. It's just that ... we could both solve our problems. I mean, we could improve our situations if we ... join forces.'

She squirmed under his stare. Why didn't he say anything? Had she been too bold? Or too late? Had he already proposed to another woman?

'What are your thoughts on that?'

Peter shook his head and blinked, as if coming to himself. When he finally answered, his expression was serious. 'Let me sleep on it.'

'All right.' She breathed a sigh of relief. 'If that's all for now, I'll be on my way again.'

Her feet started moving as soon as she had finished the last sentence. She couldn't look Peter in the eye as she whizzed past him to leave the house.

Two days later, Peter entered Father's living room in the evening. He wore his Sunday best and held a hat pressed to his chest. Since he wanted to talk to Liliana's father in private, she knew what his answer was. Her brothers exchanged astonished glances, and the farmhands pricked up their ears. But the voices from Father's room were too muffled for them to understand anything. Annelies, sensing some good gossip, sat down eagerly at the table.

Soon after, Father asked for Liliana, to talk to her alone. He led her to his bedroom, which had become more barren with each passing year since Mother's death. Liliana waited for the day when even the bed or the small window on the wall would disappear.

Father looked at her for a long time before asking, 'Did you arrange this?'

'What do you mean?'

'I'm asking, did you plant this idea in Peter's head?'

Annoyed, Liliana put her hands on her hips. 'I didn't plant anything! I asked him straight what he thought of it. And he had the decency to formally ask for your approval.'

'Aha.'

She didn't understand where this line above his brows came from. Wasn't he happy that she'd found a way to salvage the situation? Of course, the women on the back benches in the church would whisper about it if she gave birth to a child only a couple of months after getting married. But with a husband by her side and neatly wed, the whole thing would quickly be forgotten. Cases like this occurred fairly often. As long as Peter acknowledged the child as his, no one could do anything, no matter what rumours might circulate.

'You all said I should grow up already and get married.'

'That ... wasn't what we had in mind.'

'I've thought it through, Father.'

He shook his head. The furrows on his face deepened. Her misfortune worried him more than she'd previously suspected. 'I'm not going to stop you. You're old enough to know what you want to do with your life.'

She noticed that he was turning a ring over in his hands. He would have preferred for her to marry out of love, like he had, regardless of the circumstances. She swallowed and pressed her lips together. Life did not offer this luxury to everyone. For the sake of the unborn child, she couldn't afford to waver now.

'Here, this belonged to your mother. I've kept it for you.'

Liliana accepted the ring and remembered how the fused gold and silver had sparkled on Mother's finger. As a child, of course, she had grasped neither the symbolism behind it nor the value of the precious metals.

Father looked into her eyes for a long time. Finally, he sighed. 'Do what you think is right.'

With a despondent smile, she wrapped her arms around him. 'At least I won't live far from you. You'll be able to visit me any time.'

When Father stepped out of the embrace, his eyes were moist.

Chapter Nineteen

The wedding was arranged for three weeks later. Liliana wanted to talk to Valerie in person before she found out about it from someone else. She visited her uncle's farm in the evening, after dinner. Their dog, Timmy, greeted her with eager barking, and she wondered if he could sense that she was pregnant. Fortunately, her protruding belly was still easy to hide under an apron.

She suggested a short walk, because she wanted to be sure that no unwanted ears heard what she had to say. Meanwhile, Timmy leaped around them, chasing squirrels and bugs and anything else that scurried in front of his wet nose. Liliana watched his enthusiasm wistfully. Soon, he, too, would grow older, calmer, until in the end he'd just lie in the kitchen and open a tired eye when visitors came. She had hoped to find the right words somewhere between the farm and the oak tree on the small elevation behind it. But only the crunch of the dry earth beneath her feet echoed in her head.

Once at the top, they stopped and looked at the view while Timmy marked the tree. Liliana could see the Lindenbach before her, among the fields ready for harvest, and her home, which would soon no longer be her home. At their back, lay Uncle Bernd's farm, and further back, the church on its pedestal and the forest that stretched up to the mountains in the distance. Valerie, patient by nature, waited for Liliana to speak.

'I'm going to marry Peter in three weeks.' She wrapped her arms around herself, even though the warmth of the day was still brooding over the land. 'You're not angry with me, are you?'

'No, why should I be?' Valerie took the news calmly. 'You never mentioned that the two of you had something going, though.'

'We didn't. He just needs a family, and I need a father for the child I'm expecting.'

Even this confession did not upset Valerie. Liliana wished that her cousin would be shocked for once. How could she just accept that? Didn't she realise that Liliana's world was crumbling all around her? She didn't even ask about the father! Liliana felt the urge to shake her awake. Instead, she squeezed her arms tighter around herself.

'Are you happy about it?' Valerie asked, and Liliana couldn't tell from her tone whether it was an honest question or whether there was suspicion behind it. Happy? She couldn't remember what that felt like.

'I'd say I have some hope that not *all* is lost.'

Timmy yelped behind them. He ran his paws over his muzzle and jumped around, even sillier than before. Valerie tried to calm him down while Liliana continued to gaze, motionless, over the landscape.

'Timmy, did you annoy a bee? Oh, come on. It hurts a little now, but it will get better soon. You'll get through this. We are here for you.'

In a soft voice, Valerie continued to talk to the dog, looking up at Liliana repeatedly, as if she were talking to dog and human at the same time. A blood-red sun set on the horizon, which reminded Liliana of another terrible sunset. She turned away from it and pushed the memory down so hard she almost feared the child might slip out of her womb. Then she hurried back without waiting for Valerie and Timmy.

On the eve of the wedding, Peter led the bridal carriage to his farm. Although his household goods were already complete, in addition to the chest of Liliana's belongings, Father packed up the linen that had been stored in her closet, as well as two chairs and four chickens. Grandmother spread out Liliana's dowry so that her work could be properly admired during the procession through the village. Cedi drove Viola, the cow that Father had assigned her, and six sheep beside the wagon. Halfway through, they were stopped by children with a fence made of branches and garlands. As custom demanded, Peter paid a toll of sweet rolls and fruits.

Liliana lay awake late, the last night on her father's farm. She'd always imagined getting married in her mother's silver dress. But now she felt like she had somehow betrayed her and didn't deserve it. No, she would get married in traditional Sunday dress like all the other girls in the village. If she tied it smartly, nobody would notice the growing curve of her belly underneath.

The next day, the church was overflowing. Since half of Liliana's family was estranged, and Peter hardly had any family except for an older half-sister, the guests consisted mainly of the villagers and some of Father's acquaintances. Annelies stuck around for the occasion, and Grandmother had collected a bouquet of yarrows, sunflowers and goldenrods. When Liliana said 'Yes,' her eyes stung, but her voice was firm.

On the church forecourt, bread, sausage and cheese, as well as beer and even some wine, were served. The villagers were particularly cheerful. Their fear that *he* might show up to take revenge on them had been unfounded so far. Liliana endured the endless handshakes and hugs. She hadn't wanted a big gathering, but Father thought that a little food and music couldn't be missing. While she sipped from her cup, she watched her brothers: Cedi, who had been surrounded by girls since the Spring Celebrations, and Frederik, who followed Mathilde everywhere. Hopefully, the two of them would be bestowed better luck in terms of love.

No one heard her sighs over the fuss of the guests. Peter seemed to be an honest and kind man. There were wrinkles on his weather-tanned face, but she could have had it worse. She listened to the music, and the little creature in her belly listened too and moved along to the beat. Weren't they somehow allies in all this madness? Both victims of their circumstances, born into an environment they would never quite fit in. Was it selfish of her to keep the child? To cleave to her hope that she was doing the right thing, this once?

Her gaze wandered over to the north, to the edge of the village. The slope of the hill, on which the church stood, was not suited for graves. Therefore, the dead were handed over to the earth, that had nourished them all their lives, on the fringes of the forest, where the land was flat. Priest Mathias scattered seeds in due season. The flowers served as a symbol of the fact that people also blossomed when they strove towards the Light.

Later, Liliana was accompanied by Peter and her family to her new home. Cedi seemed in a good mood and listed to Father the many reasons why he should inherit Liliana's room. When the family said goodbye, she felt less ready than ever to part with them. Everything had happened so suddenly.

'Good luck and blessings in your new home,' Frederik said, patting her back, as he would have done with one of his close friends. Cedi, flashing a grin at Father, promised to treat her room well. Father held Liliana in his arms for a long time, as if he wanted to give her one last bit of refuge. Grandmother also squeezed her warmly, and Liliana breathed in the familiar herbal scent that had been nesting in her hair and clothes for years.

Although the two farms were only a short walk from each other, and Liliana, as she had recently assured Father, could visit them at any time, there was something final about this farewell. She didn't just watch the people closest to her disappear around the bend in the road. With them, her familiar surroundings, her childhood, her whole life up to this point, disappeared.

To dispel the unease from her heart, she went into the kitchen and looked at the stove and the sooty pots. She asked Peter what he wanted for dinner, and he replied that Grandmother had left them the remaining cheese and bread from the wedding. They sat down at the small dinner table, and Liliana was relieved that Peter spoke of his own accord for once. He described the livestock, how far along he was with the harvest, what plants he grew and what seeds and provisions he had in stock. Liliana ate without tasting anything. She tried to delay going to bed by asking him questions about everything, but as it got darker and darker, there were no excuses left. Of course, she knew what was expected on a wedding night.

She followed him into the bedroom and combed her hair thoroughly before sitting on the edge of the bed in her undershirt. The bed was freshly made and smelled strange. Peter silently blew out the tallow light on the windowsill and undressed in the dark, whereupon Liliana also undressed, with trembling fingers. She felt his calloused hands first on her arms, then on her bare breasts. What had it been like between him and Elisabeth? She had heard his late wife's name several times today. Had it remotely resembled what she had experienced with—

As much as she struggled against it, the face, *his* face, slid over Peter's shadowy features, as *his* hands caressed her body. Her heart failed her, and her eyes overflowed with tears. Why? Why had he sneaked his way into her heart, just to betray her? Why had he done this to her?

'Are you crying?' Peter's voice sounded as rough as his calloused hands.

'No,' she sniffed. 'I ... It's too much. Too much all at once.'

He withdrew his hands, and for a while, Liliana heard nothing but her sobs. The tears left wet marks on her cheeks and dripped down her chin onto her bare, round belly. She clenched her fists around the sheet she was holding, hoping someone would tear this unbearable feeling out of her chest.

'It's been a long day,' she finally heard Peter say. 'Take the time you need. I can wait until the child's here.'

With that, he lay down and turned on his side with his back to her. She wanted to thank him for his consideration but couldn't utter a single word. Instead, she cried until she fell asleep, depleted from exhaustion.

134

Chapter Twenty

Autumn announced its arrival with a violent storm. Everything that was not well stowed away or secured flew off and was scattered in all directions. The rain pattered against the walls of the house, and Liliana would have given a lot to be able to stay in bed. The few steps to the stable were enough to loosen her hair from the knot and soak her dress. But she resolutely tore open the barn door and started milking, while Peter took over the feeding and mucking. She couldn't feel sorry for herself forever. This was her place now. Of the options that life had left her, she had chosen this one, and none of the tears mixing with the rain on her cheeks would change that.

Whether the unaccustomed tiredness was due to her advancing pregnancy or to the fact that her daily work had become much harder, she couldn't say; probably both. She was already in her eighth month, and every Sunday someone new approached her about the growing centre of her body. Cedi mocked her by saying she looked like a skewered apple. Presumably, this was also the reason Priest Mathias urgently wanted to talk to her and Peter. After the animals had been cared for, they set off together towards the church. Priest Mathias lived in a small hut right next to it. Peter supported her whenever an acutely strong gust caught them.

Priest Mathias quickly let them in and offered tea. Liliana stood in front of the open fireplace to dry herself at least a little bit. As she took in the comforting scent of chamomile, she glanced at the small table and crooked kitchen shelves, with solitary pots and books standing around. Priest Mathias' cottage was far less exciting than she had imagined it to be as a child whenever she'd caught a glimpse through the door. Nowhere did religious artefacts or dusty scrolls peek out. Perhaps the rumours that the priest was hoarding writings in a forgotten language weren't true after all.

He explained that he wanted to talk to them both individually. Peter was the first to follow him into the adjacent room, where his bed stood. Liliana took the opportunity to skim the leather spines on the shelves. Most of them were dusty, but one looked as if it had been in use only recently: *Sacred Prayers and Dedicatory Blessings*. Her ears pricked when she thought she heard Peter say something about a child. She had guessed right. The men came back, and it was Liliana's turn to talk to Priest Mathias in private.

'I will be direct with you. Liliana, who is the father of your child?' He folded his hands over his white robe, and his green eyes focused insistently on hers. The room seemed too cramped for two people. Serious as he looked, Priest Mathias appeared older than his recently greyed hair indicated.

She'd experienced Peter as a humble and sincere man. He had definitely told Priest Mathias that the child wasn't his. This meant that the most convenient solution, namely claiming that she and Peter had been together and decided to get married when it became clear that they were expecting a child, wouldn't do. Thus, only Hans was left as a father, which happened to be what her family believed anyway. She steeled herself inwardly to appear as believable as possible. Fortunately, Priest Mathias wouldn't know whether her shame came from her lying or from the fact that she had gotten herself pregnant unmarried.

'Hans,' she said softly. 'Even Peter doesn't know that. But he has agreed to take the child as his own.'

Priest Mathias bowed his head and put a paternal hand on her shoulder. 'I just had to make sure. You shouldn't have been able to set foot in the church with a vampire breed inside of you anyway.'

She tried to smile while continuing to breathe calmly. The damp dress still stuck to her body, accentuating her barrel of a belly. She wished she still had the tea cup in her hands to hold on to.

'He was with your family in his human form for a long time. You took care of him ... and are now expecting. Thanks be to the Light, I've never seen a vampire before. They are supposed to possess demonic powers, and who knows what those might entail.'

She gave a dull nod and tried to make sense of what she had just heard. 'Why wouldn't I be able to enter the church if that were the case?'

'When a church is built, we consecrate the designated plot of land, as well as the finished building.' Priest Matthias lowered his hand to reunite it with the other. 'This protective blessing drives away everything demonic. Consequently, a demonic creature cannot enter the place.'

So ... her unborn child wasn't dangerous, especially seeing as she was able to enter the church without any problems? Or was the consecration not as effective as Priest Mathias assumed? However, *he* had avoided the church. In hindsight, a lot of things made sense. Surely, that had to mean that the being inside her was not a demon! She rejoiced inwardly and the relief surpassed her guilty conscience about having lied to Priest Mathias.

The next question slipped out of her mouth by itself, 'Vampires hunt humans?'

'They drink our blood to keep themselves alive.'

'What else is important to know about them?'

Priest Mathias sighed. 'Unfortunately, there are mainly rumours and hardly any reliable reports. Thanks to the aforementioned demonic powers, they can change their appearance. They fly, see in the dark, and are said to be warded off by sunlight. But we have learned that the latter is not true.'

He shook his head. 'I wondered for a long time why the Saint who appointed me a priest attached so much importance to us learning protective blessings, for which I saw no need at the time. That should have served as a sign to me to be more vigilant. As I now know, these demonic creatures do exist. They can even sneak into our very midst.'

Liliana shuddered and reflexively put a hand on her belly. She was unsure whether she wanted to learn more or not. Talking about it intensified the heartburn, which she already felt thanks to the growing child. Priest Mathias interrupted her inner conflict by abruptly ending the conversation.

'I'm glad we've clarified that.'

Satisfied, he pulled open the door, and Liliana followed him into the larger room, where Peter was waiting. She was about to say goodbye when Priest Mathias gave her a small bottle with a clear liquid.

'I still had some of the holy water left over, that I used to protect the houses. As I said, it keeps away the demonic. If you want, you can take it with you ... as a precautionary measure.'

She accepted the bottle with gratitude, and Priest Mathias dismissed the couple with many good wishes. Only later did it occur to her that she didn't know what to do with the holy water, seeing as their house was already blessed. She made her way back without Peter's help because, meanwhile, the wind had died down. The rain, however, remained.

Liliana welcomed the never-ending work in the coming weeks, as it left hardly any breaks in which she could long for her old home. Nevertheless, every now and then her thoughts drifted off to a dark place, where grief and loss flooded her shores and washed up confused questions. How could she have ruined her life so thoroughly with a single decision? Or had this always been her destiny, and she had simply been lulled into hoping for something better by her silly dreams and *his* flattery?

Priest Mathias had hinted at her having been seduced by some kind of demonic magic, but Liliana knew that this was not true. Still, the uncertainty haunted her. Had it all just been pretence? Then why had it felt so real? His interest, the warmth in his eyes, in his voice ... The memories rolled over her in a painful wave. She dropped her needlework. No! A monster like him could not harbour such feelings.

The Harvest Festival came and went. Despite Father's occasional help, the amount of hay and grain they collected and stored seemed pitiful to Liliana. Of course, they also had fewer mouths to feed. The weather was getting colder, and her belly was getting bigger. She began to talk to the being inside her, making sure that Peter was never around. Surely, he wanted a strong boy who would soon be able to lend a hand on the farm. Liliana, on the other hand, hoped for a girl. Although gender wasn't half as important as the absence of claws and teeth.

One Sunday, Father invited them both for dinner. Cedi really had moved into her old room. Liliana was taken aback by how much of a mess he had managed to create with his few possessions. Where her chest had stood now lodged a pile of dirty clothes, bread crusts, finds from the forest, carvings and smaller tools that apparently needed mending. She sat with Grandmother on his bed and talked about the imminent birth. Liliana would send Peter to fetch Grandmother once the contractions continued at short, regular intervals.

'Let him fetch me also if you feel like something isn't quite right. I take that seriously.'

Expecting a child of her own had made her think more about her mother again. What would she have thought of the events, and Liliana's decision to keep the child and marry Peter? What had her pregnancies been like? Father liked to tell them how happy she'd been, carrying her children, seemingly forgetting about details like lower back pain, bloating and swollen ankles.

Liliana couldn't help thinking of Cedi's birth and the complications that had not long thereafter led to Mother's death. All she had left of this memory were the stifled screams and the ominous feeling that something horrible was happening to Mother. And that had been the birth of a normal child ...

She felt Grandmother's hand on her arm. 'Are you listening to me?'

'Yes.' Liliana made little effort to hide her discomfort.

'Good. Continue to drink your raspberry leaf tea. The first child is the hardest. But think about how many women have done it before you. Nature has created us for this.'

Grandmother continued to encourage her as she led Liliana into the living room, where she called everyone to dinner. The get-together reminded Liliana of times when life had been carefree and put her in a mood that was equally peaceful and nostalgic. No matter what herbs she added to her stew, it never tasted as aromatic as Grandmother's.

'Frederik had a picnic with Mathilde yesterday!' announced Cedi with a raised spoon. 'Imagine, in this weather ... What a stupid idea!'

'When it's cold, she seeks your warmth,' Frederik replied, eliciting a knowing grin from Jakob. 'That was the whole point, you dimwit.'

Cedi shook his head, and Peter took the opportunity to thank the family for the meal. Then he started talking about the mushrooms Liliana had collected in the forest. 'Fortunately, she can distinguish the edible ones from the poisonous ones. I think—'

'I wouldn't trust everything Liliana brings back from the forest!'

Liliana froze. She was glad that the angry looks were directed at Cedi and not at her. Father cleared his throat audibly, but the new farmhand, Walther, didn't read the mood.

'What do you mean by that? Did she almost poison you once?'

Liliana put down her spoon and moved back to get away from the table, whereupon Grandmother, without looking up from her food, put a reassuring hand on her knee. But Cedi wasn't done yet.

'Isn't it funny how we thought he'd been attacked by a beast in the forest, when actually *he* was the beast?'

No one laughed.

'All right, pretend it never happened! That doesn't change anything! We just didn't know who or what he was, and now we do.'

Cedi rolled his eyes, pushed away his half-empty plate so that the pumpkin pieces spilled over the edge, and walked away from the table. All of a sudden, the farmhands ate faster, as if they wanted to follow his example as soon as possible. For the first time, Liliana realised that the rest of her family felt partly responsible for Hans' violent death. Of course, it had also been due to his overzealous courage. But the question of whether they could have prevented his untimely demise if they'd been more careful would always linger.

Indirectly, the same was true for Marie. She wanted to believe that Marie had brought her misfortune upon herself by bedding any man who wanted her. And yet, she, too, would still have been alive if Liliana and her family hadn't nursed *him* back to health. Assuming that Marie wouldn't have caught syphilis, of course ... No, she had no right to think like that. Under other circumstances, it might just as well have been Liliana herself who was sucked empty and left dead in the woods. When mothers now warned their daughters to not end up like Marie, the meaning of the words had changed completely.

Then Father cleared his throat again and turned to Liliana.

'I've got something for you.'

'Oh, thank you very much!'

'You haven't even seen it yet!' Father's laughter dispelled the heaviness for a moment. He walked around the weaving loom, where wooden legs peeked out from under a blanket, and pulled the fabric off, revealing a cot. It had high walls and curves notched into a pattern on the sides. Liliana waddled over to take a closer look.

'How beautiful! Did you make this for us? There was no need for that.' She ran her hands over the smooth-sanded wooden surfaces. It smelled fresh and slightly resinous. Suddenly, tears welled up in her. How did she deserve this? Why was she given so much, when she ruined everything she touched?

Father put his arm around her trembling shoulders. 'It'll be fine. You'll see. You'll be delighted once the little one's finally here.'

Chapter Twenty-One

The first snow had powdered the ground and hidden a thin layer of ice underneath. Despite her heavy belly, she only bumped her buttocks and scraped a hand when she slipped on her way to the stable. In the days that followed, she repeatedly felt painful pulling and cramping in her abdomen, each time believing that the anxious wait had finally come to an end. But the child tarried.

When labour truly began, Liliana was feeding the chickens. This time, however, she knew they were real contractions. She writhed and dropped the grains. Peter didn't notice until she sat down and started whimpering. He, too, instinctively knew that this was it, and he hurried to her side.

'Come, I'll help you into the house. Then I'll get your grandmother.'

Although Liliana had only helped Grandmother with one birth, the experience had left a lasting impression. While Peter ran out of the house as if it were on fire, Liliana gathered several sheets and cloths. Then she set about reviving the embers in the oven and filling a saucepan with water. She made slow progress because she had to crouch on the floor every few minutes. Filling the pot with collected rainwater was one thing, but she didn't manage to lift it again. So, she crouched on her heels beside the trough, panting, rocking back and forth until her hands and feet became numb. She almost enjoyed the paralysing feeling of the cold, as opposed to the convulsions. At some point, Peter came running with Grandmother. She pulled Liliana up.

'Dove, what's this nonsense? You're supposed to relax. Let's get you inside and warm you up!'

The next few hours passed slowly. Grandmother made her walk back and forth around the house and instructed her to squat in different positions and circle her pelvis. Liliana cursed her inwardly for not letting her rest. She cursed Peter for standing around uselessly, and her mother for giving birth to her. She cursed those women who let dozens of children pop out of their wombs as if it were nothing. And she cursed *him*, who had put her in this position in the first place. Instead of killing her immediately, he'd obviously intended a lengthy, agonising death for her. Most of all, however, she cursed herself. For believing that fate had rewarded her by placing love right at her feet. How could she have fallen for such an illusion? What a fool she was!

'It won't work like that ... relax!'

'How?' hissed Liliana.

She tasted sweat on her lips. In the meantime, she was as nauseous as she had been at the beginning of her pregnancy. Where did all the foul smells come from at once? Breathing through her teeth, she staggered to her bed and curled up on her side, exhausted. But there was no recovery. She dug her fingers into the edge of the bed when another wave swept over her.

'Remember, every contraction brings you closer to your goal.'

Grandmother waved lavender oil in her face, and Liliana vomited forcefully. She barely noticed the taste of bile in her throat. Every time she thought the pain couldn't get any worse, that was exactly what happened. She felt her strength seeping away like water in dry earth.

'The cervix is open a few fingers wide, but it's come to a halt. You need to relax. Otherwise, it will take too long. We don't want you to run out of strength. Should I bring you a warming pillow?'

She cried out as a demon hand clawed into her stomach and squeezed her organs to liquid. Did the child reveal its true nature after all? Hot fear pierced her heart. She could have sworn it wanted to eat its way through her abdominal wall. She had to warn Grandmother, who was bending over her with a worried face. But she couldn't produce anything other than groaning and gagging. She would die in childbirth like Mother, only in a more gruesome way.

It was probably for the best if her miserable existence ended here. If she died, she would no longer have to endure this torture, and her terrible secret would forever be disclosed. Against her better judgement, she had clung to the idea that at least one thing in her life would work out well. That was her last mistake. The whole village would now pay for her stupidity. Had that been *his* plan from the beginning? Had he intentionally impregnated her, so that his revenge could brood in her belly until the right time came? Perhaps vampires were parasites that couldn't reproduce on their own and needed a host.

She screamed and threw her head back, while her body writhed and twitched. If only she could finally die! Then it would all end. The pain, the guilt, the grief, the shame … She stared down at herself and waited for the vampire spawn to pluck itself out of her flesh. When nothing of the sort happened, she closed her eyes. Was the child normal after all? But that didn't matter any more. Her body was depleted. Her senses faded.

She felt the pull in both directions. It would be so easy to give up, to slip into nothingness, and secretly say her goodbyes. And yet, there was a spark. It was not necessarily the will to live but rather a defiant joy, a kind of pride in the fact that she existed, that she was in the world and could act on it. She screamed, but this time it was an affirmative scream. Yes, she wanted to give birth to this child! Yes, she would find the strength to keep going somehow! Her life was not over yet.

'Good. Keep at it, dove!'

She felt something pressing against her anus. Was the vomiting going to be followed by diarrhoea? Oh well … as long as this child finally got out of her!

'There's the head!'

Liliana almost laughed. That pressure was the child? Everything was on fire as her core muscles pushed. She sounded like a rutting bull. Then a new little voice joined in.

'It's a girl!'

Trembling, Liliana turned on her back and stretched out her hands. Grandmother dabbed the newborn and gently rubbed the vernix into its skin. Then she put it on Liliana's chest. She put a hand on her daughter and forgot about everything else.

Peter entered the room timidly. He stood by the bed for a while before he spoke up. Meanwhile, Grandmother was pushing on Liliana's abdomen.

'I would have preferred a boy, of course. But a healthy child is wonderful.'

None of the women answered. Peter must've noticed he'd said something wrong, but he obviously wasn't sure why. So, he added awkwardly, 'I'm glad everything went well.'

Grandmother eventually took pity on him and gave him the order to brew Liliana her tea blend of fennel and fenugreek, and to bring some food.

Amazingly, the baby girl was comfortable with Liliana and immediately fell asleep. She felt too faint to do anything but lie there. Nevertheless, she didn't sleep; her mind was confused and overwrought. So many feelings and impressions resonated within her. She lived ... the child lived ... It was so tiny, with its scrawny arms and legs. And so human! Nothing about it indicated a demonic heritage.

Grandmother watched her with tears in the corners of her eyes. Was it the joy of seeing her first great-grandchild, or was she relieved that the girl didn't possess pointed teeth? Although Grandmother hadn't mentioned anything, Liliana wondered if she wasn't secretly doubting that Hans was the father. Especially since she was the only one who knew that Liliana had been alone with *him* that evening.

Later – Liliana must have dozed off – she found tea, bread and soup on a stool next to her. Grandmother gave her shepherd's purse to stop the bleeding and promised she would take care of Liliana for the next few days. She showed her how to massage her breasts and squeeze out yellowish milky drops before having the newborn latch on for breastfeeding. Her daughter turned out to be a hungry and skilful drinker. Liliana was glad that she liked her milk and showed no appetite for blood. She was *her* child.

Valerie visited them two days later and brought a small cap and a hand-sewn doll. She helped Grandmother make wet curd wraps for Liliana's breasts, which had swollen to angry, throbbing balls due to the onset of mature milk. Although she picked up the newborn with a lot of tenderness, Liliana was reluctant to let her out of her arms. She couldn't shake off the fear that her daughter might suddenly bite, or that she would be taken away from her because someone had uncovered her secret. Holding her daughter now, she couldn't fathom why she had wanted to stab her while she was still in her womb. She was perfect, with her big blue eyes and pitiful little voice.

Father came by in the evenings several times. He held his first grandchild with a calmness that did Liliana good, too. Grandmother, or rather Great-grandmother, sang lullabies. The women from the sewing bee dropped by and brought freshly baked bread and pie. Although they did this more for Grandmother's sake, Liliana wouldn't refuse food as a gift, no matter the motives for giving it. She soon realised that it was wise to sleep whenever the opportunity arose. With Grandmother's active support and her supply of remedies, she soon recovered. By the time her brothers showed up to see their niece, Liliana was already back on her feet. Frederik asked to be allowed to hold the little one, which surprised Liliana. Was he already thinking about becoming a father himself? Meanwhile, Cedi tried to tickle her; his reward was a big yawn.

She began to tie her daughter to her chest with a large piece of fabric, or placed her in a soft basket next to her so that she had her hands free to work. In a quiet moment, Liliana searched for the wooden figurine from her chest that Hans had given her. She held it out to the newborn and explained that a good friend had carved it for Mummy. Then she put it on the windowsill, where she could see it from the bed.

For the naming ceremony, Grandmother conjured up a little dress from the depths of her closet that Liliana and her brothers had already worn for the same purpose. When Liliana entered the church with her firstborn in her arms, her chest swelled with pride. She knew what the unspoken question mark on their faces meant. Everyone wondered who her daughter looked like. As the child would grow older, it would become more and more obvious that she didn't resemble Hans or Peter. But she would deal with that when the time came.

Priest Mathias sprinkled the small forehead, wrists and ankles with water sanctified for this purpose and announced the name Liliana and Peter had chosen: Annie. She'd resisted the temptation to name her daughter after one of the characters from her favourite stories and instead made a point of listening to Peter's opinion: he had wished for a pretty, traditional name. As she triumphantly observed, Annie felt extremely comfortable. No one would have ever guessed she might not be fully human.

Chapter Twenty-Two

The first few months with Annie passed in a blur. Liliana was trapped in an endlessly spinning wheel. Sleeping, breastfeeding, cooking, eating, sleeping. Nevertheless, she cared for her newborn with a devotion that surprised those around her. She had no time left to herself. The books were gathering dust in her chest, as were the dreams and longings that had once evolved around a certain well-read stranger. She only noticed it was spring by the fact that Cedi received a black eye in the ball game and was celebrated for weeks for his contribution to the renewed victory of Heidenried. This was considered very important, because the village had to prove that they could win without demonic teammates.

In the summer, she had to help Peter with the harvest, which, combined with the constantly interrupted nights, was so draining that Liliana wept from pure exhaustion. Peter reacted with helplessness when Annie cried for hours instead of sleeping. He, too, had never raised a child. In the end, Grandmother came to the rescue and took the baby at least for a few nights. This broke Annie's rhythm, and she finally began to sleep longer at a time. Liliana, on the other hand, continued to sleep restlessly. She often dreamed that a vampire appeared at her bedside and kidnapped her daughter, and then woke up drenched in sweat. Sometimes the vampire first showered her with rapturing kisses, before the mood suddenly changed and he massacred the entire village in order to snatch the infant from Liliana's arms amid the ruins of her burnt home.

More than once, she thought she'd seen the outline of a man at the window. But when Peter looked, no one was there.

Accordingly, Liliana approached the front door with caution when there was a knock, even though she wasn't expecting visitors. Peter would not knock to enter his own house when he came back from chopping wood outside.

'Who's there?'

'It's me, Frederik!'

'Oh!' Surprised, Liliana opened the door and nodded towards the bedroom to indicate that Annie was asleep and shouldn't be woken up by sudden noises. 'What brings you here?'

'May I come in?'

His unusually stiff behaviour itched her curiosity, which in turn temporarily drove away the tiredness. 'Yes, of course.'

He pulled the door shut behind him, looked around, and sat down at the table. Under his arm, he held something furry. Liliana also pulled up a chair. If she listened intently, she could hear the rhythm of the hatchet on the wooden peg through the windows. She didn't waste words on anything superficial but waited for Frederik to speak.

'I thought you could give me some advice.'

The big brother, who knew everything better, was asking her for advice? Amused, she leaned forward.

'What kind of advice?'

'It's about Mathilde.' Frederik's ears turned red. 'I want to ask her to marry me.'

'It's about time …'

'I'm just unsure how to do it. And I thought you would know better what a girl thinks is romantic.'

'Maybe.'

She nodded and felt her smile widen to a grin. Although Frederik knew pretty much every lad between here and the city, he had never been confident talking to women. Cedi would have enjoyed this moment, and Liliana, too, was desirous to let him stew a little longer. She couldn't remember the last time she had spent time alone with Frederik. Even from her childhood, she had few memories of playing with her older brother. While Cedi found everything his older siblings did exciting, Frederik had been too grown up and manly to hang out with his younger sister often. Perhaps it was to some extent Father's fault, for raising Frederik from early on as the responsible son who would one day take over the farm.

'What do I need to do?'

Frederik looked at his hands, which he had folded on his lap. Liliana's heart softened.

'What have you come up with so far?'

'We could go for a walk. But I didn't know if I should ask her father for permission first ...'

'The fact that you officially ask her father for her hand in marriage is part of good manners. But I would ask Mathilde first. After all, you want to marry *her*, not her father.'

'Ah?'

'A walk isn't bad.'

She looked up at the ceiling and imagined what she would have liked the marriage proposal she'd never received to be.

'Or ... You're a good rider. You could arrange to meet her, or have her brought somewhere if you put one of her sisters up to it. When you arrive, you jump off your horse and get down on one knee in front of her.' Slowly, she began to like this idea. 'Is there a place that has a special meaning to you? Where you saw each other for the first time ... the first dance, the first kiss, that kind of thing.'

'The first dance was at the Spring Celebrations. The first kiss behind the stable.'

'Hmm ... well, that's not exactly exciting.' She wiggled her fingers as she thought. 'What were you doing when you decided you wanted to marry her?'

'I was in the wheat field … this morning.'

He had come directly to talk to her after the work was done? Was she the first to know about this? The realisation moved her.

'Oh, yes! You can meet her there in the field. She won't have any idea why this place is special. Explain it to her as part of the proposal!' She almost regretted that she wouldn't be there to witness it.

Frederik nodded eagerly. 'Sounds good.'

'You should also have a gift. It doesn't have to be an engagement ring if you don't have one. Just something that makes her happy.'

'Flowers?'

'You should know what she likes!'

'Hmm. I'll think about it.'

'And before – or after, it doesn't matter – you have to tell her that you love her, of course, and why you love her.'

'I'm sure she already knows.'

Liliana coughed. 'I doubt it. And even if she does, she will want to hear it. Why do you love her?'

'Well, you know what Mathilde looks like. The eyes, the freckles, the shape of, uh, her body …'

'What else?'

'She's the only girl who makes me laugh.'

'And …?'

'She's hardworking, and … when I see her play with her nephews and nieces, I know she's going to be a good mother.'

A good mother … Liliana smiled wistfully. She hardly knew Mathilde, but talking to Frederik about her made her feel like she was getting to know her future sister-in-law through his eyes; like he'd invited her to be part of his life a little more.

'Do you believe she'll say yes?'

Embarrassed, he scratched his head. 'I think so.'

At that moment the door sprang open, and Peter walked through the room, carrying a basket full of firewood. He nodded to Frederik in passing, who left the table and threw on his coat.

'I'd better go then. Oh, I almost forgot.' He pulled the fluffy bundle from under his arm and spread it out on the table. 'We found this jacket that Mother made, of rabbit fur. I thought you could make good use of it.'

'Thank you!' She reached out to stroke the soft material.

Frederik stood up. 'And, um, please don't tell anyone what I've just told you until we've announced it.'

'Sure.'

In the doorway, he hesitated. 'Liliana?'

'Yes?'

'I ... I'm sorry we pushed you to get married soon, and ... and all that.'

Was he sorry because she seemed unhappy? Or because, being in a similar situation now, he'd realised it was a serious decision to make? She swallowed and buried her hand deeper in the small fur jacket. Then she smiled.

'It's all right.'

When Cedi excitedly broke the news of Frederik's engagement at the beginning of autumn, Liliana acted surprised. Since Mathilde came from a large family, and Frederik had many friends, the wedding turned into a feast rivalling the Harvest Festival. She thought that this was far more in line with Father's idea of a real wedding than her little celebration. There was food, games and dancing until late. Liliana couldn't banish the jealous tingle she felt as she watched the beaming couple step out of the church. She'd rarely seen Frederik so exuberant.

His hair was elegantly waxed; he could have passed for one of the fine gentlemen of the city. His friends dared him to hop on a table and shout a toast to the beautiful bride.

Meanwhile, Liliana felt disoriented, likely owing to months of lacking sleep. The twirling silhouettes and the music dissolved like colours reflected on the surface of effervescent water. Nevertheless, she liked the diversion. She handed Annie over to Grandmother, along with the doll Valerie had given her. Annie liked to cuddle her doll and had been chewing on it relentlessly for about a week. Her first teeth would push through soon. Teeth ... She sighed inwardly and pushed that worry aside. All she wanted was to fill her stomach with ham and cake and not think about anything else for a while.

Cedi strolled past her, a girl on each arm. While Frederik was a younger version of Father, and Liliana was entirely her mother's daughter, Cedi's face combined the narrow, dark eyes of one side with the broad cheekbones and pointed chin of the other. She followed Cedi with her gaze and spotted Karina, who ogled at Jakob near the dance area. At first, she thought it inappropriate for Karina to try and get in with Valerie's admirer. But she had to admit that she hadn't done much better when she arranged her marriage to Peter. But what else was she supposed to do? Such entanglements were almost unavoidable in the countryside, where everyone knew everyone. No wonder the narrow world of the village had always seemed a bit of a trap to her.

Unfortunately, Annie soon became restless from all the noise and began to cry. Liliana took her and assured both Grandmother and Peter that she didn't mind putting her to bed alone, because she was tired anyway. As Annie grew up to be a chubby bundle of joy, she was getting noticeably heavier to carry, and it took Liliana a while to reach the farmhouse.

After Annie had fallen asleep, Liliana didn't immediately lie down. The feast had put some life into her. Although it was already dark, she set out to check on the animals. The wind gently brushed her neck, and the stars sparkled pensively.

The occasional call of an eagle owl floated through the silence. She stopped, and for a moment she thought she heard *his* voice.

'*There is the hare. And that is the diamond. Do you see this elongated triangle? That is the tip of the big sickle. Its handle points westward. This allows you to orient yourself at night. Once you have found the North Star as well, you cannot get lost.*'

The memory faded, and Liliana's heart was knocked down to earth. How could a creature like him have left such a tear within her? Why could she not banish him from her memory?

Somewhere out there, he flew through the night and maybe looked up at the stars, just as she was, to find his way. Did he ever think of her? Did he sometimes tell his demonic friends about the stupid young human he'd fooled? Or did vampires live alone? And – this had been on her mind for some time – how come she had survived the whole thing? After all, he'd had plenty of opportunities to drink her blood. It was almost as if he'd spared her life because she had saved his. This, in turn, would mean that he felt some sort of gratitude or had a sense of justice, which did not fit the nature of a beast. The conversations they'd had indicated a sensitive personality. Liliana couldn't possibly reconcile this with the image of the claws from which Hans' blood dripped.

The air gradually became cooler. The shrubs on the other side of the vegetable garden rustled. She rubbed her arms as if she could rub away the goosebumps that were spreading on them. It had to be a fox. Nevertheless, she felt uncomfortable. Since she was regularly plagued by nightmares, she always carried Priest Mathias' small bottle with her.

Moments ago, she had almost wished she knew where he was now and what he was doing. Now she dreaded the idea. Was he planning something out there, or was he now completely indifferent to what had happened to her and the village? What if he ever found out that Annie was his child? Hopefully, she wasn't doomed to suffer for her mistake over and over again; to forever drag the people around her into danger ...

She pulled herself together when she saw Peter approaching the house. Such thoughts only stirred up paranoia. If he hadn't shown his face by now, he'd simply forgotten her.

Chapter Twenty-Three

Just over a year after Annie's birth, Peter's patience was running out. He reminded Liliana that intercourse was part of married life and that he wanted a child of his own. Her period of grace had expired. As little as the thought excited her, she couldn't blame him. After all, that had been one of her arguments for the agreed marriage. If she hadn't experienced how it *could* be, she might have been satisfied with the somewhat monotonous but efficient act of love. She'd heard stories about violent and overbearing husbands, and Peter certainly wasn't one of them. He may not have been the most sensitive, but he demanded little and always behaved respectfully. Still, the knowledge lay dormant in her heart that this was not an expression of shared passion. It was not like *then*, not like it had been with ... *No.* She forbade herself the thought whenever it came up. Her role now was to remedy her husband's pent-up arousal and to conceive his child in the process.

Another year went by, and still they waited for a second child. Fortunately, Peter didn't blame her. He hardly spoke about having a child of his own any more. Since neither his first nor his second wife had conceived so far, he apparently suspected that he was the reason. Still, Liliana wondered if she had somehow become infertile after getting pregnant by a vampire.

Was Peter secretly comparing her to Elisabeth? Had he loved his first wife, or had that marriage also been one of convenience? Whether out of sadness or out of politeness towards Liliana, he hardly ever mentioned her. Only when Liliana asked directly where a cloak or a crocheted blanket she found in the corner of a cupboard came from, he answered 'Elisabeth', as if her name explained everything.

Meanwhile, Annie developed into a cheerful toddler. She followed Liliana's every step, Valerie's doll in her arms, which she had named Lisi. When Liliana milked the two cows, Annie wanted to climb onto her lap. When she fed the chickens, Annie tried to grab them. And when she sowed seeds, Annie picked up the grains and stuffed them into her mouth. Liliana was impressed every time she learned a new word. Annie's laughter gave her bright moments in the dreary everyday grind. Peter had also grown fond of her. His dwindling hope for further offspring prompted him to make even more of an effort with her. She often rode on his shoulders or had him explain to her what he was working on.

Although Liliana had taken everything she owned with her, the feeling remained that she'd left something important behind in her old home. She told Annie abridged stories from her books and then sent her over to Peter because she suddenly felt a lump in her throat. Those were the stories she'd read to *him*.

The rosy, chubby cheeks still hid the shape of Annie's face, but the blue of her eyes had now given way to a rich brown. A faint pain burrowed into her chest when Liliana thought she could already spot *his* nose and *his* eyebrows. Annie might have passed for Peter's daughter, but she looked less like Hans with every passing month. Liliana had already had to cleverly redirect several of Cedi's comments, by pointing out how much faces changed with age or that she, too, had had slight curls as a child.

Once, Annie spat out her vegetable stew, threw the spoon away and emptied her bowl on the living room floor.

'No! No want! Want eat meat!'

Liliana was scared and rebuked her until Peter intervened.

'We'd also rather have meat,' he said amicably, 'but look, if we eat our chickens, they won't give us eggs any more.'

Annie continued whining for a while, and Liliana left her to Peter, who had inexhaustible patience for stubborn little beings. To calm herself down, she sat outside in the sun. It probably didn't mean anything. Young children refused to eat certain kinds of food for no reason. Nevertheless, the fear that Annie might have an appetite for blood gnawed at her.

Another time, Annie claimed she could fly like a bird, and Liliana told her to stop immediately. 'You will not say that again. Understood?'

There wasn't a single soul in the village who didn't like Annie. On Sunday mornings, she walked through the rows of benches and gave away beautiful stones, leaves or snail shells she'd found during the week. Valerie had formed the habit of bringing her a flower or an apple in exchange. Annie was now big enough to wear Mother's rabbit fur jacket, and she beamed whenever she got to show it off.

One Sunday, after the sermon, they found Valerie outside the church, pale as a bed sheet. She'd been waiting for them.

'What's wrong?' Liliana asked, startled, and put Annie down. Peter kept a couple of steps behind them.

'My mother is dying.'

'You've been thinking that for a long time, and she's always kept on going.'

'No, this time it's different ...' Valerie fingered the birch branch Annie had brought her earlier. 'Priest Mathias has been giving her blessings of healing ever since she first got sick. But he told us today that he won't do it any more because he fears he's only prolonging her suffering.'

Valerie swallowed, and tears began to run down her cheeks. 'He thinks there's nothing more he can do for her. Other than praying. She will leave us soon. Only a real miracle can save her now!'

Liliana was sorry to see Valerie, who was usually never rattled by anything, so desperate. She had spent most of her time caring for her mother for the past few years. One might have thought she was prepared to let go now, but that didn't make it any less painful. Clearly, Valerie had never completely given up hope that Aunt Clara would be restored to her former self.

She pulled her cousin close and held her tightly. 'Maybe Grandmother knows a secret remedy.'

'No, she … All she says she can do … is to … numb the pain a little.'

Annie looked up at them anxiously, and Liliana saw Peter beckoning her over out of the corner of her eye. His unassuming calm magically spread to the people around him. She smiled gratefully at him. In such moments, he reminded her of Father.

'You did everything you could. No one could have taken better care of her …' She stroked Valerie's trembling shoulders. 'Would you like to join us for dinner today?'

Valerie continued to weep without saying a word until all the churchgoers, including Uncle Bernd, had dispersed. Her sobs slowly subsided and she finally raised her head to answer the question Liliana had long forgotten she'd asked.

'That would be nice. But I can't stay long because my mother still … needs me.'

At home, Liliana served yesterday's soup. While she had tea with Valerie in the kitchen, Peter kept Annie busy outside. He was sparing with words but readily stepped in when there was a need for practical help.

Liliana felt a little out of her depth, even though she had lost her mother too. It seemed so long ago now. Nevertheless, she thought she remembered that the exact words that were said didn't matter too much at the time. Rather, it had been the presence of her loved ones and the space they'd given her to mourn that had made a difference. The inner struggle couldn't be sped up from the outside. Perhaps knowing she wasn't alone already comforted Valerie. In any case, she seemed more composed when she left Peter's farm.

While the family was preparing for Aunt Clara's death, Mathilde gave birth to her first child, a boy who was named Kaspar after Liliana's deceased grandfather, on the very day of the Harvest Festival. One life withered while a new one blossomed. Liliana, Peter and Annie visited both of them in one afternoon. Aunt Clara was hardly responsive, and Valerie endured her last days, possibly even hours, with a brave face. Then they went to Father's farm, where Frederik had moved in with his bride after the wedding.

Annie's interest in the newborn was limited. She preferred to tug at Cedi's trouser leg, climb up on him, and try to pluck the fuzz that grew on his upper lip and chin. When he'd finally had enough, he chased her all over the house, and both were reprimanded by Frederik for waking Kaspar. Grandmother did not miss this opportunity to cook meat dumplings for everyone, while Liliana introduced Annie to the animals she still knew by name. Good old Elisa was slowly getting both lame and blind; Father would have to buy a new horse soon.

At dinner, Father shared the news of two missing girls from Oberdorf and Hubelmatt, the village beyond Krambach. Neither of them had been seen for two nights.

'Benevolent Light!' Annelies exclaimed. 'You'd think that no one would dare to go out alone in the dark since we had that monster with us. We know what those things are capable of. But some have to find out the hard way ...'

'It's shocking how quickly everyone is forgetting what happened,' Frederik agreed. 'Many have thrown caution to the wind. People don't go everywhere in groups any more, and I see less holy water and skewers in circulation.'

Cedi uttered what everyone was thinking. 'Do you think it was *him?*

Liliana shrugged her shoulders with feigned indifference, whereupon the others muttered 'Who knows' and 'I don't know' to themselves. But something scraped at the edge of her consciousness, scratching until the hole was big enough for it to slip through and jump at Liliana. That evening ... hadn't he spoken of revenge on his brother, and of coming back to get her? Was it possible? She felt the blood drain from her cheeks.

'What?' cried Annie.

'Well, the horrible vampire!' Cedi growled and reached for her across the table with bent fingers, whereupon Annie giggled and squealed.

'I'm telling you, since that demon disappeared, the cases of rabies have also decreased,' Father grumbled.

Peter leaned towards her. 'You don't look so good ...?'

'Everything's fine.'

Mathilde entering with her newborn at this moment was great timing. Liliana loudly offered to hold her nephew so that his mother could join the table and grab a bite. The conversation immediately turned back to Kaspar.

Her thoughts, on the other hand, remained in turmoil. Did the disappearance of those girls have anything to do with her? Could *he* be behind it? Were there any other vampires in the area? Or was it just a coincidence that two girls had disappeared at night? She'd thought she could leave it all behind. But she was fooling herself. She would forever fear that someone out there might be coming for her and her loved ones. He may have just been waiting for the right moment to ... to what? To get her? To kill her, after all? To demand his child from her? What did these other girls have to do with it? Had they also been seduced, or would they soon be found dead and void of blood in the forest?

She rocked her nephew for a while, then urged Peter to leave. Darkness was already creeping in through the windows. The conversation earlier had made her nervous, and she wanted to be home as soon as possible. Before they stepped outside, Liliana spontaneously hugged everyone in the family.

'I'm sure it's nothing, but be careful anyway and don't dawdle,' Father warned as she pulled a hat over Annie's head.

She smiled anxiously, waved and followed Peter, who held up his lantern. As soon as they left the farm, she felt like they were being watched by hundreds of eyes. She took Annie, who had been walking beside her holding her hand, into her arms and quickened her steps.

'What's wrong?' Peter hurried to keep up.

'Nothing ... Let's make sure we get home quickly.'

Not for the first time, she fervently wished she lived even closer to her family, or that her family didn't live so close to the edge of the forest. The outlines of the trees rose menacingly into the sky. The undergrowth cracked and rustled. More than once, she heard footsteps behind her but couldn't make out anything when she looked back.

Peter, at her side, looked stubbornly straight ahead, but she knew him well enough to know that he didn't feel comfortable in his skin either. Why did Father have to tell them the gruesome news late at night? She didn't like what she'd heard about the missing girls. She wouldn't calm down until she was in her bed, with the blanket pulled up to her chin, and heard Annie breathing peacefully near her.

They had walked about halfway home when they heard creeping, uneasy movement from forest on their right. Something was in the air; the animals felt it too. Liliana looked over her shoulder again and again. The moon was almost full, but smoky clouds dimmed its brightness. If only the light from Peter's lantern could reach a little further. Someone could be standing right over there in the field, and they wouldn't notice him unless he moved. They, on the other hand, were a shining target, recognisable from afar. Although that didn't really matter if vampires, as Priest Mathias had said, could see in the dark.

The next time Liliana glanced over her shoulder, she registered a movement, as if something sinister was flying against the cloudy night sky. She peered up intently. Was it just a figment of her imagination?

Suddenly, the haze in front of the moon disappeared, and Liliana was certain: there was a shadow, and it was coming towards them. All her instincts sounded the alarm.

'Q-quick! Run!' Liliana's voice jumped with fright. She hugged Annie tightly and ran like she'd never run before.

But where to? In open combat with a demonic creature, they had no chance; not if it resembled in the slightest the monster *he* had turned into. They had to find shelter somewhere. It would take them too long to get home. They'd never make it! Father's farm was too far behind them. The next house was Uncle Bernd's farm, or the one on the other side of the woodlands. The former was where Peter started heading.

Liliana looked back. The shadow was already close enough that she could see glowing eyes. She turned frontwards again and saw something flash to her right. In her horror, she hadn't noticed which hill it was that they were rushing past. Of course, there was no better place of refuge!

'Peter, the church!'

She turned, slid, and began to sprint up the steep slope. Her heart drummed in her ears. Her lungs were burning. Behind her, she heard huge wings beating. She lowered her head and kept sprinting. Peter followed her call and changed direction. Since the path ran along the other side of the hill, her feet scrambled across loose earth and wild grass. A film of cool sweat covered her skin.

She had almost reached the top of the hill when she felt air whip past her head, and a figure landed in front of her with outstretched wings – a woman with black, knotty hair and an evil grin Liliana could see even without the light of the lantern. Her face was distorted, as if her head had grown and then melted towards the pointy ears. Crooked teeth shimmered moistly in an oversized mouth. She narrowed her glowing eyes to slits and kept her dark, leathery wings open in a threatening gesture.

'This time, I'm sure. You're the one!'

Annie clung to her in fear and buried her face in Liliana's chest. The vampire took a leisurely step towards them. The hair on the back of Liliana's neck stood up. She couldn't take her eyes off the sharp claws. Everything about this woman was wrong, like she didn't belong in this world.

'The other girl thought I'd let her live if she willingly told me where the family lives that so infamously took in a vampire. How stupid ...'

Something hit the vampiress in the head. A stone? Further up, Peter stood with the lantern and hurled a second projectile. He had apparently overtaken them from the side and was trying to distract the vampiress from them. The creature turned, hissed angrily and flew in a direct line towards the lantern. Despite her shaking knees, Liliana started moving again and stumbled up the last section of the hill. The church was their only hope.

She heard the creature's angry exclamations over her own panicked gasping. Her foot buckled, and she stumbled in the dark. In the process, she almost dropped Annie, whose stiff little arms were wrapped around her neck.

By the time she'd caught herself, the light of the lantern had gone out. The vampiress had pounced on Peter! Liliana ran on and finally reached the church, fervently praying that the gate wasn't locked. She threw herself against it – and it opened! She staggered inside and set Annie down on the floor. The girl began to cry as soon as she was no longer in her mother's arms. Liliana mumbled a few soothing words and hurried back to the gate and outside, where Peter, lying on his back, was doggedly fighting off the vampiress. Her claws pressed in on his neck. But Peter still held the extinguished lantern in his hand, and smashed it against her head. Glass shattered with a clattering chink, whereupon the vampiress shrieked and Peter freed himself with a kick to her chest. He crawled, gasping, towards the steps in front of the church gate.

Liliana took a step forward, but the vampiress jumped at Peter with such force that his head hit the edge of one of the stone steps. She grabbed him with both hands and bit his neck. He went limp, except for his hand, which was still groping around. It found a large shard, closed a fist around it, and plunged it with desperate strength into the evil creature's heart. At least Liliana assumed it was her heart, because the vampiress made a terrible sound and a violent shudder ran through her body. She knelt on Peter's stomach and gawked at the shard, still lodged in her ribcage. Her face was inhumanly contorted with rage and pain. She certainly hadn't expected to meet such resistance.

It had all happened so quickly that Liliana could hardly react. Fear urged her to run back into the church, but she didn't move. If there was still life in Peter, she had to help him! The vampiress' eyes flickered dangerously as she turned to face Liliana. What could she do? Frantic, Liliana searched her surroundings.

Then she remembered the holy water. She had no idea what it would do, but it was the only thing she could think of. With trembling fingers, she reached into her apron, uncorked the bottle, and poured it over the astonished vampire's face and chest. As soon as the liquid touched her, it etched her skin off. There was hissing, joined by the smell of burning hair. The vampiress howled and screamed. Where the water had come into contact with the bleeding wound, a whitish coating formed. Shock filled her now disfigured face as her limbs began to twitch uncontrollably. The pupils in the glowing eyes widened; the lips darkened. Liliana recoiled from the sight. This was how Grandmother had described the effect of the toxin from a yew tree; just not in such rapid succession. Finally, the vampiress' eyes rolled upwards, and she collapsed over Peter.

Liliana didn't dare to touch the creature with her bare hands and pushed her to the side with her foot, so that she rolled off Peter. Not only did he have a deep bite wound on his neck, but he was also bleeding badly from the back of his head. She moved his head gently and placed it on her lap. On her knees, her fingers, the gate, the steps ... there was blood everywhere. She began to doubt that he would survive the next few hours, or even minutes. She had to do something!

He groaned, opened his eyes and blinked, confused.

'Peter?'

His gaze darted around with dizzying movements. 'Get ... yourself and Annie ... to safety.'

'I will, I will. You saved us!'

'I'm so ... cold.'

Peter closed his eyes. His breathing got faster. He had to be in great pain. Liliana swallowed her tears. She had never loved Peter as she should have loved her husband, and yet they'd developed an affectionate bond of friendship.

He began to jerk so violently that Liliana was jolted along with him.

'Peter!'

He reared up and screamed in agony. His voice had taken on an inhuman tone.

Liliana slid away from him, unable to take her eyes off his wildly rolling, golden eyes. What was happening to him? Were vampire bites poisonous? Was he ...? Was he becoming a vampire himself?

Peter screamed again – no, roared, at the top of his lungs – then went limp. His head rolled to the side, as if he were simply falling asleep.

'No! Peter!'

She stared at the now motionless body. Finally, she dared to crawl closer and reach out a hand to nudge him.

'Peter?'

He didn't respond.

'Peter, wake up!'

She shook him; first gently, then more violently. He remained motionless. She slumped beside him and sobbed. How could a person simply cease to be, from one moment to the next? Why? *Why?* How many more innocent people had to die?

When she heard footsteps, she instinctively crawled backwards until she felt the church gate at her back. A whimper came from inside. Annie!

'Who's there?'

'It's me,' said the voice of Priest Mathias, whose face was now hovering around the corner, illuminated by a lantern. In the other hand, he held a shovel. The sounds of the horrible encounter had woken him.

'For Light's sake, what happened here?'

Chapter Twenty-Four

'We were attacked on our way home!'

'This doesn't look good.' Priest Mathias leaned on his shovel and bent over Peter with a sorrowful expression. He touched the uninjured side of his neck to feel for a pulse and gloomily shook his head. 'His soul is gone. Unfortunately, there's nothing I can do for him.'

'But you ... can't you ...? With a blessing of some kind ...?'

'Even the Light can't resurrect someone once the soul has left the body.' He sought eye contact, but Liliana couldn't bear his sympathy.

'I'm sorry.'

When she continued to avoid his gaze, he sighed and started to inspect the lifeless vampire instead.

Liliana shakily got to her feet and pushed the gate open. Annie needed her now. She staggered to her daughter and took her in her arms. 'Mummy's here. Everything will be fine.'

Annie sniffed for a while until Priest Mathias walked in. He went right past them and pulled on the rope at the back of the church to ring the bell. Usually, the sound called the villagers to a joyous occasion such as a sermon or a wedding. It seemed ironic that the same bell was used to warn of danger.

Afterwards, Priest Mathias lit the long candles along the central aisle, quickly but not necessarily frantically. The flickering lights danced across his bright robe. His footsteps echoed off the walls. She would not have thought that the church could seem so solemn and oppressive without visitors. Only now, as her racing heart slowly calmed down, did she notice a dull pain in her ankle. She must've pulled a muscle or tendon when she tripped.

'At least everyone should stay inside after that,' said Priest Mathias, once all the candles were burning. 'Did you see any other vampires?'

'N-no.' *Peter ... dead.*

'The dead one out there isn't the one we feared might come back and take revenge on us. Which could mean we will be facing a broader attack. However, I'd expect more noise and unrest in the village if that were the case. We've never had attacks from vampires before, but now ...'

Priest Mathias stopped several arms' lengths in front of them and studied her, sitting with Annie on the cold stone floor. 'It could be two isolated incidents ... a coincidence. But why do I have a feeling that you're hiding something from me, Liliana?'

She squirmed inwardly.

'The vampire wanted *me*,' she said after a tense pause. Or had she meant Annie? As soon as Liliana said it, she was no longer sure. Had she wanted both of them? Had *he* sent her to take Annie away? Or had he decided, after all this time, to finally follow through on his promise to bring Liliana to him? Whatever he was up to, it couldn't be anything good. As it turned out, he would stop at nothing to get what he wanted.

'How do you know that?'

'She said it.'

'The creature? Did it say why?'

Liliana shook her head. She didn't like the way Priest Mathias' gaze wandered to Annie. If she confessed to him what Annie was, he would force her to abandon her daughter ... or worse. But as long as she didn't admit to anything, he couldn't seem to make sense of it, not least because Annie seemed so thoroughly human.

'I'm afraid ...' he began, 'I'm afraid that if you stay here, you'll put the whole village, including your family, in danger. It would be best if you could go somewhere else for a while. There must be a reason why you attract these vampires, why they want you. If it really is you they want, hopefully, they'll leave Heidenried alone if you're not here. You must understand, I have to consider the good of everyone. In other words, it is safer for the village if you leave as soon as possible … and safer for you, if you make it harder for them to find you.'

This thought had occurred to Liliana, too. The assumption that more vampires could make the village unsafe in search of her was not plucked out of thin air. No, she couldn't allow more people to die around her. Plus, she didn't like the idea of sitting around and waiting for whatever bad thing was coming her way.

'Yes, I agree.'

Annie looked up at her with big, reddened eyes. She took the thumb with which she'd comforted herself out of her mouth. 'Mummy go?'

'Don't worry, you'll come with me. We will stay together.'

Her own words made her swallow forcefully. They should have stayed together. As a family. With Peter. The tears came back. Could he truly be dead? So suddenly?

Priest Mathias gave her a short respite by peering through the church door to make sure that there weren't any other vampires gathering out there. Liliana hugged Annie so they could give each other a little bit of comfort.

At last, the priest came back and sat down next to them on the stone floor. He seemed calm but in a forced way. 'I see you have used the holy water successfully.'

Liliana's voice was still shaking. 'I didn't know it would work that way.'

'Neither did I.'

'Is it just normal water that has been consecrated with a blessing?'

He shook his head. 'Basically, yes. However, a blessing, in this case a protective blessing to ward off the demonic, is not as simple as you probably imagine. A priest must learn to bind a small part of his own life force – the Light that is inherent in all living things – to water. The words give it a specific effect.'

'How can protective blessings kill vampires?'

'The defence against the demonic seems to harm them when they come into direct contact with it. I guess that, just as death is the separation of soul and body for us, a separation from the demonic is extremely harmful, if not deadly, for vampires. However, I would have expected that they'd need to be completely doused with holy water to achieve this kind of effect ...'

'You use your own life force to create holy water?'

'That's right. Just like with a blessing of healing, where I bestow some of my strength onto another person. A vampire prolongs his own life by robbing others of their life force in the form of blood. I give my blood for the good of the village.'

'Oh ...'

Priest Mathias drained himself, possibly shortening his life span, with each blessing he gave, and the villagers didn't even know. No wonder he used those blessings sparingly. Her guilt welled up again. But no, she couldn't give up on her daughter. *Never.* She had planned to ask Priest Mathias if he'd give her more holy water. Now this request seemed wrong.

'Can anyone learn to give blessings? Wouldn't it be useful if we could help each other with this? Then you wouldn't have to do everything at the expense of your own life force.'

'In theory, yes. However, the use of blessings requires many years of practice, sacrifice, and a certain purity of thought and way of life. Priests live alone and often meditate. Apart from the few vegetables I grow, I depend on the support of the village. And so, we couldn't all live like this. Maybe it used to be different in the past ...'

Priest Mathias let out a long sigh. He stood up, spread his arms, and the church filled with his words. No matter what was going on outside these walls, in here he was in his element. 'There was a time when the Light flowed more abundantly into the world, but people corrupted it and it retreated.'

He fell into a kind of rhythmic speech that sounded as though he was quoting a passage he'd read so many times he knew it by heart. 'Since the dawn of time, this world has been a melting pot of Light and Darkness, bound to the eternal cycle of life and death. Without life, there would be no death; without death, there would be no renewal of life. We observe this in nature and in ourselves. Light and Darkness are suspended in a delicate balance.'

His gaze wandered into a non-existent distance. 'As humans became more aware, they understood that they could influence life and death, intentionally create or end life. This gave them a sense of control. What could be more powerful than having a say in the cycle of life and death? However, creating life is harder than ending it ...'

Focusing on Liliana again, he smiled painfully. 'As a mother, you know how much of your substance, how much care and nurturing goes into a single new life, and how comparatively little effort it takes to destroy it – in any case, killing was quickly used by those who sought power. In this pursuit, they were willing to do anything, even summoning otherworldly, demonic forces. Thus, they opened the door to the Darkness that had always been waiting to spread throughout the world. New creatures emerged: humans with demonic powers, so-called vampires. They spread across the world and threatened to swallow it whole. But surrounded by the deepest Darkness, the Light shines brightest. Despair-driven hope, on the other hand, paved the way for the sacred, life-giving Light to come into our physical world. Mankind almost succeeded in banishing the demonic power. But little by little, they began to use the Light in ways that were contrary to its nature: namely, for the sake of their own gain. They corrupted its use, and the Light receded until both sides arrived at the weakened state we see nowadays.'

He put his palms together. 'The blessings are what's left of that time. Many of you may assume that my sermons merely serve to strengthen our sense of community, which is, of course, important. But there's more to it than that. In the constant struggle between Light and Darkness, we must never cease to nourish the Light within us, to invite it in, to hope for it. I repeat it, Sunday after

Sunday. *Pray. Take care of one another.* The more the Light can dwell within us, the more protected we are from Darkness.'

Abruptly separating his hands, Priest Mathias sighed again. 'Wherever you go, don't forget that. Tonight, you will be safe here. I'll get you a horse as soon as the sun rises.'

Mother and daughter watched Priest Mathias as he walked past them, stuck his head out and looked around thoroughly.

'What about ... Peter?'

'He was a good man. His soul is now united with the heavenly Light,' said Priest Mathias, as if he sensed her doubts. Of course, he hadn't seen the golden madness in Peter's dying eyes. 'We will bury him as a community. As much as I would prefer to stay within the safety of these walls, I need to check on the others in the village ... just to make sure,' he added. Then he closed the gate behind him.

It was going to be a long night. Although Annie snuggled up close to her, Liliana kept shivering. She had sat down in the corner of a bench, and its back cut into her spine. The church seemed reluctant to tolerate her within itself. It smelled strange; musty. Apart from the occasional rustle of a rodent on the floor, an unnerving silence surrounded them.

Where would they go? How would they survive? Priest Mathias was right. She couldn't stay here. Still, how could he expect her to fend for herself while looking after a small child? She could ride to Uncle Herbert and Aunt Charlotte in Oberdorf. But that was too obvious, too close. If more vampires came searching for her, they would quickly find Liliana only a few villages away. Her thoughts wandered briefly to Aunt Jana but hastily abandoned that corner of her mind again.

She'd assumed that Annie was asleep by now. But the girl suddenly raised her head.

'Where Daddy?'

'He's gone on a very, very long journey.' She whispered without intending to. The fright still sat in her limbs.

'Why?'

'He was ... very tired.'

'Why?'

'Because he fought with the vampire.' She stroked Annie's dark curls. 'You and I, we are going on a trip together, too. Tomorrow.'

'With Daddy?'

'No, we're going on a different kind of trip ...'

Annie dropped her head forward, as if reminding herself that she wanted to sleep. Liliana felt sorry for her. She would have to try and explain to her why they had to leave everything they knew behind ... How could a small child understand, when she herself barely understood what was happening? One day, she would have to tell her the truth about how the man who had been a father to her during her early years died ... The man who had taken them both in and given them a new home, without ever asking who the secret father was. With his quiet but reliable manner, he would leave a gaping emptiness at their side. He had not deserved to die like this.

She would tell her that he had saved them; that he had fought bravely to the end. Liliana closed her eyes and cried silently. The pain in her ankle flared up again.

What was that sound? She bolted upright and looked around. The candles were half burned down. She must have dozed off, despite her overstimulated nerves. Fortunately, the sound didn't repeat itself. All of her limbs felt stiff, but she didn't dare move in case she woke Annie.

She couldn't make up her mind whether to drop by Father's farm to say goodbye when she left the village. She didn't think she had the heart to do it. Her family would want to persuade her to stay.

The first rays of sunshine peeked through the church windows, filling the interior with a friendlier atmosphere. Almost all the candles had burned down by now. A short gust of wind swirled the last threads of smoke around as Priest Mathias opened the gate and called for them.

Her heart pounded as she stepped outside, a yawning Annie in her arms. She covered the girl's eyes for a moment as she hurried past the bodies of Peter and the vampire. The horizon shimmered in the same orange-red tones as the remaining leaves on the trees. Frost crackled beneath her feet as she walked towards Priest Mathias. Autumn was about to turn into winter. The horse he'd brought was her own, or rather Peter's, horse, Silo.

'I've taken the liberty of getting some things for you.'

Presumably, he wanted to avoid her changing her mind if she went home to pack. She had filled the former holy water bottle with drinking water and put it in the saddlebag that Priest Mathias had stuffed with food. In addition, he had tied a rolled-up woollen blanket to the saddle.

'If possible, avoid the cities. There are no churches there because the influence of money and worldly pleasures is too strong, and – here!'

Silo snorted nervously as Priest Mathias slipped Liliana a handful of coins. She asked him to pass her farewell on to her family.

'Write if you can. So that your family knows how you're doing. And once everything has blown over, you should be able to return, hopefully.'

He held Annie so Liliana could mount and then put the girl in the saddle in front of her. Liliana looked back at the small farmsteads on the other side of the hill, the church, the two corpses on the steps, the priest with his robe fluttering in the wind like a white flag. He raised his hand.

'I will pray for your welfare. Now ride and don't look back!'

Chapter Twenty-Five

This was where she left behind everything she'd ever known. Just like her mother all those years ago, she had to turn her back on the place she called home. From now on, new places, new opportunities and new dangers waited around every bend in the road. Liliana paused at the crossroads. The road on the right led to Roinnenstadt. In the distance, she could see the fortress on the hill and the countless pointed roofs that climbed like thorny vines down to the river. The road to her left led south, along the water.

They had made slow progress, especially since she was not a skilled rider and Silo was a plough horse. The fact that she had to hold Annie didn't make it any easier. Midday had already passed. Every now and then, the dull pain in her ankle made itself known. Travelling by stagecoach would have been faster but cost more than she could spend.

Liliana got off Silo's back and encouraged her daughter to pee while he drank some water. She then let Annie carry a stray worm from the road to the grass and used the break to rub her hands. If only she'd taken gloves with her in addition to the scarf. She had left too hastily to notice the melancholy in her chest. The burnt face of the vampire and the empty eyes of her bleeding husband haunted her.

Ever since she could read and think, she'd wanted to see more of the world than the village and its surroundings. Now that she was forced to leave, it seemed cruel and unreal. Would she ever see the brown fields and the forest with its leaves waving in the wind again? How long before she would be able to hug her family again? Of course, that opportunity would only exist if they survived the days, weeks, months or even years ahead. The vampires searched for her almost four years after *he* had been chased away. So who knew how long it would take for them to abandon their hunt?

She made cheerful chatter for Annie's sake as they climbed back onto the horse. 'Do you see the river? That's the Roinne.'

Annie peered through the willows and alders that separated them from the shore. 'Where goes?'

'That's what we're going to find out now.'

Taking a deep breath, she steered Silo south. They weren't heading for a specific destination. The simple plan was to put as great a distance as possible between herself and her home village. She had imagined living on the riverbank as being romantic. But here, where the Roinne flowed wildly and freely, it ruled over the landscape. It dug valleys in which the banks rose steeply on both sides. Later, the area flattened out and the pastures were still swampy from the last flood. Nevertheless, people had always ventured onto the moss-green masses of water to transport goods. As far as she was aware, boats also stopped in smaller towns, for example, Grünau or Sasselheim, and she wanted to inquire about that if the opportunity arose.

The river marked the border to the Lowlands, and the thought of fleeing there had a certain appeal. Although no one was allowed to cross without the right papers, the border guard couldn't possibly control every spot of the riverbank. Then again, if she managed to get there, whoever was chasing her would, too – especially if that someone had wings at his disposal.

Like Liliana, Annie couldn't get enough of their ever-changing surroundings at first. After a while, however, she became restless. Liliana sang songs to her and looked for a place where they would be able to sleep. Whenever someone rode towards them or overtook them from behind, she kept her head down. She tried to avoid people as much as she could so that she wouldn't leave an easy trace to follow. Priest Mathias had sent her away primarily for the good of the village, but also for *her* safety.

If only she knew what these creatures wanted from her … Perhaps they could somehow be reasoned and negotiated with. Unless they wanted Annie. She would never give up her daughter. She couldn't imagine a life without her. Annie was the only good thing she had left. Or maybe the vampires were driven by revenge, or the ominous promise *he* had made to her.

They passed an inn, but the bustling activity made Liliana hesitate. The thought of staying there with Annie filled her with unease. Since it was too cold to spend the night outdoors, and they couldn't find another inn, she was forced to ask for shelter at a farm off the busy road. The farmer and his wife didn't seem too pleased but let them sleep in the hay after she assured them that they had brought their own food with them and would be off again at dawn. Silo was allowed to be fed and penned up with the farm's horse.

After they had made themselves comfortable with their woollen blanket, the farmer's wife appeared with a bowl of soup anyway. Liliana thanked her, and Annie happily told her about all the water they'd followed today. The farmer's wife sat down with them.

'Where do you come from then?'

'Oberdorf.' She would have liked to retract her answer right away. It was too close to the truth.

'And where are you going?'

'Harderwil.' This was a place from one of her books that, to her knowledge, didn't exist.

'Never heard of it.' The farmer's wife scratched her head. 'Is it far?'

'Yes, far!' interjected Annie, who had slurped up all her soup.

'Three days.'

'Why are only two of you on the road? A journey like this can be dangerous.'

It was still less dangerous than the alternative … 'My mother is dying, and we want to see her. Unfortunately, my husband can't leave the cattle unsupervised.'

She hoped that this tragedy would prevent further questions. Indeed, the farmer's wife nodded with a sorrowful expression and was silent for a moment before starting again.

'Good thing you aren't staying at the drinking hole up by the heron field. There's a lot of dodgy stuff going on there. Not a safe place for a young woman with a small child.'

'What hole?' asked Annie.

Liliana stroked her hair and smiled. 'A drinking hole is not actually a hole but a house, where you can drink, eat and spend the night. Not a nice house though.'

'Why?'

'Because sometimes bad things happen there, my child,' replied the farmer's wife. 'We have travellers with us from time to time. You wouldn't believe the stories they tell. Of wild brawls, masked figures, and people who disappear without a trace at night. And this isn't even the worst place on this north–south axis: you'll find all sorts, gambling dens and brothels.'

Although she would have liked to have listened to these stories herself, Liliana was glad that they hadn't ended up in any of those places. She was also glad that Annie didn't ask what a gambling den or a brothel was. The farmer's wife left with a meaningful nod.

'So be careful.'

'Absolutely.'

She snuggled up with Annie. A straw repeatedly poked her arm, but she was too tired from the journey to pluck it away. She'd never spent a whole day on horseback before. Her legs and buttocks hurt in places she never usually noticed. At least she had almost forgotten about her sore ankle.

'Mummy?'

'Yes?'

'Daddy back?'

'No, he's not coming back.'

'Why?'

'He's dead, Annie. He's gone … He's gone on a long journey, and he's never coming back.'

Annie pulled the corners of her mouth down and sniffed. Liliana hugged her tighter, but she soon wriggled out of the embrace, rolled to the side, and demanded Lisi. Liliana explained that Lisi had stayed home because someone had to look after Viola and the other animals. She stroked Annie's back until the little girl fell asleep. The familiar scratching and snorting sounds in the stable calmed them both down. Nevertheless, they missed Peter's constant presence. Liliana lay awake for a long time, twirling the ring she had worn on her finger ever since the wedding.

In the morning, as they were leaving, they met the farmer and his wife, who were getting ready to do the milking. She thanked them again. The fact that she had not yet had to spend any of the two copper and ten iron pennies she carried with her would certainly be helpful later on. Once she ran out of money, she would have to interrupt her journey and find work. If the Light favoured her, a wealthier family might take her in as a maid, despite her bringing a small child with her. If not, the near future looked grim. She would only sell Mother's ring if there was no other way.

Outside, thick fog enveloped the world. They followed the path back to the road. It could have led them directly into the open mouth of a giant; Liliana wouldn't even have noticed. Her skin felt clammy. When they reached the road, it was mysteriously quiet. Not even Silo's hooves made a sound on the ground, as if he were floating. Even the Roinne was barely audible.

Was Annie still too sleepy, or did she not dare to talk? Liliana decided to tell her a tale about talking trees. It was difficult to determine the time of day without the sun. So they stopped to eat according to Annie's hunger pangs. Back in the saddle, she noticed a low stone wall running along the riverbank. After some time, it turned into a bridge. Was there a village on the other side? A border post?

She made Silo stop and peered across the river but couldn't see anything. Above the water, white vapour swirled. Her heart was beating faster. Should she try to flee to the Lowlands, ignoring the law?

Silo neighed in fright, and immediately, the fog spat out a carriage with four mighty horses, which overtook them at breakneck speed, came to a halt at the beginning of the bridge and blocked their way.

The carriage door flew open, and someone leaped out in a high arc, rolled over on the ground, and landed unerringly on his feet. She registered light blond hair that stood up in all directions and, paired with the pale skin, created a stark contrast to his dark clothing. The horses puffed and wheezed in the background. Another person got out of the carriage much more leisurely, a young man with black hair and a delicate face. She puzzled over what seemed strange about him until he began to speak, and she realised it was a woman in an elegant men's suit.

'I see we found you just in time. This bridge is where our territory ends, and that would have made everything more complicated.'

The woman approached. Her thin lips spread out into a ready smile. 'I am Lola. And you must be Liliana.'

Her stomach contracted painfully. Hastily, she snapped at Silo to move off. The woman with the short haircut cursed like someone who'd had a lot of practice in it.

'It's no use! You're much too slow, with your rusty horse and a child in your arms!'

Although she realised that the woman was right, she stubbornly rode on. What else was she supposed to do? Give up? Behind her, there was a muffled gallop and the crack of a whip. The carriage overtook and pushed them against the wall that continued on this side of the bridge. Her knee chafed against the stone, and Silo neighed nervously.

'Mummy, watch out!' Annie's arms clung to her.

She yanked at Silo's bridle. The carriage rushed past them and scraped briefly along the wall, before steering back into the middle of the road. The blond man was holding on to the back of the carriage. He jumped off nimbly and grabbed her wrist. Liliana tried to shake him off, but he was much stronger. She released her foot from the stirrup and kicked him. Unfortunately, the kick was inaccurate and only grazed the side of his head. While he twisted her arm, Lola appeared and snatched Annie from her.

'No!' Her desperate scream got lost in the fog. 'Annie!'

Annie shrieked, fidgeted with her legs, and arched her back in an attempt to escape the grip of the stranger. But she was taken straight over to the carriage.

'Annie!'

'Get off if you want to keep the child!' hissed the blond, tightening his grip.

She slipped off the horse and landed on her sore ankle. She didn't care about the pain. If they harmed Annie ... At the thought, nausea overcame her. She would do anything for Annie. She had known this ever since she first held her daughter. And now, staring at the blond man in his fine suit, trembling with fear and anger, this knowledge was confirmed. Whatever they asked, she would do it so as to not lose Annie.

'What do you want?'

He grinned and pulled up his upper lip in a way that meant she could well imagine him with pointed canines. 'That sounds so much better. What we want is simple: come with us!'

'Fine!'

Finally, the blond let go. Liliana grabbed her reddened wrist. She forced herself to move slowly and unfastened Silo's saddlebag, to maintain at least some semblance of control. With suppressed tears and a resolute chin, she marched towards the carriage, which perched on the road like a fat, black spider.

'In you go!' he shouted after her.

Annie knelt crying next to Lola, who was holding her by the collar. She squirmed away as soon as her mother got in. Liliana hugged her tightly.

'Mummy's here.'

The blond squeezed himself onto the bench next to her, and Liliana slid away from him until she touched the vehicle's wall. His chin and strong nose protruded from his profile. Meanwhile, Lola, who was sitting opposite them with her back to the coachman, gave the signal to continue the journey and slammed the door shut. The carriage started moving, and the occupants were shaken vigorously. Everyone was silent, enveloped by the patter of hooves and the groans of axles.

The deformed face of the vampire ... Peter lying in a pool of his own blood ... She held Annie as tightly as she could without hurting her. Her arms trembled as if she were freezing. Who were these people, who attacked a defenceless mother with a child? Demonic creatures that, like *him*, were able to transform into humans? Where were they taking them?

They followed the road to the south for some time before the carriage made a turn eastward, which pressed Liliana, and Annie in her arms, against the wall. They seemed to more or less maintain this course. She tried to memorise the direction, in case an opportunity to escape should arise later. Now and then, she peered out of the window behind the dark curtain. But apart from the blurred outlines of trees and larger boulders along the way, nothing stood out from the foggy soup that would have given her any clue as to where they were. Later, the backward slant told her that they were going uphill. The horses puffed with exertion.

Poor Silo was now wandering all alone along the riverbank somewhere. Annie barely moved, sucking her thumb with her eyes half closed. Suddenly, the landscape outside the window shone. She removed the curtain so that Annie could see. The little girl straightened up on her lap in amazement. The fog dispersed into threads until it disappeared completely, revealing steep meadows and hilltops. They stretched out of the white surface like the first spring flowers out of the snow. Above it, the sun was enthroned in all its glory.

'Oooohh, Mummy, look! Sun!'

'Yes, I see it too.'

The blond turned away with an irritated sound and put his hand in front of his eyes. 'Why do we have to be out during the day?'

'As you may have noticed, we got her just in time.' Lola narrowed her eyes but didn't complain. 'Or were you out to provoke a fight?'

'I would never.'

'Our instructions were to move quickly and unnoticed.'

'Yes, yes ...'

She listened to the conversation as she toyed with the idea of rolling out of the moving carriage. However, she didn't think it would have been of much use. She had to wait for a better opportunity. The two had to be vampires; she was convinced of that now. How had they been able to find Liliana so soon? She'd been careful! The fact that they hadn't pounced on her right away, like the first vampire, could only mean one of two things. Either daylight prevented them from doing so, or they were working for someone who wanted to get their hands on Annie and her alive.

The carriage stopped abruptly. The blond swung open the door and fanned his hand.

'Hup, hup! All out!'

Chapter Twenty-Six

Liliana, holding Annie, climbed outside. The road ran through a sparse forest of beeches, sycamores and rowan trees. Between their discoloured leaves, the dark green branches of silver firs peeked out. She'd never breathed air fresher than this before. The carriage stood in front of a cottage with a spacious barn. It looked neglected, but little puffs of smoke rose from the chimney, and in the front yard two pygmy goats plucked at sparse grass.

A scrawny man, whom she hadn't noticed before, hopped down from the coachman's trestle, his beard bouncing along with him. He opened the barn door and led the horses and carriage inside. Meanwhile, Lola took her by the arm and led them into the house. As they got closer, Liliana noticed traces of woodworm in the vertical beams.

They entered a room furnished with a table, a corner bench and a fireplace, where a wrinkly-faced man was fanning flames. He hummed a greeting, not even looking up. The wood had to still be damp, because the smoke scratched her throat. The blond man, who had followed them, coughed and dropped money into the man's hand before shooing him outside. As evening was approaching and it was getting colder, Liliana dropped Annie onto the floor and stood with her next to the fireplace, despite the smoke.

'Why not? Smoke is still better than cow dung.'

She suspected that the blond's words were meant as a disparaging comment directed at her and did not answer. Lola, on the other hand, laughed and sat down at the table. 'He's right. You're a pretty one, but you stink like a whole herd of cattle.'

When Liliana didn't pay attention to her either, she turned away with a roll of her eyes. 'We're just trying to be nice. There is no need for us to scare you.'

Annie found a rod and poked the burning logs with it. At home, Liliana would have stopped her from doing that, but at this moment she was just glad it entertained the girl. Out of the corner of her eye, she watched the two vampires. While Lola rested her head on the table, yawning, the blond walked up and down. Animal skulls hung on the wall, and three cuckoo clocks, whose hands didn't match, filled the already narrow space.

'Can you stop that, Tripp?'

The blond, Tripp, clicked his tongue, but he interrupted his rounds anyway and took one of the skulls off the wall to inspect it. He ran his finger over its well-preserved teeth. 'What do you think, a fox?'

Lola shrugged, looking bored.

'Are the others back yet?'

'I doubt it.'

Tripp threw the skull up in the air and caught it again. On the next few throws, he reached under one leg with his arm, spun in circles, or did the whole thing with his eyes closed. In passing, he remarked, 'Travelling without flying is like a lake without water.'

'Dry?'

'Useless!'

Liliana was distracted by a tug at her dress. She bent down to Annie.

'I'm hungry.'

'Hungry?' She picked out a cloth bag from the saddlebag she had brought with her, which was filled with dried apple wedges. Annie nibbled contentedly.

'Speaking of hunger ...' Tripp caught the skull upside down and leered at her with a devious sparkle in his eyes.

Lola sat up straighter and furrowed her brows. 'Don't even think about it!'

'Do we really need both?'

'Shut up, straw head! Do you know what the word *unscathed* means?'

'Pfff ... I'm just kidding.' With another long glance over at Liliana and Annie, he resumed his game with the skull. 'What does he even want with those humans?'

'What do I know? Maybe he needs them for one of his experiments with Albert. In any case, it must be important, or he wouldn't have sent us.'

Soon, they would end up like that fox whose skull Tripp was playing with. Liliana's heart was racing. She tried not to show her fear so that she wouldn't infect Annie with it. Hopefully, the girl didn't understand what was being said. Could this unknown ordering party be Annie's real father? The idea of facing *him* again after all that had happened created a nervous turmoil in her stomach. What did he want? Was he keeping his promise so as to get her blood after all? Who knew what gruesome rituals vampires arranged for such occasions ... How else could she imagine these *experiments* Lola had mentioned? She'd never heard the word before, but it sounded dangerous. She wrapped her arms around her torso and gave Annie a frantic smile.

So far, she'd only come up with one idea to escape that was even remotely promising. She picked Annie up and walked to the door. Tripp promptly blocked her way and braced his foot against the frame. The leather of his shoes shone, freshly waxed.

'Where do you think you're going?'

'I need to relieve myself.'

'Then I'm sure you won't mind if I come along,' Lola said and stood up, whereupon Tripp let all three of them pass.

Just before sunset, the leaves on the trees looked as if they were on fire. An uneasy feeling crept over Liliana. Since she couldn't find an outhouse anywhere, she hid behind a tree. Lola stood by her the whole time, her legs spread in a ready stance. Without an element of surprise and some kind of weapon, Liliana's chances of overpowering her were dim.

She also made Annie pee and searched the forest floor for sharp-edged rocks or heavy branches. But when she turned to the vampiress with a testing glance, she knew it was too late.

The moment the sun finally sank behind the horizon, Lola's eyes started gleaming, and sharp teeth grew out of her mouth. Although she still looked very human – her face was not animalistically distorted towards the back of her head, as it had been with the first vampiress – Liliana felt her frightening demonic power. She grabbed Annie and stumbled backwards, her eyes fixed on the demonic creature, that could jump at her at any time.

'Leave us alone!'

Lola laughed hoarsely. 'Don't be so scared, sweetie! We can finally get going again.'

Liliana started to run – her legs seemed to move of their own volition – but Lola quickly caught up with them and dragged them back to the house.

'Come along now, and nothing will happen to anyone.'

Every fibre in her body was screaming that this was a lie. But she had no way of fighting the vampiress. *Holy Light, help us!*

Lola pushed them forward to the black horses the coachman had just led out of the barn. Even they had been transformed. Their mouths were sharper and longer, their eyes glowing coals, their flanks and legs imbued with monstrous strength.

'Hoh-sey have wings!' cried Annie, with more enthusiasm than fear in her voice.

Liliana's tongue refused to form words. 'Mh-hm.'

The coachman also dragged long chains from the barn and tied two of the vampire horses together. The tips of sharp, white teeth peeked out from under his beard. The way the metal rattled across the floor tugged at Liliana's already brittle nerves.

Tripp stuffed the skull into his suit pocket as he walked out, and sprang, light-footed, onto the monster closest to him. If at all possible, his hair stood up in even more of a mess. His eyes sparkled, patina green.

'Come on, human, take this one! She's the tamest.'

Liliana swallowed. 'How am I supposed to hold on to that with my daughter? We'll fall to our deaths!'

Tripp turned to the coachman. 'Do you have any more chains?'

'You want to chain us to it?'

'Why not?' He grinned, flashing his teeth in the light of the last, weakening rays of the sun. He clearly enjoyed teasing a reaction out of her.

Lola sighed. 'Herder must have a rope somewhere. Henry, would you be so good as to look in the dugout?'

The coachman did find a rope, which Lola tied around Liliana and Annie and then knotted to the saddle. She climbed onto the chained partner of Liliana's vampire horse and chirruped. The horse roared joyfully, galloped a bit and beat itself upward with its leathery wings. Without any instructions or warnings, the coachman gave Liliana's horse a brisk clap to the side, whereupon she also rushed off.

Liliana threw herself forward to keep as close to the horse as possible and wedged Annie between her arms. She grabbed the straps, which were not tied around her head but around her neck and chest, so tightly that they cut into her palms. Annie squealed a few words, but Liliana didn't understand them over the sound of the wings. As they lifted off the ground, her stomach plunged into some kind of void; she felt as if she'd just lost a vital organ.

Each flap of the wings threw them up and down. In a fit of dizziness, she closed her eyes, but she immediately tore them open again, as not seeing confused her sense of balance even more. Shady treetops and the outline of the mountainside rushed past beneath them. Nothing else surrounded her: left, right, and below there was nothing but thin air; dark emptiness. Only the horizon had received a fine, golden coating, which traced the curling lines in the clouds and illuminated the layer of fog from which wooded ranges of hills jutted. But the view soon faded with the last remnant of sunlight.

'Fly!' Annie, sandwiched between mother and horse, stretched her neck to see more.

'Yes!' cried Liliana, trying not to think about how far they would fall.

Lola was a good distance ahead of them, yet the chain between the two vampire horses wasn't fully stretched. The freezing wind brought tears to Liliana's face. She hoped that the trip would end soon. Unfortunately, they stayed in the air for what felt like an eternity, and she couldn't get used to the jerky rocking. Annie, who should've been asleep long ago, squealed with excitement.

Suddenly, Liliana saw a spire in front of them. The castle attached to it had almost escaped her in the dark. It seemed like a continuation of a rock formation, rising vertically from the forest. The shape reminded her of a crystal cluster. From the main part, towers, outbuildings, and walls grew in different directions, and someone had inserted stairs and doors at will.

Annie must have noticed it, too, because a shred of a sentence reached Liliana's ears.

'... we there?'

Just as she was about to answer, she saw something plummet in front of her. That had to be the other horse with Lola. Did that mean—? Before she could finish the thought, her horse also folded her wings in and dropped.

She choked on her scream and clasped the straps tighter. For a moment, she thought she'd lose consciousness. But the wings expanded again, and they slowed down with a blow that drove through her entire spine. Her stomach was pushing up into her throat, despite its lack of contents. The horse trotted out with a rattling chain and stopped next to its fellow.

'Ouch, Mummy!'

Groaning, she straightened up. Her innards couldn't possibly still be all in the right place. She'd squashed poor Annie against the horse's neck out of sheer fright. Thankfully, the girl was unharmed and wriggled impatiently.

'I'm sorry.'

Behind her, she heard the other vampire horses landing. While she looked around in a daze at the stony forecourt, which dropped steeply on all sides except towards the castle, Lola was already undoing the rope. She quickly helped them off the horse and threw a cloak over them so that Liliana's face was mostly covered. Annie kicked in her arms while Lola pulled her along.

A single torch burned at the entrance gate. Two figures landed in front of them, but she could only see their lower halves due to her low-hanging hood. After a brief exchange of whispering voices, they were allowed to continue. Lola and Tripp smuggled her through a side entrance and, after a few steps, across a cobbled courtyard – she caught a glimpse of an elaborate fountain and a few trees – and then immediately through a door into a narrow corridor. As far as she could tell, they met no one else: everything was gloomy, and noises only came to her from further away.

Liliana shuddered. She could've tried calling for help. But what good would that have done? The climb up to this castle was too steep for anyone who couldn't fly ... except maybe with the help of a pickaxe and at risk of one's life. In other words, they had landed in a vampire nest.

She was pushed up more corridors and stairs, to a spiral staircase that went on and on. At the top, she stumbled into a dark space, and a heavy door was closed behind them. Before silence set in, she heard footsteps and muffled voices moving away from them.

'Job done. That was child's play.'

'Don't you go bragging about it now! That would mean we could have saved ourselves the secrecy ...'

Chapter Twenty-Seven

She pulled the cloak off her head. Milky moonlight fell through a single, small window in the wall. Liliana could make out a table with two chairs, a bed, a fireplace, a single shelf with four books and a cupboard. Had they ended up at the top of that tower she'd seen from afar, of all places? She put Annie down, turned to the door, and shook it. Locked!

The window was covered with a grille made of fist-thick rods. She could just about fit her hand through the gaps. On this side of the tower, the forest stretched over edged rocks, and white mountain peaks shimmered in the background.

'Want to see, too!'

'In a bit.'

Next, she opened the closet. It was empty except for a few clothes and shoes. They would be able to put on extra layers to keep warm in a pinch. Although the air felt dust-free, the cold suggested that the room had been uninhabited before. In the fireplace she found a pile of wood that could have made a considerable fire, only there was no equipment to start said fire. Hadn't Frederik once wanted to show her how to get heat by rubbing a wooden stick really fast?

'Where Daddy?'

'He's gone, Annie. He's not coming back.'

'Where Lisi?'

'She stayed at home.'

'I want be home, too!' Annie's voice took on a shrill tone.

'Me, too, Annie. Me, too. But look!' She pushed down the door handle, as before, in vain. 'It's locked.'

'Lisi! Lisi! Daddy!'

Annie started wailing violently. Snot came running out of her nose. She hit Liliana, who lacked the strength to deal with a tantrum adequately. Silent and helpless, she stood there until Annie finally lost her balance and remained, sobbing, on the floor.

Several moments passed until Liliana broke free from her stupor and picked Annie up. She spoke softly to her, promising that they would go home as soon as possible. As she did so, she knocked back the blanket on the bed. It didn't stink, and nothing moved underneath. She lay down with Annie, who first angrily pushed herself away and almost fell off, then crawled closer under the covers and curled up.

Liliana hummed and stroked her fingers through Annie's curls. At last, a sleepy, peaceful expression settled on her daughter's face. She looked lovingly at the long eyelashes and the little nose. The nightmare come true receded a little into the distance when they snuggled up like this.

It had become comfortably warm. The stiffness in her limbs had given way to unexpected ease. Liliana bolted up in bed.

Who had started the fire? She searched the room, but no one was around. There was, however, a plate on the table, as well as two cups and a jug. The smell of food triggered her hunger. She slipped out of bed without waking Annie. Meatballs, potatoes, carrots and leeks were waiting for them. From the jug, the steam of sweet tea wafted over. She hesitated for a moment. Was this part of those demonic experiments? Serving them poisoned food seemed pointless. A calf intended for slaughter was not fattened with poison.

Her stomach gurgled insistently. Whatever the intention, it was better to face the coming evils on a full stomach. She grabbed the cutlery and ate greedily, taking care to set aside a good portion for Annie.

A noise outside the window made her wince. She knew this sound well by now: the flapping of wings. Her maternal instinct answered. She jumped up and reached the bed at the same time as the attacker crashed into the wall and a clawed hand closed around the bars.

The face of a vampiress appeared next to the claws, framed by waves of dark hair. She quickly assessed the round room before she fixed her eyes on Liliana, who had placed herself tensely in front of the bed. The bronze shimmer in her eyes looked oddly familiar. She swallowed but withstood the wordless stare. What did she want? Had she come to pry on the prisoners?

The vampiress shook the bars, as if to test their stability. But they resisted her demonic strength – thank the Light! After a few more fruitless attempts, the creature flew away. Liliana lay down next to Annie and remained there, with eyes open, until dawn.

When she heard footsteps, she rose and accidentally gave Annie a slight push. The girl stretched and went back to sleep. Outside, the new day dawned. A key turned in the lock, and a young, skinny woman with a tray entered. She wore a black uniform, comprising a thin jacket and a skirt that reached only to her knees, both with a line of silver buttons in the middle. Her hair was tightly knotted back, and a small stubby nose rounded off her otherwise pointy face.

'Breakfast, Mylady.'

Liliana must have been staring at her in disbelief, because the girl blushed and curtseyed. 'I'm Martha.'

What was that? No one had ever curtseyed before her; except, perhaps, when dancing. And what did she mean with *Mylady?* Well, she was in a castle, and there were probably servants around. But why was she sent a maid instead of a jailer?

Martha checked the fire and added wood. Then she curtseyed again.

'Have a pleasant day, Mylady.'

'Wait!' Liliana jumped after her before she reached the door.

'Excuse me, Mylady. I almost forgot.' She pulled out a bunch of keys from the inside of her jacket and took one of them off the ring. 'This one is for this door, so you can use the water closet a few steps down. Please always lock it behind you afterwards.'

'Uh, thank you.' Liliana put the key on the table. 'Why am I here? What do they want from us?'

'I can't say, Mylady.'

'You don't know, or you don't want to tell me?'

Martha smiled regretfully.

'Why not?'

'I do not know. And I was explicitly instructed not to talk to anyone about this task.'

Martha turned on her heel, scurried out of the door and locked it with another key.

'Instructed by whom?' Liliana shouted after her.

Instead of an answer, all she heard was the tapping of moving feet. Stunned, she looked at the key. So ... they weren't trapped after all? Then she should immediately wake Annie and make a move. She had no hopes of being able to climb down the rock formation on which the castle stood. Then again, she could steal one of those flying horses.

'Wake up, Annie! We're leaving.'

Liliana nudged her several times. While Annie rubbed the sleep out of her eyes, Liliana turned the key in the lock and heard a satisfying clack. Out of curiosity, she hopped down the first steps and found the door to the water closet after the second turn. It was a simple arrangement, similar to most privies from the village, only made of stone. Next to it lay a silver bowl filled with water and a soft cloth.

'Mummy!'

She dashed back and picked Annie up from the ground. Before leaving, she stuffed bread, cheese, and grapes from breakfast into her little hands. She overcame the many twists and turns of the staircase in such a hurry that she felt dizzy. Since fist-sized openings were regularly embedded in the walls, Liliana could see well where she was treading. When she thought she'd reached the end of the tower, a grid appeared, or more precisely, a grid door. She sighed and turned back to fetch the key still stuck in the door at the top. Out of breath, she got back to the grid door, rammed the key into it and found that it didn't fit. She put Annie down and fiddled with the key. It was no use. She plopped down on the step next to Annie, who had already devoured all of the grapes and was biting off a large piece of bread.

Had Martha tricked her? She sighed and glared at the key. No, it worked for the first door. And why warn a prisoner that her path to freedom was blocked by additional doors?

'Break, yes?'

Unsuspectingly, Annie kept chewing her bread.

'No, no break. This is the end. We're not going anywhere!'

'Mummy sad? Food?'

Annie held out the cheese, which she'd already given a thorough lick over.

'No, cuddle bunny. But thank you.'

Torn between her angry disappointment and Annie's attempt to comfort her, she pulled herself up and tried to see around the bend. How many more doors came after this one? She couldn't remember them from when they'd been brought here because she'd been hidden under that hood. She had seen the key as a sign that someone was sympathetic towards her after all. But it had turned out to be a vain hope. What now?

There was a bright chime as she grabbed the rods and her wedding ring slammed against the metal. Peter ... The memory of his pale, lifeless face still hurt. For the sake of his sacrifice, she couldn't allow herself to give up.

'More eating!'

Annie beamed expectantly at her and held out her cheesy hands.

'Maybe we'll get something to eat again later.'

She planted a kiss on Annie's forehead, took her by the hand and helped her climb back up the long spiral staircase. Until noon, they passed the time by looking at the books on the shelf. They seemed to tell fantastic adventures and love stories in which the characters were all vampires. One of them had illustrations Annie could look at. Liliana had her point to different letters and made the corresponding sounds to amuse her. She especially liked P, T and S.

Liliana hadn't opened a single book since the night she found out what *he* was. Since he had disappeared from her life. Although ... had his influence ever truly left her? And now she was trapped in the same vampire castle that he was probably lurking around somewhere. Or was she wrong, and they had fallen victim to a completely different breed of vampires? Why had they bothered to provide warmth, food and even books?

Noon passed, and no one came. Annie hopped around on the bed and plunged face-first into the pillows. Meanwhile, Liliana stoked the fire and ran her fingers across the walls and floor. It was likely a futile endeavour, but she had nothing else to do. Who knew, maybe there was something hidden under a loose stone; a secret door, ideally. She tried to explain to Annie that the people in this new place were not normal but were called vampires and could grow long teeth and wings. And that they were not to be trusted. Of course, Annie had picked up the word 'vampire' before, yet she probably couldn't connect the monster that was spoken of in the village with what was currently happening to them. Liliana didn't want to scare her, but she needed to help her understand what she'd experienced.

Towards the evening, Annie began to get bored and wanted to be held up to look out the window. 'Want go outside!'

'I'm sorry, cuddle bunny, we can't do that.'

'I want to!'

'It's not possible.'

'Mummy, look, mountain! Mummy, trees! Mummy, Mummy, look! Birdy, trees!'

Liliana thought her head would boil over.

Only when the sky started to change colour, did Martha finally appear. She placed another tray on the small table and cleared away the dirty plates. Liliana put Annie on her own two feet, and the girl immediately walked towards the maid.

'Hello!'

'Good evening, Miss, Mylady.'

'I need to know what's going to happen to us!' Liliana straightened up and stepped in front of her. She was close to grabbing Martha but realised that getting violent didn't come naturally to her. Would she be able to overpower the maid if necessary? Forcibly take away her keys? Surely, she, too, was a vampire in disguise ...

'Why do you take care of us when we are held as prisoners? Do you want to fatten us up or something?'

Martha respectfully retreated the same distance that Liliana had moved towards her. 'Mylady ... I believe I can tell you this much: it is not in my Lord's interest to inflict suffering upon you.'

'Lord?'

'You vampire? What that?' Annie stretched the tip of her nose over the tabletop to eye the food.

'Yes, Miss, I'm a vampire. That's vegetable rice with pheasant.'

'Vegetable wise?'

'Rice, Miss.'

'Who is this Lord?'

'I had the impression that you were already acquainted with Lord Eldric.'

Martha bowed and slid out the door.

Lord Eldric ... *El*. Liliana slowly sat down on one of the chairs. He *had* brought them here. She noticed how Annie was scooping the long white grains out of the plates with her index finger and embellishing the table with them, but she didn't have the presence of mind to stop her. Although she'd suspected that El was behind all this, the confirmation stirred her insides. Because that meant there were personal reasons.

Did he know Annie was his daughter? Did he want her to become one of them? Her innocent Annie, with the concentrated expression on her face, her brows pulled together over her big brown eyes ... Or did he want to turn them both into bloodsucking monsters? She'd heard rumours that vampires could turn humans into their kind. The golden glow in Peter's eyes at the moment of his death wouldn't leave her mind.

In order to avoid the pain and chaos, she'd suppressed the memories, the moments they had shared together, to the best of her ability. But now the situation forced her to brood over the being she had saved. The badly injured stranger had turned out to be an eloquent, reserved man with whom she had fallen in love – who then turned into the monster that brought death to Hans, Marie and Peter. The thought of standing face to face with him filled her with panic.

She rested her head in her hands. Had it all been pretence? The long conversations, the feelings and thoughts he'd revealed, the affection they'd shared? Had he been planning, in the back of his mind, to attack her and the villagers all that time? What had he been doing for the past three, almost four years? Why had he kidnapped her *now*?

His voice echoed in her head. *'Do you want to...? With me...?'* Her arms began to tremble in a bout of weakness. What had she done? She'd thought she knew what his question meant; had willingly agreed to it. But now those events took on a sinister hue. Had she, without comprehending, coalesced herself with him through a demonic bond? Had she entered into some kind of pact that he'd now demand she fulfil?

'Mummy, do you want wises? Loot, they all many!'

Forcing a smile, she turned to her daughter and noticed what had happened to the food. She had to get a grip and not let Annie feel her fear. Deep breaths ...

'What are you doing? The rice is everywhere ... on the table, on the floor, in your hair ...'

Annie grinned and blinked innocently. She knew perfectly well that Liliana didn't like it when she played with food. Nevertheless, she continued to shape the rice into lumps and placed rosettes of cauliflower on top as hats.

Liliana finally got up. Since she didn't have a rag present, she scraped everything together with her hands. She'd heard of rice but had imagined it differently, especially less sticky. Annie helped by moving the rice from the different surfaces directly into her mouth.

After that, Liliana washed Annie's dirty strands of hair with the water from the bowl in the water closet. Annie resisted and it took much longer than necessary for them to go to bed. As Liliana sang bedtime songs, she looked up at the dark, obstructed square of night sky in the wall. She thought of how the vampires were probably circling the castle now, and her voice gradually became quieter.

Chapter Twenty-Eight

The days passed and nothing happened. She read the books to Annie, but the girl soon got bored of them. So Liliana let her spread out the clothes and shoes from the closet everywhere and try them on. She had expected El would soon show up or ask for his daughter, but they remained cut off from the outside world. Although the maid, Martha, took good care of their physical needs, she always seemed in a hurry and never stayed longer than she needed to serve food or restock firewood.

It felt as if Liliana was just holding out in this cell until her death sentence was handed down. She didn't believe Martha that she wouldn't be harmed. Yes, maybe El would let her live. However, she could imagine a whole host of other sinister things that vampires could do to her. No doubt a bad fate awaited her. Instead of jumping at her, though, it lurked out there until the fear of the unknown wore her down.

They were used to working or playing outside every day, and Annie got so cranky that Liliana walked up and down the spiral staircase with her countless times just to tire her out. In between, she tried unsuccessfully to break the lock on the grille door at the bottom using the silver cutlery.

More days passed, days with more than enough to eat, but without proper sunlight; days without trees, without the earth under their feet and the wind on their faces; days without conversations that included more than 'Unfortunately, I can't tell you, Mylady'. They sang, counted and clambered about on the bed and the table. When Annie, out of sheer agitation, began to tear pages out of the books to watch them burn in the fireplace, Liliana didn't stop her. Although she flinched at the sound of the paper tearing, she even encouraged Annie to crumple it into balls and throw it against the wall.

Whether she screamed, begged or threatened, Martha always remained frustratingly polite and apologised for not being able to give her any satisfactory answers.

Eventually, Annie just cried and stamped her feet and hammered against the wall. Liliana felt like crying out of frustration, too. She longed for her family, for the meadows and the animals. So far, no one had harmed them, but if nothing bad was to happen to them, then why didn't El show his face? Was the experiment to see how long humans could be locked up before they went mad? Was he waiting for a very specific night, when the full moon and the stars were aligned just so, to summon power for his ritual? She almost wished he would come to get her blood or her soul already, or whatever he was after, to put an end to this miserable wait.

Had she been alone, she would have been tempted to cut important blood vessels with a knife to speed up the course of events. Then she would either have bled to death, or the vampires – especially El and Martha – would have finally been forced to do something. But she wasn't alone. She had Annie. She couldn't take that risk. Neither could she afford to completely lose her head or fall into dull indifference.

No ... she had to wait for the right opportunity to escape. She probably wouldn't get more than one. And she had to find out where the flying horses were kept and where castle guards were stationed. Then they wouldn't run the risk of immediately being recaptured and punished. But where was she supposed to get this information, if she couldn't talk to anyone but Martha? If she'd inherited Father's inventive spirit, she might have been capable of building a snare to kill or trap the maid ...

At first, she blocked out the knocking, assuming it was Annie or a figment of her battered mind. But then Annie tugged at her dress and gestured to the door. Was someone there? Martha always stepped in on her own, and she always came around dusk or dawn. *Could it be El?*

Distraught, she smoothed her dress and hair. The dreaded moment had finally arrived. 'Hello?'

She heard a faint scraping and whispering.

'Who's there?'

'Zac and Zic! May we come in?'

Annie held on to her leg and looked up in amazement. Zac and Zic? Who was that? And why did they ask to be let in? Liliana clasped her fingers.

'Who are you?'

'Open the door for us! Can you do that?'

Since Martha had instructed her to lock the door behind herself every time she visited the water closet, Liliana weighed up the potential danger on the other side of the door. However, the pressing desire for a ray of hope, for some interruption of the eternal waiting, quickly prevailed. This could be her opportunity to talk to someone who finally gave her answers.

She whispered to Annie to hide in the closet as a surprise and to not come out before she said so. Only then did she turn the key in the lock and peer through the crack. On the stairs stood two young men, barely older than Cedi, who looked confusingly alike. Both had short, dark curls, bronze eyes, narrow noses and dimpled cheeks. One immediately pushed the door open and squeezed through.

'Zac at your service! And that's Zic.' He made a bow and looked around with open curiosity. 'So ... you're hiding up here! What are you called?'

'Liliana.'

She exhaled. There didn't seem to be any imminent danger. With their slender physique and comfortable clothing – consisting of trousers, white shirts, and dressing gowns made of a green patterned material she would have rather expected to see on an elegant curtain – they didn't exactly intimidate Liliana. There were no teeth or claws in sight, and genuine enthusiasm spoke from Zac's voice. Nevertheless, she took a few steps back to position herself between them and the closet, to be on the safe side.

'Very pleased to meet you!' said Zac, sniffing around the room and rubbing his hands together with interest. 'And? What did you do to him, to be locked up here?'

'Nothing.'

'Don't be modest! We won't mess with you.'

'If it were really bad, she would be dead already,' said Zic with an emphatically uninvolved expression on his face. He picked up one of the paper balls and smoothed it out.

'True, true.'

The confidential tone of these young vampires unsettled Liliana. 'What are you doing here?'

'We just wanted to uncover the secret.' Zac grinned broadly. 'We knew something was up! Whispers of a search and an intruder, a covert mission ... And a remark of our mother's. She didn't know that we were listening, of course.'

'That *I* was listening,' Zic interrupted, looking up from the randomly torn page he had begun to read.

'That one of us was listening.' Zac leaned over and nodded contentedly. 'Indeed, you do have big blue eyes!'

'Which she couldn't have known without seeing you,' Zic added.

'Therefore, we concluded that the secret revolves around firstly, a person, secondly, a human, and thirdly, a woman.'

She shook her head. 'I don't follow.'

'She wanted to tease him, and said something about him not being able to resist those big blue eyes.' Zac raised his index finger. 'Meaning, he had found the person he was looking for, brought them here and left them alive. All we had to do was track you down.'

'What ...' She swallowed. 'What does he want with us?'

'We have no idea!' Zac announced on behalf of both of them. 'Humans aren't normally kept at Finsterwald Castle.'

'Then how did you know I was human?'

'Vampires don't have blue eyes.' Zac laughed and nudged his brother with his elbow. 'Or have you ever come across one who did?'

Zic shook his head and shrugged at the same time.

Liliana looked at the twins and thought quickly. 'In other words, you shouldn't be here ...'

'No.' Zac winked at her. 'And yet, here we are!'

She heard a rustle behind her – Annie was getting impatient – and quickly asked, 'How did you do it?'

'With the help of this little friend!' Zac pulled a key out of his coat pocket. 'We borrowed the original, got a clay imprint, and made our own key. It doesn't look great, but it works. Of course, we didn't know that we would find another locked door up here. Hence why you had to let us into your room.'

'If Uncle El finds out ...' Zic grimaced.

Uncle El ... Against her will, she had to smile at the absurd image this designation conjured. All the while, her gaze was glued to the copied key that had disappeared into Zac's coat pocket.

Zac shrugged. 'But enough of that. Where do you come from? Why are you here?'

'I'd like to know that, too. Unfortunately, we've only met Martha so far, and she doesn't want to tell us anything.'

Before she realised her mistake, Zac was already raising an eyebrow. 'We? Us?'

'I thought I heard noises ...' Zic took a step forward, and Liliana quickly knocked on the cupboard before he could reach it. Annie pushed the door open and hopped out.

'Tada!'

'A tiny human!' exclaimed Zac, laughing as his brother stared at Annie in bewilderment.

'I'm Annie.'

'I'm Zac, and that's Zic!'

'Yes.' Annie nodded eagerly.

Liliana flinched as Zac crouched down, but he simply winked at Annie. 'You hid well!'

'At night, you would not have fooled our noses like this.' Zic crossed his arms.

'Now you, Mummy!' Annie waved her hands, excited about the unexpected visit.

When she shook her head, Zac jumped in. 'Should I hide? But you mustn't look!'

Obediently, Annie covered her eyes, and Zac rolled silently under the bed. Zic also rolled, but only his eyes.

'I'm coming!'

Annie peeked through the closet door and opened her mouth, surprised she didn't see anyone behind it. At first, she looked around the room, perplexed, but then concluded that there was only one other place where someone could hide. With a triumphant 'There!' she stuck her head under the bed, from where Zac screamed in feigned fright.

'Aaahh, you found me!'

Liliana watched the brothers, puzzled. Was this how bloodthirsty vampires acted? They seemed to have nothing in common with the fury that had killed Peter. Could it be that day and night brought about such a drastic transformation? Or weren't all vampires equally terrible?

'Again!' Annie demanded, giggling.

'We shouldn't stay too long, or Martha might catch us.'

Zic glanced at the door, and suddenly Liliana had an idea. It wasn't exactly a plan, and maybe it wouldn't lead anywhere. Still, she had to try.

'Why don't all three of us hide, and you look for us?'

Annie clapped. 'Yes!'

'All right,' said Zac, crawling out from under the bed.

Immediately, Annie closed her eyes. Zic sighed listlessly and held the smoothed book page in front of his face. Meanwhile, Zac climbed into the closet, and Liliana quickly followed him. Her heart was racing as she squeezed herself next to the young vampire and pulled the closet door shut. A musty smell went up her nose. Would she manage to steal the key from his coat pocket without him noticing? Could he see her searching fingers in the dark? The fabric was so close to his hip that he would surely notice her touching him when she reached for the copied key.

'I'm coming!' Annie announced from outside.

She had to act! Liliana brushed Zac's hip from the side as if she'd lost her balance and was looking for support. As she did so, she placed one hand in front of his chest as a distraction and stretched the other deep into his coat pocket, hoping that he wouldn't be able to tell which part of his coat she specifically tugged at. Her fingers had but that one moment to find the key before she had to pull them back. Cold metal!

'There!' Annie opened the closet.

She managed to make the key disappear into her sleeve. As she stepped out of the closet, she raised her hand and fiddled with the shoulder part of her dress so that the key slipped down to the elbow.

'You've found us!'

She laughed nervously and turned to Zac, who climbed out of the closet behind her. Had he noticed what she was up to? He adjusted his clothes and gave his brother a furtive look but didn't say anything.

Trying not to lower her arm too much or make it look oddly stiff, she turned to Annie. 'Did you find Zic, too?'

'Yes, there!'

'But he hid so well.'

Zic lowered the paper. A quick grin deepened his dimples before he recovered his indifferent expression. 'We have to go now.'

The twins waved at Annie, to which she shook her head earnestly. 'No, not go.'

'Yes, yes! We can come back another time.'

Annie pouted and stretched her arms out to Liliana to be picked up.

'In a moment, cuddle bunny ...'

She didn't dare to move her arm until Zic and Zac had left. Then she locked the door behind them and shook the copied key out of her sleeve. Where to put it? Behind one of the books? Under the pillow? She had not yet decided on a suitable hiding place when she heard trampling feet.

'Liliana, open up!'

'What's the matter?'

'Open up!'

Should she leave them locked out? No, the only way out was through this door. She would have to get past them somehow. She stuffed the copied key into her neckline and unlocked the door. Zac and Zic rushed in at the same time.

'The key is gone! I had it just a minute ago!' Zac ran to the bed and peered underneath. 'If we don't find it, we're done! Martha is coming any moment now.'

'Of course, something was going to go wrong,' Zic said, putting his hands in his pockets and watching his brother grope around under the bed.

Thinking they had started a new game, Annie rolled a paper ball at Zac, which went past him unnoticed. He stuck his head out from under the edge of the bed and looked up at Liliana.

'Where's the key?'

'Are you sure it's not there?'

Impatiently, Zac blew a stray curl out of his eyes, slid forward, and pushed himself up from the floor with his hands. 'It's not! The only other possibility is that you stole it. Where is it?'

She bit her lower lip. 'Do you want me to check again?'

'No!' Zic set himself up in front of her, and Zac stood next to him. They barely towered over Liliana. 'Give us back the key!'

'I don't know where it is,' she said, casting a worried glance at Annie. Hopefully, the girl wouldn't say anything suspicious now. Liliana hadn't had time to warn her. She also hadn't had time to ask about the horses, or think about what to do if the twins noticed that their key was missing. 'Keep looking. Or come back later, once Martha's gone again.'

'We can't do that because the grid is locked!' Zac glared at her. 'Cough it up already!'

'You are welcome to search me,' Liliana said, spreading her arms provocatively. Inwardly, she prayed that she hadn't misjudged the situation and was about to end up as vampire fodder.

If the two of them behaved similarly to the adolescents from the village, she still had a chance. Even Cedi, who was accustomed to the company of girls, would rather have sunk into the ground than pat down the bosom of a respectable and somewhat attractive woman in front of others. Although ... maybe they just looked young and were actually several centuries old. Or maybe vampires knew no such inhibitions. Just a few weeks ago, she would've never dared to try something like this. She'd probably lost her mind on account of the endless waiting!

Uncomfortably, she looked from one to the other. Annie, still hoping for a game, also spread her arms. Zic avoided Liliana's gaze and remained silent. Zac pressed his lips together. He hemmed and hawed for a moment and then took a deep breath. Before he could act, footsteps approached from the staircase.

'Martha!' whispered Liliana. 'Quick!'

The twins threw themselves to the ground and crawled under the bed together. Liliana grabbed Annie, who wanted to follow them. She would have preferred for them to have chosen the closet, where she could've trapped them.

'Mylady!' Martha's eyes widened when she saw the mess of torn-up books in the room. 'What ...? Lord Eldric will not—'

She broke off, indicating her disapproval with a soft sigh. Then she knelt and began to collect the pages. From this position, all she had to do was turn around and she would spot Zac and Zic. Annie giggled and pointed to the bed, whereupon Liliana quickly pulled her close and picked her up.

'There's no need for that. I'll put it away myself later.'

She put a hand on Martha's shoulder. Confused, the vampiric maid stood up. 'Mylady?'

'Really, I have more than enough time to do it myself. If you would please leave us alone now so we can eat ...'

If Martha found this wish suspicious, she didn't show it. 'As you please. Good evening, Mylady, young Miss.'

She dutifully smiled and curtseyed. When she left, Liliana flinched. That was the opportunity she had been waiting for! It was now or never!

'Wait for my sign ... until Martha is fully gone,' she hissed at the twins and listened at the door.

She gave Martha plenty of time to descend the long flight of stairs and waited until the twins became restless to fiddle the room key out of the lock. As soon as she saw them starting to move out of the corner of her eye, she scurried through the door with Annie in her arms and slammed it shut. With trembling fingers, she rammed the key into the lock and turned it only moments before the handle was thrust down from the other side.

'Hey!'

Pushing aside a hint of guilty conscience for tricking Zac and Zic, even though she'd liked them right away, she hurried down the stairs. They were, after all, vampires. If only Martha didn't hear the dull knocking and decided to come back! She crept on, with a galloping heartbeat.

'Mummy?'

'Shhhh!' Liliana held Annie's head against her chest with her free hand. She listened carefully but heard neither the maid nor the twins. 'We're going to win this game of hide and seek. We will hide so well, no one will find us. And then, we can go home.'

Annie nodded, confounded, and put her thumb in her mouth. They had successfully taken the first step on their way to freedom.

Chapter Twenty-Nine

Owing to the copied key, they passed through the grid door and reached the end of the tower without any further obstacles. There they met what appeared to be a walled-up exit. She dropped Annie and studied the stones. There had to be a passage here. At first glance, nothing stood out to her, so she ran her hands over the rough surface, especially over the cracks between the stones. Then she noticed the empty torch holder on her left. Was the solution that simple? As if taken from one of her books!

With a little bit of effort, she managed to push it back, and something started to rattle. Soon, a crack appeared on the side of the walled-up exit. She braced herself against the wall, which now slowly opened outwards.

'Come!'

They slipped into a long corridor, lined with pointed, arched windows and heavy curtains on one side and pedestals with stone sculptures of forest animals on the other. Liliana turned her head frantically and looked through one of the windows onto the courtyard. There was a section of exposed rock with a few trees and shrubs in the middle – she recognised pines, junipers, and wild roses – that looked as if it had been deliberately preserved during the construction of the castle. Behind it, she could make out the fountain, which was adorned with a long-tailed, golden figure. The courtyard was, as far as she could tell, empty. She assumed that there had to be stables adjacent to it, so this was their next destination.

She scooped Annie up as she ran. Although she tried not to let her footsteps echo, they seemed unmistakable to her in the eerie silence of the sleeping castle. She slid around the corner on the polished floor but caught herself again. Behind it stretched another corridor with doors at regular intervals. One of them was embedded in the wall facing the courtyard. However, when Liliana tore it open, she almost fell onto the cobblestones several stories beneath her feet. She clung to the door frame and leaned back to make up for Annie's extra weight on the side. Of course ... Vampires didn't have to rely on stairs.

She gasped for air for a few moments. Annie didn't say anything; just looked at her wide-eyed. No, there had to be a staircase down here somewhere. She pushed aside the rising panic and kept looking. What else could she do? Without stairs, she would have to climb down the outer facade with a toddler in her arms.

Maybe she'd started running in the wrong direction? Who built a castle with such a convoluted layout? She turned around and passed the hidden exit of the tower again without initially recognising it. Perhaps the stairs were also hidden. On this side, the corridor didn't lead around the corner, as on the other side, but ended with a door. She put her ear against the lacquered wood, hearing nothing but the throbbing of her own heart. Warily, she pushed the handle down and peeked through the crack. It wasn't until some of the sparse daylight fell on the steps that she comprehended her luck.

Her feet moved almost of their own accord and she rushed forward. The staircase ran along the wall in an angular spiral, creating a shaft in the middle, a drop into the dark with no parapet or railing. The further they went, the more impenetrable the darkness got. With wobbly legs, she climbed on, pressing Annie to her chest and running her other hand along the wall.

Around the next bend, she felt emptiness instead of stone, and then wood and a handle further back. An equally dark room followed. She noticed narrow streaks of light on the floor. Thankful that she didn't encounter any obstacles while passing through, she tried the first door. Behind it stretched a kitchen that would have fit Grandmother's kitchen at least four times. The faint light gave the long tables and the huge stove an abandoned look, although there was coal glowing in a lonely cooking alcove. She hurried past squeaky-clean pots and ladles, the dimensions of which suggested that food for giants was prepared here. Why did vampires even need a kitchen? Hadn't the twins claimed that there were never any humans here? Hopefully, they hadn't been able to free themselves from the room in the tower yet.

She stumbled out into the cold air at the other end, and squinted at the abrupt brightness, although the sun was only just hovering over the mountain ridges.

'Outside!' Annie's face was beaming.

'Shush ... yes, we're outside.'

She searched the different sections of the buildings: the balustrade of a covered passage; the mostly darkened windows; the decorative bridges and the spires; but nothing moved. The vampires had to be so convinced of their superiority that they hadn't set up any guards. Either that or they were very well hidden.

She broke away from the arch and ran to the overgrown rocks, where she crouched behind a bush with Annie. No one had noticed them. Everything seemed deserted. But she couldn't let her guard down.

'Hiding?'

'Yes. No. We want to look for the horses. Do you remember the horses with wings?'

Annie nodded.

Where were they? Stables usually had a gate that a horse with a rider could pass through. There were only two gates that met this condition: the entrance gate in the fortress wall and the gate to the main body of the castle. Then, not far from the entrance, she discovered an arch, under which a path led around the side wing of the castle, although it didn't look like there was anything behind it; no buildings, just the abyss.

Liliana put Annie back on her hip and ran off, hounded by the fear of shouts, roars or flapping wings. She hardly noticed the stinging of the cold air in her throat and lungs. The path under the arch was a single steep curve carved into the rock, with a dizzying drop on the other side.

She pressed herself against the wall. On the one hand, so as not to be discovered, and on the other hand, to keep as much distance as possible between herself and the drop. Her heart stopped at the sight of the tiny trees beneath them and the jagged cliffs in the landscape. There was nothing to stop her fall, only all-encompassing nothingness. She tore her gaze away and turned to the left, where there really was a gate. It was exactly the kind of gate she'd been looking for, except that it was set directly into the stone.

Little by little, she crept with Annie along the wall towards the gate. Pushing it open lit up a long cave with rows of chambers, from which dark, sleepy horse eyes squinted at her. Whether she was waking up the animals or whether they would have begun to stir anyway with the imminent twilight ... she didn't care too much. Some of them rose and growled hungrily. What did vampire horses eat? Was she crazy? How had she thought she could fly away on one of those beasts?

'There! Look! Hoh-sey!'

Annie pointed wildly around the cave. Her voice bounced back from the smoothed walls. Something was stirring in the dark heights of the ceiling. Liliana shuddered. Why didn't Annie seem scared by the deadly heights or the fierce beasts? Was it her vampiric side? She bit her lips. It was now or never ... Now or never ...

She had to take advantage of the remaining time and tie herself and Annie to one of the horses – while they didn't yet have their demon eyes and wings – so that they would be ready when the sun went down. The vampires would wake up at the same time, and their prospects of actually escaping from this place would dissipate quickly. If only she knew which one was the mare that had flown them here. All of them had the same perfect, shining black coat. She walked past the animals and decided on one that was still sniffing tiredly. Each chamber housed only one horse and was equipped with tack on the outside of its shoulder-high swing door. She remembered how the straps had been fastened and, in addition, used those of another horse to fix herself and Annie in place. The chosen mare simply let it happen.

Unsure whether the makeshift knots would hold their weight, she fiddled with them for a long time until she noticed that the light from the gap at the entrance had turned reddish. Time was up. Opening and closing the chamber door from the horse's back wasn't as easy as she'd hoped. However, she didn't have to convince the animal twice to trot off. No sooner had it escaped the chamber than it squeezed outside, as wings sprouted on the side of its back. A chirping swarm of bats fluttered over their heads into the open air, and she ducked in fright. The next moment, the mare neighed a gleeful farewell to her friends, shook her mane and, without Liliana asking her to do so, jumped over the edge.

She was too surprised to scream, and clung to Annie. They fell briefly and then were carried up by powerful wings. Her stomach rushed to her throat, like on their first flight, this time filling her with an intoxicating relief in addition to the nausea.

'Hold on tight!' she instructed Annie, rather late. She couldn't see her face; nevertheless, she felt that the little one enjoyed flying, which annoyed her somewhat.

She slid her forearms under the first strap for stabilisation and held on to the upper one. Only then did she dare to take a look back at the castle. In the lustre of the evening, it looked almost fairy-tale-like as it sat there, enthroned on the giant rock formation, and crowned by its towers and bay windows. As far as she could tell, no one had followed them. Ideally, their disappearance – and the missing twins – would go unnoticed for some time longer. She could hardly believe it. They'd got away!

Chapter Thirty

'What its name?'

She had to bend over to understand Annie.

'What's whose name?'

'Hoh-sey.'

'I don't know.'

'Nana?'

'Yes, why not …'

Liliana looked at the nocturnal landscape. Nothing but forest. As on the flight there, they were shaken with every flap of the leathery wings. The white mountain peaks at her back, which she could see even in the delicate moonlight, served as a rough guide. However, they slowly faded as the stars above their heads shone brighter.

Loosening her muscles to adjust to the strange ups and downs on the horse's back, she scanned the sky for the North Star. And the sickle – there it was – pointed to the west, as a certain someone had taught her. Now she would use his advice to escape from him.

She pressed her thigh to the side of the vampire mare and steered her more to the west. If they drifted too far westward, she would know as soon as the Roinne came into view. If, on the other hand, they oversteered to the east, they could stray dangerously far from their destination without realising it.

In hindsight, it would have made more sense to take the exact opposite course, cross the icy peaks and try their luck on the other side of the mountain range. The likelihood that they would be followed there seemed much lower. But she had involuntarily steered the mare – which never fully ignored her orders, yet followed them with obvious delay – northward, the direction in which her home lay.

Was it foolish to want to see her family? El would easily find them there. Still ... She would gain so much strength if she could only enjoy Father's strong arms, Grandmother's herbal scent and the laughter of her brothers for just a few hours. After that, they would continue their journey, further and further north, this time across the territorial border into the Moorlands.

Her fingers hurt and her face felt numb. She should've taken more clothes from the closet. How did Annie's little hands endure the cold?

'Home going?'

Liliana hesitated for a moment. She didn't want to promise Annie anything she couldn't keep to. Then again, she could hardly put her family in any more danger than they already were in. El knew where they lived anyway.

'Yes. But then we'll have to continue our journey.'

After flying for a considerable period, the mare began to huff restlessly. Had she smelled something? Liliana looked around but heard nothing except the whooshing of wings, and she didn't see anything suspicious either. Or was it because the mare was hungry? What were they supposed to feed a vampire horse? All she could do was land and then hope that the horse was self-sufficient ... and had no appetite for humans. When the mare finally lost more and more altitude and disregarded her orders to stay in the air, Liliana directed her to a clearing in the dense carpet of leaves and needles below.

They landed abruptly, and Liliana untied the knots with stiff fingers, yet, she kept the strap in her hand when dismounting. If the horse – Nana, or whatever her name was – were to run away from them now, they'd be in trouble. At first, it felt like the earth was still rocking. She placed Annie next to her in the wild grass.

'Are you tired? Show me your fingers.'

She rubbed Annie's hands. Riding in the air was more strenuous than on solid ground. She would've liked to lie down, but the grass was damp. So, she crouched and took Annie into her arms; the child pressed a cold nose to her neck. Had she fallen asleep earlier?

A jerk went through the strap she'd tied around her hand. Nana puffed discordantly and sniffed around in the grass. Her eyes glowed greedily. Liliana wanted to retreat, but the horse was stronger. With Annie still in her arms, she stumbled after Nana, who grabbed something from the ground with her teeth and devoured it with her neck thrown back. A hairy tail dangled from her mouth, and then disappeared without a trace. Liliana shook herself. Her insides recoiled from the sight of this monstrosity of a horse chewing on another animal and merging with the shadows of the trees in the background – except for those glowing eyes. Nonetheless, she was glad that its hunger was not directed at her or Annie.

Nana caught two more rodents and swallowed them, fur and all. Liliana shivered with fatigue. But the fear of possible pursuers urged her onwards. As soon as the mare shook herself contentedly and became calmer, Liliana looked around for a way to get back onto her. Much beckoning and tugging at the straps convinced Nana to get close to a tree stump, from where she first lifted Annie and then climbed onto the horse's back herself. Having given her a name diminished the animal's abnormality a little. Perhaps it was because they always gave their cattle back home names, or perhaps it was the need to imbue everything with human characteristics.

She tied the knots around her and Annie's waists while Nana was already stretching her wings. The vampire mare trotted across the clearing and jumped. This time, the departure demanded a lot from her. Her wings fluttered violently and she scraped her legs over the treetops. As they continued to rise into the air, Liliana thought she could see a silver loop sparkle through the landscape in the distance. Could this be the Roinne? Her heart skipped a beat. This meant that they would soon encounter offshoots of human civilisation. It also meant that they had to turn sharply to the east.

For a while, they flew on, until Liliana noticed a movement – hopefully only owls or other nocturnal birds. She urged Nana to fly faster, but the vampire horse was not impressed. Liliana looked over her shoulder repeatedly. At first, the birds seemed to have disappeared. Then she saw three moving spots in the sky.

'Faster!'

Annie flinched and whimpered. 'Mummy?'

'Everything's fine, cuddle bunny.'

The spots grew to winged figures that were quickly catching up to them. *No!* Liliana clung to the mare. If she could see the pursuers, they could see her. What to do? In flight, they offered an easy target. She had to land. They could continue on foot and hide under the trees.

'Whooaa! Stop!'

She pulled the strap and increased pressure with her knees. Was this the right command? Now that Nana herself didn't feel like landing, she slowed down instead.

'No, not in the air! Stop on the ground! Land!'

Liliana began to sweat despite the icy night air.

'Quick! Stop! Land!'

'Stop!' She heard her command echoed from behind her. 'Don't you dare fly away again!'

From the corner of her eye, Liliana saw the vampire horses catching up and encircling them. She barely recognised the faces, but the dressing gowns blowing in the wind were sign enough. Then the third rider appeared in front of them, and Nana flew even more slowly.

'You will come back to the castle with us right away!'

She assumed that the darkly distorted voice belonged to Zac. His gleaming eyes stared at her from the side. She'd hoped to never see the twins at night; and not just because she wanted to leave the castle with all its trappings behind her.

'No! We've been locked up long enough! Kidnapped and imprisoned for no reason!'

'Oh, and what did you lock *us* up for?'

Was she imagining it, or did his response sound a little snubbed? She glanced left and right and at the vampire in front of her, a stout figure crouching in the saddle.

'That was different! Look at how quickly you've freed yourselves!'

'Don't force us to use meaner methods!'

If only she had more control over Nana, she could try a dive! Should she jump off the horse with Annie? She squinted down and dismissed the thought. While she feverishly searched for a way out, Zic leaned over in flight, grabbed Nana's reins, and manoeuvred her around in a wide curve.

Liliana, who had been busy holding herself and Annie, tried to loosen his hand. Zic just grinned at her with his pointed canines and continued to hold Nana quite effortlessly. Zac and the strange rider locked them in with their animals from the side and from the front.

'Let me go!'

'And have Uncle El rip our heads off?' cried Zac. 'Fat chance!'

'Did you hear that?'

The third rider turned around. He sniffed the wind. Zac and Zic looked anxiously in all directions, and even Liliana paused her frustrated resistance.

'Should we land?' the unknown vampire asked.

'Where are they?'

'There!'

A deep rumble escaped Zic's throat and Zac shouted, 'No, back! This way! If El has sent someone, we'll come across them soon ...'

Zic had briefly let go of Nana's reins, and Liliana saw an opportunity. She leaned forward and pressed her elbows and knees against the mare. This time, Nana reacted according to her wishes and plunged towards the trees.

'No! What are you doing?'

'Stupid human—'

The voices broke off. She adjusted pressure just above the trees, and Nana flew horizontally, as if she were galloping over the treetops. Annie kept unusually quiet, but Liliana had no time to ask her how she was doing. Her fear of flying had been overshadowed by a different, more urgent fear. Behind them, someone howled angrily, followed by roars and other sounds of combat. She kept her head down. Perhaps the attacking vampires, whoever they were, wouldn't pay attention to a single rider moving away from the battle.

A shadow shot down and caught hold of her. It hadn't expected her to be tied to the horse, however, and its claws didn't carry her off but scraped across her right side, ripping open her clothes and skin as she tipped over. The strap cut into her stomach. Her hands desperately sought support, and Nana's frantically fluttering wing slapped her in the face. Annie was dragged along by her weight and shrieked in fright.

Just as Liliana got hold of the reins to pull herself up, Nana dodged another attack. Liliana's body swung out and was held back by the strap so jerkily that she thought her spine would snap. Suddenly, the pull disappeared – the knots had come loose! She lurched about, sliding over the wing and reaching for empty air.

'Mummy!'

A fir tree swallowed her, the twigs and needles scraped her, branches swung at her. She lost all orientation, only knowing that she was falling from branch to branch. Something hit her head. Lights flickered before her eyes. Filled with panic, she tried to hold on to something – and came to a sudden stop. Her dress had become hooked on a thick branch! For a moment she dangled like this, her head and feet down, her buttocks up. Then the dress tore, and she fell again, tossed back and forth, and hit the ground with such force that it took her breath away.

She lay motionless until the air returned to her lungs. Her horror inhibited the pain that poured in from all her limbs. It felt like one of her ribs had impaled her insides. Was it broken? Panting, she crawled to the trunk of the fir tree and pulled herself up. Her head protested violently, and her right leg slumped, but she pulled it up and finally stood. She tasted blood in her mouth. Blood! The vampires! *Annie!*

Fear for her daughter whipped through her veins. Where was she? Still in the air? Hanging in another tree? *By everything that's Light and whole, if only Annie survives this!*

The canopy muffled both the moonlight and the sounds from above in the air. Down here on the forest floor, she heard nothing but her own breath. She was surrounded by gloomy outlines in a strange, hostile environment. If the vampire from before ambushed her ... This was his hunting ground, and she was a blind chick right in front of the muzzle of a hungry predator. As soon as she detached herself from the tree trunk, he would see her movement in the dark, and immediately perceive an unintentional rustle or crack with his superhuman senses. Even if she didn't move, and waited, he could probably smell her ... her terror and the blood dripping from her side.

How, on the other hand, was she to find Annie, lost in the dark? Her cries would give away her position. But she had no other choice.

'Annie?' she whispered. 'Annie?'

No answer. She steeled herself against the rising dread and limped off. Her back and the right side of her body, where the claws had torn her open, burned, and her left rib seemed to pierce her with every breath.

Although she might as well have closed her eyes, her head swirled here and there, her overstimulated senses scanning the gaps between the trees. Everything was threatening. Behind every tree trunk, one of *them* could be waiting – for her to run straight into their clutches. She stumbled over young plants, roots and ferns, and held her hands outstretched in front of her so as not to collide with an unseen obstacle. They could approach at any moment, from any side – and what if they found Annie before her?

'Annie!'

She ducked under a fallen tree, which emanated a mouldy smell. There was a rustle. Quickly, she hid back under the trunk and remained there. Was that a vampire? Or was it an animal? Could it be Annie? No, she'd call for her.

Liliana tried to calm her heart. Renewed rustling came from the undergrowth. But from which direction? She didn't dare move, hardly allowing herself to breathe. Nonetheless, the desire to find Annie, to protect her ... Of course, it was wishful thinking. Facing what they faced, she was as helpless as a toddler. Hopefully, Annie, too, was hiding somewhere! She had to find her, take her into her arms and run, run, run, until all of this was over, until the impenetrable forest spat them out, in a place where there were no monsters.

She took a cautious step forward, straightened up – and looked directly into two eyes glowing from the darkness.

Chapter Thirty-One

She stumbled backwards, ducking just in time to avoid hitting her head against the almost horizontal trunk. While doing so, she slipped, crawled, clambered and groped for twigs, and pulled herself back to her feet. The slavering and laughing at her back made her turn around. The glowing eyes rose as the creature jumped over the fallen tree with ease, landing in a crouch. As it drew closer, a faint remnant of light fell on the contours of a bestially distorted face and bared teeth.

'Here's our hostage. And she smells so ... appetising ...'

There was no scream that could express the horror that gripped her. Before she could take a single step back, he was already on top of her. His claws pinned her to the ground, his open mouth hovered over her face and moved to her neck. She felt his hot, moist breath on her skin. Suddenly, his face disappeared from her sight. The vampire was pulled away. He rolled off Liliana and gave the newly appeared figure a blow in the stomach with his elbow. The figure turned out to be another vampire, who proceeded to kick at Liliana's attacker. But he dodged away.

She crawled backwards, her eyes fixed on the combatants. None of them used their wings; presumably the trees were too dense here. Instead, they duelled with their claws like knives, stabbing at eyes and slashing each other's arms. She could barely see what was happening. The taller one looked more delicate and seemed to be wearing some kind of coat, no, a dressing gown! It had to be one of the twins. He grabbed the other vampire's arm, jumped against a tree as if he wanted to run vertically up it, bounced off, and used the arm as a lever to fall onto his back. The other roared in pain: that arm was probably broken or dislocated.

But before the twin could fully take advantage of his trick, a female vampire pounced on him out of nowhere and bit his shoulder. The twin's attempts to shake her off were not successful. Where was his brother?

The first vampire escaped the twin's grip and struck at him with his healthy arm. The twin grabbed the vampiress behind him, got down on his knees, swung her over his shoulder and hurled her against her comrade-in-arms. Then the twin jumped at both of them, and they all landed in a heap. Liliana shuffled further away from the scramble.

Another pair of demonic eyes appeared among the trees. They only briefly took notice of Liliana, which was enough to make her blood freeze, before they turned to the fighting vampires. The newcomer snorted condescendingly.

'What are you? Maggots? You can't even handle this little boy?'

His booming voice would have scared off a wild bear. He trudged over, grabbed the first vampire and carelessly threw him into some shrubs, then grabbed the vampiress and pushed her into a tree. She groaned and slumped. The twin jumped quickly to his feet, one hand pressed to his hurt shoulder. Liliana saw a flicker in his eyes and swallowed. The behemoth of a vampire laughed. Then he grabbed Zic or Zac by the collar, heaved him high into the air and smashed him to the ground. The young vampire gasped in pain, and Liliana gasped, too. He tried to get up, but the behemoth placed a foot on his throat and pressed.

'Today I will feast on every Finsterwaldean I find!'

The twin choked and desperately shook the monstrous leg that relentlessly crushed his neck. Liliana trembled. A wave of cold washed over her as another shadow fell from the treetops and landed light-footed in front of the behemoth vampire. As soon as he touched the ground, the darkness deepened around him, and an invisible frost crept over the carpet of moss, roots and needles. She couldn't see his face, but she instinctively knew who it was.

The giant vampire, who was standing on one of the twins, turned his head and grinned so that the teeth flashed in his brutishly distorted face.

'Look at that ... the high Lord himself. This must be my lucky night!'

He lifted his foot briefly, intending to finish off the wheezing vampire on the ground. However, before the foot touched the maltreated throat, El moved. His demon claws drove across the behemoth's torso. In the surprised silence, Liliana heard the soft sloshing of blood on the fern and wood around her. She felt something warm running down her forehead and wiped it away in disgust. When she looked up again, she felt even more nauseated.

El thrust his claws into the open torso again and again, tearing out anything he could grab. Parts of organs and intestines flew through the air around them. The other vampire gurgled in agony, and Liliana threw up.

This answered the question of how the shreds of skin and flesh had ended up in the trees at the place where she'd found El, back then. She choked and spat and crawled like a panicked beetle behind the nearest tree, where she leaned her head against the bark. Her thoughts remained empty until a familiar voice pierced them.

'Catch the fugitive! Then bring Zac back. We're done here.'

'Sure.' That sounded like Tripp. 'The others are dead. Tiomon, too.'

El sighed. 'An unnecessary loss. Oh, and bring this head along, will you?'

Liliana clasped her knees. She sat there with her ears pricked up but trembling and completely immobilised. They were leaving. Perhaps ... they'd forgotten about her? But what about Annie? Had anyone found Annie? Was she one of *the others*?

A gentle crunch sounded at her side, and she recognised the outline of a human: no, a vampire who looked like a human. His eyes were no longer glowing, and the icy shadows had disappeared.

'Get up!'

She pulled her knees closer to herself. Bile burned in her throat.

'As you can see, I don't mean to hurt you.'

He stretched out a bloodied hand. Liliana stayed silent. She knew no words that could possibly do justice to this situation.

'As you wish,' grumbled El. He picked her up and threw her over his shoulder as if she were a sack of straw.

She felt another burst of cold as he pushed his way up between branches and trunks, summoned wings, and took off. Her upper body was crammed between his wings; her head dangled disoriented over the shrinking trees. Everything hurt. She thought she was going to vomit again. Only her fear for Annie gave her strength.

'No!' she cried hoarsely. 'Where's Annie? Let me go!'

She perceived his growling voice vibrating through his back rather than through the air streaming past her ears. 'If I did, you'd fall to your death.'

'I don't care! Where's my daughter? I need to go to her!'

His hesitation made her heart stop for a moment. 'Zic flew back to the castle with her.'

She closed her eyes. Annie was alive! Everything else – the pain, the dreadfulness of the situation – was of secondary importance. She put her arms protectively around her head and spoke no more. Whether she'd lost consciousness in between or had fallen asleep from exhaustion in this uncomfortable position, the return journey felt much shorter. El landed in the courtyard of his castle, put her down and dragged her across the square behind him. She staggered the first steps, was picked up and pulled onwards. Although she didn't see anyone, she sensed the spectators peeping out from behind curtains and ornate railings.

They crossed a storeroom and climbed the same staircase with the shaft in the middle that Liliana had used to escape a few hours ago. They continued through the corridor, the hidden entrance and up the spiral staircase. Although El supported her, Liliana kept buckling and panting in pain. Finally, he stopped and glared at her from above, as if it was her fault that she'd collapsed from agony and exhaustion.

'Very clever to make a target of yourself like that ... Was that necessary? Now everyone knows you're here.'

She looked up, distraught. He was the one who'd locked them up here, and he was reproaching *her*?

'You monster! You have no right to imprison us!'

He crossed his arms. His tone remained calm but irritated. Who knew what was going on inside a demon like him?

'I had to keep others away from you! You've just experienced for yourself the reason why.'

'We were locked away like criminals! You wanted to wear us down, didn't you? To let us rot! What have we ever done to deserve all this?'

'It was by far the simplest and most effective solution.'

Apart from the splashes on his neck and face and the blood-soaked spots on his once elegant suit, there was nothing left to indicate the beast she had observed in the forest. How dared he look so normal? To breathe like a person, to wear clothes, to speak, to argue like a rational being? He knew exactly what he was doing; what he *had* done!

She'd spent nights wrestling, waiting for what felt like an eternity for this confrontation – to throw everything at his head that had accrued inside her; to find the reincarnation of evil, a demon who, with derisive laughter, would declare that he had planned everything from the beginning, to bind her soul to himself and consume it along with her blood; or to meet a creature plagued by inner conflict, driven by the craze of a curse at night and overwhelmed by unbearable remorse during the day. But she found nothing of the sort, only an apparently stable individual, so painfully similar to the man she had nursed back to health, and yet so different ... while she knelt in front of him on these stairs, confused and lost.

'You killed Hans and Marie!' She pulled herself up along the wall. Her fists trembled, this time not with weakness. 'And Peter! Was that *simple and effective*, too?'

'Pfff; that Marie tried to impose herself on me at the wrong time. Hans, for his part, would have happily impaled me if I had given him the opportunity.'

'And Peter was probably to blame himself, too?'

'I don't know of any Peter.'

'My husband!'

El's gaze slid to the gold and silver ring on her finger. Did he know the meaning behind it? He wrinkled his nose. 'That wasn't me.'

He knew. 'You sent this vampire woman to look for me!'

'Lola?'

'No, the other one!'

Frowning, he leaned against the opposite wall. 'We thought she was a stray. And it was only because she seemed to go after you that I felt compelled to act.'

'So you're saying that this vampire who killed Peter ... wasn't sent by you?'

'You just said she was looking for you. Had I sent her, I would have given her specific instructions. I know very well where your family lives.'

She had to admit she hadn't taken that into account. Even if El had sent the vampiress to Father instead of Peter's farm, she wouldn't have had to look around for Liliana and attack women in other villages.

'Who then? Who sent her?'

He shrugged, still scowling. 'One of my countless enviers and arch-enemies.'
'Why?'

Without breaking eye contact, he released his arms and took a step away from the wall. 'You look frightful.'

Liliana didn't care that she was staring at him with her mouth gaping open. 'What ...? *I* look frightful? You're the monster here! *You* just had claws, and all the guts flying around and ... and ...'

'It seems that we are frightened by different things,' El said with a smile. 'Come, I'll carry you.'

He stretched out his hand, but Liliana backed away, suppressing a pained whimper. His smile died. Wiping his hand on his trouser leg, he growled,

'Anyway, you have to treat your injuries and get rid of all the blood that's on you. Especially your own.'

He was probably right. It bordered on a miracle that she was still alive. More superficial wounds could heal if they were properly cared for. She would have to wash out the deep scratches so that they didn't get infected and begin to fester. Something in her leg had to be pulled, and a rib was probably compressed or broken – maybe even two ribs. As long as her internal organs, lungs and heart, had remained intact ...

Gritting her teeth, Liliana set out to climb the tower along the outer wall. She put one foot on the next step and pushed herself up, then went over on her ankle and staggered back. El caught her and carried her. She didn't protest any more. She wouldn't make it by herself. And Annie was waiting for her up there.

Halfway to the top, she noticed a shiver going through his body. The light peeking through the small openings changed colour. He stopped, took a deep breath, and climbed the second half with much more difficulty, so that she began to fear they might end up tumbling down the stairs together.

Martha greeted them in the tower room. El laid Liliana down on the bed, where Annie was already sleeping. Then he turned and walked away, not saying another word.

'The young miss cried herself to sleep. But rest assured, nothing else happened to her.'

Their escape had failed. They were back in the tower, back in the castle, surrounded by vampires; back to being locked up. But Annie was unharmed. She stroked her daughter's head and tears of gratitude burned on her blood-encrusted cheeks. Everything else could wait until tomorrow.

IF YOU LIKED THIS BOOK ...

Please take two minutes to write a review on Amazon – and wherever else you like to hang out!

I'm thrilled about every review as to us self-publishers, every single review counts towards making our work more visible. Plus, I am obviously interested to hear what readers think about my book.

Thank you so much for your time. Being able to share this story with others is truly a dream come true.

A BIG THANK YOU

I would like to take this opportunity to thank everyone who has supported me in any way in writing and publishing this book.

Thank you, Alex, for your unwavering support and for always believing in me. A big thank you to my parents for reading just about everything I have ever written as well as to my sister Melinda for her critical and invaluable feedback, and my sister Saphira for often being the only one to like my posts on social media;) I want to thank my mother-in-law Katie for reading my translations quicker than anyone else and my sister-in-law Rhiannon for being the first person who ever bought something I wrote.

I thank Lukas for creating such an amazing cover for me and Klaudia for her beautiful map that came with a lovely share of friendship and support. Another big thank you goes to my German editor Lauren Tebbe and my English editor Leona Skene, who helped improve this translation, as well as Phillipa Haskins, who proofread for me.

Finally, I want to thank my wonderful test readers Samantha, Greta, Manuela, Anita, Marei, Lara, and Jon for your feedback. My books would definitely not be the same without your input!

Hugs to you all, and may the Light watch over you!

WHAT HAPPENS NEXT?

If you'd like to hear when the next book in the series gets published, check out my website www.ataleofbooks.com and sign up for my newsletter!

You can also find me on Instagram as @dsmccolgan (personal profile, in German) and @ataleof_books (English).